ALSO BY SUAD AMIRY

My Damascus
Sharon and My Mother-in-Law

Mother *of* Strangers

Mother
of
Strangers

SUAD AMIRY

PANTHEON BOOKS
New York

Copyright © 2022 by Suad Amiry

All rights reserved. Published in the United States by Pantheon Books,
a division of Penguin Random House LLC, New York, and distributed
in Canada by Penguin Random House Canada Limited, Toronto.
Originally published in hardcover in Italy as *Storia di un abito
inglese e di una mucca ebrea*, by Mondadori Libri S.p.A., Milano, in 2020.
Copyright © 2020 by Suad Amiry and Mondadori Libri S.p.A.

Pantheon Books and colophon are registered trademarks
of Penguin Random House LLC.

Library of Congress Cataloging-in-Publication Data
Name: Amiry, Suad, author.
Title: Mother of strangers : a novel / Suad Amiry.
Description: New York : Pantheon Books, 2022.
Identifiers: LCCN 2021051323 (print). LCCN 2021051324 (ebook).
ISBN 9780593316559 (hardcover). ISBN 9780593316566 (ebook).
Subjects: LCSH: Jaffa (Tel Aviv, Israel)—Fiction. | LCGFT: Novels.
Classification: LCC PR9570.P343 A45 2022 (print) |
LCC PR9570.P343 (ebook) | DDC 823/.92—dc23/eng/20220225
LC record available at https://lccn.loc.gov/2021051323
LC ebook record available at https://lccn.loc.gov/2021051324

www.pantheonbooks.com

Jacket images: (man) Ranta Images / iStock / Getty Images
and Icodacci / E+/ Getty Images; (Jaffa) Historic Collection /
Alamy; (orange) Glasshouse Images / Alamy
Jacket design by Jenny Carrow

Printed in the United States of America
First American Edition
2 4 6 8 9 7 5 3 1

To my father

And all the other refugees who died in the diaspora
while waiting to go home

Contents

Part I

Subhi

ᘓ

The Best Mechanic in Town

(Jaffa, June 1947)

I T TOOK a few ascending yells—"Subhi! Subhi! Subhi! God-damn, *walak*, Subhiiii!"—before he showed signs of hearing his name. Half-heartedly, he raised his head and looked in the direction of his boss. At the entrance of the dark garage stood M'allem Mustafa with a new customer who was tall and elegant. It took Subhi a few long minutes before he silenced the deafening noise of the electrical generator he was repairing. From a distance, he lifted his palm as if to say "What?" In return, he received a beckoning hand gesture and a command: "Come here!"

Resenting the interruption, Subhi pointed to the dozens of dismantled engine pieces spread out on the smeared concrete floor under his feet. In line were other machines: water pumps, more electrical generators, and engines, all waiting to be fixed by the clever fifteen-year-old mechanic. Familiar with Subhi's "not wanting to budge" body language, M'allem Mustafa yelled at him again.

"Subhi! Leave everything. Go wash your hands and face. I want you to accompany Khawaja Michael to his orange grove, his *bayyara*. There seems to be a problem with the irrigation system or the water pump in the big cistern."

"Khawaja Michael," mumbled Subhi to himself as he stared once more in the direction of the new customer, a well-built man dressed in a camel hair suit with a light brown fedora.

Khawaja Michael was standing with the strong midday light behind him, making it difficult for Subhi to see his face. The glare formed a halo around one of the richest men in the port city of Jaffa.

Khawaja Michael, Khawaja Michael . . . Where have I heard that name before? Subhi asked himself as he bent over the stone sink, rubbing the engine grease off his hands. *Oh, of course, from my father,* he remembered, then said aloud, "Khawaja Michael himself! What an honor."

All of a sudden, Subhi recalled word for word an argument, more like a fight, he once had with his father in which Khawaja Michael's name was mentioned.

"I love my job. If need be, I'll do it for free," Subhi had said in defense of his choice to leave school and work as a mechanic with M'allem Mustafa, the owner of the garage.

"For *free?* You son of a bitch. Who do you think you are? The son of Khawaja Michael?"

Subhi also recalled how his father had made fun of him for thinking Khawaja was Mr. Michael's first name.

"*La ya ibni,* no, my son, Khawaja is not his first name. A *khawaja* is a Christian or Jewish gentleman. But of course not all Christians and Jews are *khawajat,* only the rich among them. Some are as poor as your father, if not poorer."

Subhi knew the poor among the Christians, the Jews, and the Muslims—including his Christian neighbors Abu and Um Yousef and Abu Ya'qoub, the Jewish porter at the Carmel Market—but he certainly didn't know any of the rich *khawajat*.

"And what is a rich Muslim called?" Subhi asked his father.

"A rich man, I suppose!" his father responded with a smile.

Though excited to accompany one of the city's richest merchants, who grew oranges and exported them to the whole world, Subhi was worried: *What if I fail to fix the water system in one of the city's largest and most prestigious bayyarat?* What baffled Subhi most as he pulled up his stained baggy trousers and hurriedly walked across the garage in the direction of M'allem Mustafa and Khawaja Michael was why Khawaja himself had come to the Blacksmith Market, the *Suq il Haddadeen*, one of the poorest and shabbiest parts of town, where the garage was located, and had not sent his driver or one of the numerous men who worked for him instead. Khawaja Michael must have had dozens if not hundreds of men working in his groves, and just as many working in his orange export company. It was at this point that Subhi remembered his father describing Khawaja Michael as an *isami*, a self-made man. Only then did he understand the modesty of self-made men.

Unlike his older and younger brothers, Jamal and Amir, who worked with their father planting and tending for a number of orange groves to the east and southeast of Jaffa, Subhi had followed his passion—or rather, his obsession. From an early age, he had been dismantling and reassembling everything in sight, whether it was his grandfather's Zenith radio, his father's agricultural tools, his brothers' bicycles, the neighbor children's tricycle, his uncle's horse carriage, or his younger siblings' toys and dolls. He dismembered those toys into heads, arms, hands, legs. While the children cried frantically, older family members burst into laughter as they complimented him on his newly invented creatures, where one doll's limbs were attached to another doll's torso or an animal head to a human body or the like. Subhi would always restore the dolls and toys back to their original compositions, and then the screaming and yelling would stop.

Subhi's father, Ismael—also called Abu Jamal, in reference to his eldest son—often asked him, "Why work for M'allem Mustafa when you could work with your own father?"

"The answer to your question is very simple," replied Subhi. "M'allem Mustafa pays me thirty piastres a day, while you pay my brothers nothing."

"Nothing, *ya 'ars*, you bastard? Nothing? Don't I give you and your siblings a roof over your heads and a mattress to sleep on? Don't your mother and your grandmother spend their days and nights washing and boiling your greasy clothes and cooking for you? You call that nothing? What else can a poor man like me do for his kids? Let's see how far your thirty piastres a day get you. I bet you'll end up a bachelor just like your uncle!"

"What's wrong with Uncle Habeeb? Isn't he having fun staying out late in Tel Aviv most nights?"

"Is that the kind of life you aspire to, son?"

Subhi's father was referring to his youngest brother, who, in spite of the little work he did and the little money he earned, managed to lead a rather wild life in the bars and nightclubs of Tel Aviv. He also spent most of his weekends in the Arab and Jewish brothels located along the Jaffa–Tel Aviv Road frequented by British soldiers and Jews.

"But doesn't Uncle Habeeb say he's making use of his good relationships with the British soldiers he meets in the brothels to change their government's policy toward Jewish immigration to Palestine?"

"What nonsense. We see more and more ships full of Jewish immigrants arriving at the Tel Aviv Port every week. If neither the 1929 nor 1936 revolts managed to change British immigration policy, do you think your drunken uncle and the drunken British soldiers in the same brothel could?"

"Why not?" asked Subhi, who was enjoying one of his first man-to-man conversations with his father.

"Why not? Everybody goes on strike against the British bias toward the Zionists except those *sharameet*, those whores, and their *karakhanat*, their brothels. War or peace, they never shut their doors."

"But wasn't the brothel on Chelouche Street set on fire the other day?"

"I see, my son, that you're closely following the political struggles of your city."

Subhi added, "And Jews go there as well."

"I tell you, son, every time Arabs and Jews get together, something sinful happens: prostitution, smuggling, arms sales, gangs, looters, and robbers, not to mention the informants who spy on our political leaders and fighters."

"You are telling me all this just because I want to be a mechanic?" Subhi was making fun of his father, who never missed an opportunity to bad-mouth his younger brother and lecture Subhi about the Palestinian struggle and the resistance.

"What I meant to say, is this the kind of life you aspire to live, son? Smoking and getting drunk every night and doing God knows what other sinful things your uncle does in Tel Aviv? I'm afraid that's about all your thirty piastres a day will get you. Oh well, what does one expect from an earthquake except destruction?"

Zilzal, earthquake, was Habeeb's nickname. He'd acquired it as a result of being born on the same day a catastrophic earthquake struck and devastated Jericho, along with many cities and towns in Palestine: July 11, 1927. Subhi's grandmother had gone to visit her sister in Jericho and prematurely given birth to Habeeb. "Scared to death, Habeeb came running out of his mother's womb and hasn't stopped going to other warm places ever since." This was the family joke.

Habeeb was not alone, since most members of his family had a nickname associated with a significant event: a revolt, a war, or a natural disaster, of which there were many in Palestine. Born in 1911, Subhi's father acquired the nickname *il Sakhra*, the Rock. This was a reference to the uprising and demonstrations that took place throughout Palestine against the digs that were being done, secretly, by the British under the Muslim holy site of the Dome of the Rock in Jerusalem. Indeed, Ismael was as tough as a rock, especially when it came to his younger brother Habeeb, who was sixteen years his junior, more like his son. Born in 1915, also called the Year of the Locust, one of Subhi's uncles was nicknamed Jarad, meaning "grasshopper." And since he was born in 1924, when the city of Jaffa was connected to electricity, another one of Subhi's uncles had the nickname Dhaw, meaning "light."

The nicknaming was a tradition passed on to Subhi and his siblings. Subhi, born during the big snowstorm of 1932, was called 'Assefeh, for "snowstorm." Jamal, Subhi's older brother, born during the 1929 Buraq Uprising was il Hait, the Wall. This revolt was a popular uprising against the British Mandate for Palestine, changing the status quo of Ha'it al-Buraq, or the Wailing Wall in Jerusalem. Just like fire, the Buraq Uprising spread to many other cities, resulting in the massacre of 133 Palestinians in different cities across the region, and of 166 Jews in Hebron. Except for the natural disasters such as earthquakes, fires, snowstorms, and locusts, all other nicknames were related to the many uprisings and revolts against the establishment of the Jewish State in Palestine.

The nicknaming also applied to Subhi's youngest sister, Hanan, who was born during the 1936 revolution, which lasted for three long years. Thus Hanan acquired the nickname Fawda, for "chaos." This was partly because she herself was a bit disorganized and partly because of the chaos that characterized the 1936 revolution and the general strike that lasted from 1936 to 1939 against the British and Zionist forces in Palestine. Some of the siblings did not need nicknames since their names reflected their true nature. This was particularly true of Subhi's kind, well-behaved younger brother, Amir, whose name meant "prince."

It was also true of his sister Kulthum, named after the Egyptian singer Umm Kulthum, who in 1937 had a concert in il Hamra Cinema in Jaffa. Every time their grandfather Ali heard her name, he told the same story: "To buy that ticket, I had to spend a whole year's savings, but I never regretted it. Not only listening to but also seeing il Sit, the diva, was certainly worth it. The whole city was mobilized and went out to receive Umm Kulthum. It was everyone in the city, and I mean everyone: the mayor, all the members of the municipal council, all the notables, and the *khawajat*. The peasants and Egyptian riffraff poured in from neighboring villages and Jaffa's outskirts and slept in the streets for two days in hopes of seeing il Sit, who had arrived in Jaffa Port by private yacht.

"It was the Sailors' and Fishermens' Union of Jaffa who organized her tour and paid her two hundred Palestinian pounds for each performance. Mind you, she had a total of five performances: two in Jerusalem, two in Haifa, and one in Jaffa. Umm Kulthum made a fortune on her tours to Palestine in 1931, 1935, and 1937."

Realizing that talking about Uncle Habeeb only infuriated his father and led to a political lecture, Subhi went back to discussing why he had become a mechanic and not a *bayyari,* an orange grove worker.

"You of all people should know the value of being a mechanic fixing people's machines and water pumps. I'd like to see what would happen to your orange grove if your water pumps broke with no one to fix them!"

"OK, OK, *ya shattur,* you clever boy, you win this time," said his father in a conciliatory tone so as not to upset his son any more. But Subhi carried on with the conversation.

"If sons are supposed to work with their fathers as you wish, how come you're not a fisherman like Grandpa Ali? Didn't he beg you, and doesn't he still, to accompany him every single night he goes out fishing?"

"Why venture into a rough sea at night when you can be a *bayyari* working in an orange grove?" Ismael was getting frustrated trying to explain what he thought was pretty obvious. "Son, I sense that you've got no idea what Jaffa oranges are or mean. The whole world takes pride in your city's oranges, but you want to be a mechanic! Jaffa oranges are gold, pure gold. You're obviously too young to understand the kind of wealth merchants like Khawaja Michael, or the Abu il Jabeen brothers or someone like Abdelghani il Nabulsi, achieve with these oranges. Thirty million boxes of oranges were exported last year alone. You know how much money that is? Orange groves are gold mines."

"All I see are oranges, but no gold!"

"And I'm waiting to see what kind of girl will marry a boy who works his ass off in a dark, greasy garage for thirty piastres a day!"

Not wanting to prolong this futile argument, but also, more

important, not wanting to reveal his dream of marrying a village girl named Shams, Subhi kept quiet, thinking of her shy, reassuring smile. For many months now, he had been keeping the secret of seeing her at the summer festival, Mawsim il Nabi Rubin, the year before all to himself.

Subhi had never told his father—or anyone else, for that matter— that he was head over heels in love with thirteen-year-old Shams, the eldest daughter of Khalil Abu Ramadan, one of Ismael's helpers, who was a *saqqa*, a water provider, whose main responsibility was to irrigate the orange grove. Something about that girl drove Subhi out of his mind. He could never figure out what it was about her that had made him fall for her. Was it her smile or her melancholic hazelnut eyes? The curls in her long hair made him feel as though he was trapped in a fisherman's net. Just like the fish in his grandfather's net, Subhi had flipped from one side to another, unable to sleep, the night he saw Shams on the shores of il Nabi Rubin. And what better place to fall in love than during the festival? Mawsim il Nabi Rubin took place in the open air south of Jaffa and lasted for a whole month from mid-August to mid-September. Everything flourished during that vacation month, including the love between Subhi and Shams.

Like hundreds of other kids, she was joyfully running on the beach, along with her younger sisters, Nazira and Nawal, and their many cousins. Subhi spotted Shams's white and orange dress before he came closer to admire her smile, her eyes, and her hair. Little did Subhi know at the time that the melancholy he spotted in her eyes foretold a tragedy that would befall them, their people, and their country in the coming years.

2

The Promised English Suit

S UBHI STOOD MODESTLY next to M'allem Mustafa as his employer praised him to Khawaja Michael.

"Young but clever" were the last words he heard his boss say to the English-looking client before M'allem Mustafa looked at him and said, "Go figure out why the water dried up so early in the season when the Khawaja has one of the city's biggest wells."

Confused as to whether to sit in the front seat or the back seat of Khawaja Michael's Packard, Subhi waited for a signal.

"Come on, young man, get in the car," said Khawaja Michael, pointing to the front seat as he opened the car door and slipped into the driver's seat.

In his head, Subhi heard the words of his grandfather Ali: "Keep quiet when you're in the company of older people."

Being in the company of an older person—and, more important, an affluent gentleman—Subhi just stared out the car window and stayed silent for most of the ride. Though he frequently accompanied customers to their homes, businesses, and orange groves in different parts of the city, this was the first time he had been in the company of such a celebrity: a politician, a member of the municipal council, and the head of Jaffa's chamber of commerce. In short, a very influential man. Considering how rich Khawaja Michael was, Subhi thought of the fees his boss would charge if Subhi managed to repair his irrigation system. Though an employee, Subhi knew that M'allem Mustafa charged different rates for the same job depending on the looks and status of his clients, and the neighborhood in which they lived or worked.

In Subhi's mind, and that of M'allem Mustafa, the city was geographically and socially divided into three parts, as were their rates. The highest prices were given to the inhabitants of the richest parts of the city located to the south and southeast of the Jaffa Clock Tower, one of many clock towers built by Sultan Abdul Hamid II in cities such as Acre, Nablus, Beirut, and Damascus. Such rich areas included Hai il 'Ajami, which had the city's most lavish villas and most of the city's missionary schools and churches, as well as the French and government hospitals. The highest prices also applied to il Jabaliyyeh neighborhood, where Khawaja Michael's villa stood among many other elegant villas and lush gardens, and Hai il Nuzha, by far the most modern neighborhood, with fancy villas and apartment buildings constructed along and off King George Boulevard, also known as Jamal Pasha Street. That was also where the new city hall, the luxurious il Hamra Cinema, and the prestigious Café Venezia were located.

The cheapest prices were given to the inhabitants of the Old City as well as to those living in the outskirt neighborhoods such as Sakanet Abu Kbir and il Bassa in the north and Sakanet Darwish and Tell ir Reish in the south. Most if not all of the outlying areas were on the borders of Jewish settlements and cities such as Tel Aviv in the north and Holon and Bat Yam in the south. Jaffa's poorest families, including Subhi's maternal grandmother, Farida, lived in the Old City. On its outskirts lived mostly laborers and immigrants who came to work in the booming port city. The relative economic boom during the British Mandate, particularly after the Great Depression and before World War II, resulted in a big influx of workers to Jaffa, mostly from Palestinian villages but also from neighboring countries such as Egypt, Jordan, Yemen, and Syria. The great majority of migrants worked either in the orange industry—growing, picking, inspecting, wrapping, packing, transporting, and exporting oranges—or transporting and exporting as day laborers in the city's flourishing port. They also worked in the growing construction sector, in light industry, and doing odd jobs.

The intermediate and most reasonable rates applied to the inhabitants and businesses of the northern neighborhoods of il Rashidiyyeh and il Manshiyyeh. The latter was where Subhi's family lived and was by far the biggest neighborhood in Jaffa, stretching from the clock tower in the center of town all the way to Tel Aviv in the north. Passing by the port, Subhi thought of perhaps the only exception to his boss's rule: while merchants and exporters of oranges were charged the highest fees, fishermen were given the lowest rates. This was a gesture of appreciation made by Subhi's boss to Subhi just because most if not all of the fishermen on the port were friends and colleagues of his grandfather's or uncle Habeeb's.

SUBHI'S THOUGHTS ABOUT the different fees came to an end when Khawaja Michael started a conversation.

"What's your name, young man?"

"Subhi Ismael Abu Shehadeh." Subhi gave his full name in hopes that Khawaja Michael would recognize his father's name, but obviously he did not.

"And how old are you?"

"Sixteen in October." He was actually only fifteen years old, but Subhi often liked to pretend to be a year or two older.

"Though you're still young, people say you're the best mechanic in town."

"Khawaja, let's wait and see," Subhi said, then added, "Only if I manage to identify the problem in your water system and succeed in fixing it."

"Let's hope you do. So far no one has been able to figure out why the water has dried out so early in the season."

"*Inshallah,* Khawaja, God willing, I will be able to fix it for you," Subhi replied, feeling apprehensive about the challenging mission awaiting him.

"And I promise to buy you the best English suit in town if I ever see the water flowing out of that main pipe again."

Subhi gasped.

"An English suit!" He took a deep breath and repeated, "Did you say an English suit, Khawaja Michael?"

"Yes, a Manchester woolen suit customized by the best tailor in town, a tailor of your own choice, young man."

"I thought you said an English suit!"

Realizing that Subhi might be a genius mechanic but not necessarily good at geography, Khawaja Michael reassured him, "Yes, yes, an English suit. Manchester is where the best English textiles come from."

Staring at Khawaja Michael's camel hair suit, Subhi could not resist asking one more question: "Excuse me, Khawaja Michael, but how much does an English suit cost?"

"Seven to eight pounds, something in that range," replied Khawaja Michael.

Subhi could not believe it. That was more than a headmaster's monthly salary, and much more than he could ever save in a year. Not that he could save a single millieme out of the thirty piastres he was making a day.

With such exhilarating news, Subhi's imagination was instantly at work: he, the elegant bridegroom, was proudly standing tall next to his beloved Shams, the sunshine of his life, the most gorgeous girl in the world. He in his eight-pound English suit and she in her white wedding dress, like the prince and princess on the page he'd torn from a magazine he'd found in the stacks at the library he frequented. For a few days after, he avoided going to that library for fear of being reprimanded for tearing out that page. It was now taped on the gray wall of the garage above his toolbox: one obsession hanging above another.

Subhi drifted off in thought. He and his bride were now standing in the midst of a rejoicing crowd. Everyone was singing and dancing—his mother, his father, his siblings and all their children, his maternal grandmother, whose husband had died, and paternal grandparents, members of his extended family, and their guests. He could easily distinguish the Jaffa crowd from Shams's family, which came from the nearby village of Salameh. Though Salameh was only a few kilometers to the east of Jaffa, the embroidered dresses of Shams's family—the Abu Ramadans—and their guests were very different from the urban costumes of Jaffa. It was at this point that Subhi thought about his family's anticipated disapproval of his marrying a peasant girl, especially since Shams was the daughter of one of his father's helpers.

The only redeeming aspect of this fantasy was the praise his father had for Shams's father whenever his name was mentioned: "If only I had a few hardworking and conscientious workers like Khalil, I could be a *bayyari,* the owner of another two or even three orange groves." Subhi's father, Ismael, was already the caretaker of a huge grove and was beginning to have the means to buy the oranges of other groves. In other words, he was becoming a modest orange merchant above and beyond an orange grower.

Now that Khawaja Michael would provide him with a wedding suit—that is, if he succeeded in repairing the water system—for the first time ever, Subhi thought of the need to reveal to his father that he was in love with Shams. He figured he would need a week or two, perhaps a whole month, to convince his father as well as the older members of his family to allow him to marry Shams before he could ask them to form a *jaha,* or group of elders, to formally ask for the bride's hand. They would also have to agree on the details of her dowry, but that should not be a problem since the dowry for village girls was much less than that for a Jaffa bride.

Not wanting to spoil his ecstasy about the promised English suit by thinking of his family's objections to his marrying Shams, or for that matter of the political unrest in the country as a whole and the frequent skirmishes between Jaffa and Tel Aviv that had increased in the last few months, Subhi began to calculate wedding expenses. *Now that I have the English suit, how much longer should I work to save for wedding expenses: Shams's wedding dress; her* masagh, *the gold necklace; and her dowry? And what if my father and his older brothers refuse to pay their share in an attempt to pressure me not to marry Shams?* He imagined them saying, "Out of all the beautiful Jaffa girls around you, and all your cousins, you choose to marry a stranger, a peasant, and a young girl? How old is she? Twelve, thirteen? Stop this nonsense. You yourself are way too young to marry." All sorts of arguments were bouncing around Subhi's excited head.

I only wish they could see her through my eyes, he thought, sighing.

And what if Shams's wedding dress turned out to be as expensive as his English suit? In that case, he wouldn't mind if it were a simpler dress than that of the princess in the magazine. As far as he was concerned, nothing could match the white and orange dress Shams was wearing the first time he spotted her at the annual summer festival, Mawsim il Nabi Rubin. Like a feather, she was swirling as she played and laughed with her friends. Subhi's head also swirled every time he thought of the first time his eyes fell on her.

Thinking of the little savings he could put aside from his thirty piastres a day, Subhi came to the sad conclusion that both he and the promised English suit would have to wait for a long time. *Like Khawaja Michael, I should perhaps take it one step at a time. I am also a self-made man,* he thought.

3

Jaffa's Orange Groves
(Bayyarat Yafa)

S UBHI'S HEART SKIPPED a beat when Khawaja Michael declared
they had arrived at their destination. "Here we are, young man,"
he said as he waited for someone to appear and open the gate to his
bayyara. Three workers came running out: two opened the huge
iron gate panels while the third waved them in.

"OK, clever mechanic, get your toolbox out of the trunk and follow me."

By the time Subhi got out of the passenger's seat and went to the
rear of the car, a few more workers had appeared from three different doors of a long concrete building. They came forward in order
to salute their boss but also to inquire about the call for an open
strike. They wanted to know if the strike excluded citrus growers.

Subhi had already heard the rumors from his father about a tacit
agreement, referred to as the Citrus Agreement, between Arabs and
Jews to refrain from any acts of sabotage against the citrus industry.
While waiting to be ushered to the well, Subhi overheard one of the
supervisors reporting to Khawaja Michael that two of his workers

had distributed leaflets against the Citrus Agreement. Quite keen to get his English suit, Subhi walked away with body language suggesting *Let's get started before yet another strike starts.* Patiently waiting on the hill where he stood, Subhi had a spectacular, panoramic view of his city, a view he had never seen before.

"God, what beauty," he mumbled. This was the very first time he had seen his city from the east, where most of the city's citrus groves were. Orange dotted the vast green carpet that spread in front of him for miles. Tall palm trees as well as dark green conical cypresses at times divided the view as others framed it, accentuating the perspective. Though Subhi had been to his father's orange groves and many others, nothing came close to this one in size or in organization. The attention given to every single tree in this orchard was phenomenal. What impressed the young mechanic most was the vastness of the irrigation system and how well kept the now empty canals looked.

The Khawaja must have brought not only architects to build the his mansion, the workers' houses, and the factory located at the entrance of the *bayyara,* but also agricultural engineers to design this elaborate network of irrigation canals.

Recalling his conversation with his father, Subhi now understood why Ismael preferred to be in such bliss rather than work as a fisherman in the midst of a rough sea. His father was also right about the fragrance of the orange blossoms compared to the pungency of the Mediterranean Sea. Subhi had thought he liked the odor of the sea until the moment the fragrance of orange blossoms filled his lungs.

Subhi stood there comparing the view of his city from the sea to that from the *bayyara* where he stood now: the city looked inverted. No wonder orange merchants and fishermen literally had different points of view on life and politics and never got along. It was as if they were living on two different planets. And indeed they were: while one group of men was spending the nights making a living out at sea, the other was spending long days making a living inland. Subhi had grown up listening to the arguments between his father and his grandfather. While the citrus industry flourished in Jaffa, more and more fishermen were deserting the sea in favor of the land. The same was true when it came to the control of Jaffa's port. It was now the orange merchants rather than the fishermen who were becoming the "lords of the port." As simple and as obvious as it was, in his dark garage fixing engines, Subhi had never reflected on this before.

On those occasions he had accompanied his grandfather fishing, Subhi was used to seeing the city from the west looking east. The image of the city that was stamped in his head was that of sailors and fishermen who ventured into the Mediterranean. The view was of small and big ships: big ships that feared Jaffa's rocky port and were set apart and looming, waiting for small boats moving back and forth carrying merchandise—mostly oranges—from the port's warehouses to them. The elevated warehouses right on the port looked more like a wall. From his grandfather's little boat, he was used to seeing the steep hill upon which stood the Old City where his grandmother Farida lived; also the castle from the Crusaders times, which according to his schoolteacher, "Governor Abu Nabbout, the father of modern Jaffa, used as his seat"; and the Armenian and Greek convents where many Christian pilgrims stayed on their way to Jerusalem. From the sea, Subhi could also see the square tower of Saint Peter's Church located on the very top of the hill, the small il Bahr Mosque next to his grandmother's house, the red lighthouse, and parts of il Mahmoudiyyeh Mosque, the site of one of the city's best public libraries, where he frequently borrowed books or tore pages from magazines. It was also from the sea that Subhi and his grandfather saw the big ships that smuggled Jewish immigrants into the port of Tel Aviv, while the British authorities claimed otherwise.

Though he could not recognize most of the buildings from such a distance and strange angle all in reverse, he guessed that the built-up area to his far left must be il Jabaliyyeh neighborhood that bordered the Jewish city Bat Yam. To the north of it was the rich neighborhood of il 'Ajami. Subhi suspected that the row of buildings in the foreground was in Hai il Nuzha, the newest and most modern neighborhood built along King George Boulevard. On this street stood one of the city's most elegant and expensive cafés. Unlike the modest Café il Tious, or Fools' Café, which was located in il Manshiyyeh, Café Venezia was the exclusive or "in" place. Subhi wondered if he would have the courage to walk into it if he ever received the promised English suit. Subhi's mind was making a list of all the "in" places he would like to go if he ever got that suit.

But until that happened, he would continue a visual journey of his city. The one thing he recognized immediately was the Ottoman clock tower that stood in the middle of the square: the city's main landmark. To its left was Saint Peter's Church, elongated with its distinct square tower. Subhi was trying to figure out if the minaret to the left of the clock tower belonged to il Bahr Mosque or il Mahmoudiyyeh Mosque when he heard his name.

"*Yalla ya,* Subhi, let's go!" yelled Khawaja Michael, and then he instructed one of his workers to assist Subhi. "OK, M'allem Marwan, I've brought you a mechanic to figure out the water problem. I tell you, if this lad can't figure it out, no one can. And you know what that means? We're in big trouble." Khawaja Michael was trying to impress M'allem Marwan, who seemed to be skeptical about the experience of such a young mechanic. Though the Khawaja's flattering words gratified Subhi, they burdened him with a greater sense of responsibility.

"In that case, should I have him check all the wells and all the ponds, or should I take him directly to the main water cistern?" asked M'allem Marwan.

"What's wrong with you? Take him directly to the big well, the east well where the main pump is." Khawaja Michael was taken aback by the detour in M'allem Marwan's mind. Perhaps that was the reason they hadn't been able to figure out the problem. However, Khawaja Michael kept the negative thought to himself.

"How deep is the biggest cistern?" inquired Subhi, hoping it wasn't too deep. Though he'd been up and down all sorts of wells, Subhi felt claustrophobic in those that were deeper than ten meters. Having heard so many tragic stories about deep wells, Subhi always inquired about safety conditions.

"Don't worry; it's only eight meters deep."

"Does it have a fixed metal ladder or a collapsible one?"

"I can see you're quite fussy—Apologies; I meant to say that you seem to be a cautious young man. It was installed by German engineers, so it should be safe," replied the superintendent.

"I want to make sure that I live long enough to wear that English suit on my wedding day." M'allem Marwan had no idea what Subhi was referring to, but Khawaja Michael responded with a smile, "*Inshallah,* you will."

"OK, let's go, then."

Only when he walked through the long rows of perfect orange trees that extended for miles on end did Subhi realize what it meant to be a *khawaja.* He also understood why big orange merchants like Khawaja Michael were in favor of the Citrus Agreement, for he himself wouldn't want to see such a heaven burned down or damaged. Subhi started to see why Khawaja Michael was also against the call for an open strike, which would cause great losses for the orange industry. Subhi recalled his father's words, "Jaffa oranges are gold, pure gold."

4

To Have or Not to Have the Promised Suit

BEFORE VENTURING into the darkness of the well, Subhi went around checking all the aboveground parts of the irrigation system. He inspected the main pipe in order to make sure there was no blockage there. He placed his muscled arms on the iron wheel and pushed it. It spun around, as it should. He examined the rope and the washer thoroughly; nothing seemed to be wrong with them. Having checked those parts, he now had to venture into the well to check the main riser pipe and the guide pulley at the very bottom.

With a firm grip on the metal ladder, Subhi climbed down. Though his light and slim body permitted him to go fast, he did not. He went slowly, so as to get his eyes accustomed to the darkness. Once he was deep into the well, he used his flashlight to check the situation. To his surprise, he saw his reflection and that of the flashlight on the surface of water below him. Relieved that the water had not dried up, as Khawaja Michael had suspected or assumed, Subhi concluded that the problem was mechanical. He now hoped that the issue would be in the riser pipe above water level and not in the guide pulley immersed in water at the very bottom of the well.

It did not take Subhi long to go up and down the ladder to check the riser pipe and discover that the problem was indeed in the casing of the main pipe. He could not help but giggle aloud and shout, "OK, Shams, get ready. Here I come with my wedding suit!"

"ANYTHING WRONG?" asked M'allem Marwan, who was waiting for Subhi.

"No, nothing wrong. On the contrary, I think I've figured out what the problem is."

Coming up the ladder into the light, Subhi could not help but think of the color of his suit. Should it be gray or blue? Should it be dark or light? Was he to get married in the winter or in the summer, as most people did?

By the time Subhi emerged from the well, Khawaja Michael had heard the happy news and come back running to hear Subhi's explanation.

"The good news is that the water has not dried up. The well is more than half full."

"I am so relieved. The last thing I want is to lose this year's crops."

"God forbid," said Subhi, then added, "The problem lies in the main pipe casting. It's rusted and worn out. So I will need to go back to the workshop and make new pieces to replace the rusted ones. They're the ones allowing the air to get into the pipe and preventing the water from rising."

"May I conclude that you can fix it, young man?"

"With God's help, yes, Khawaja, I can."

"M'allem Marwan, why don't you drive Subhi to M'allem Mustafa's workshop and stay with him as long as it takes to make or buy the necessary spare parts. Stay with him even if it takes the whole day."

"*Hader,* sure, Khawaja."

Eager to accomplish the mission, Subhi and M'allem Marwan hurriedly got into the latter's modest car and drove along the King Faisal Street constructed by the British Mandate government to facilitate transport between the orange groves to the east of Jaffa and its port. They drove along the Jerusalem Road and into the narrow streets of il Manshiyyeh neighborhood.

WHEN THEY GOT to the garage, Subhi briefed his boss about the problem. Proud of his young mechanic, M'allem Mustafa gave him a hand by getting on the job right away. And thus all necessary pieces were made in a couple of hours.

Back to Khawaja Michael's orange grove and back to the darkness of the well: under the direct supervision of Khawaja Michael and with the help of M'allem Marwan and another worker, Subhi managed to replace the worn-out and rusted parts with the new ones. Once all was in place, Subhi started ascending the ladder.

By the time he had made it aboveground, the good news had spread around the *bayyara,* and dozens of workers surrounded Khawaja Michael and Subhi. The festive mood felt like an inauguration ceremony where young Subhi was about to cut the red ribbon, and indeed Subhi rose to the occasion: with a theatrical gesture, he extended his arm and switched the water pump on. After a couple of puffs and a few strong shakes, the water gushed out from the main pipe. "Hurray!" screamed the crowd, bursting into applause as they congratulated their boss and themselves for having the water back.

Some hung around for a bit, others went back to work, especially *il saqqaiyyeh,* whose primary responsibility was to irrigate the orange trees, something they had not done for a week. Subhi could not help but think of Shams's father, Khalil, when he saw *il saqqaiyyeh,* the water providers, run away faithfully to do their jobs.

Once Khawaja Michael, superintendent Marwan, and Subhi were left alone, Subhi hoped that Khawaja Michael would say a few words about the logistics of fulfilling his promise. But to Subhi's great disappointment, Khawaja Michael did not mention the one and only thing that was on Subhi's mind.

"So, young man, you do deserve the reputation of being the best mechanic in town after all. You certainly proved it today."

"Thank you, Khawaja."

"Tell M'allem Mustafa I'll come by his workshop sometime tomorrow to settle the account with him."

"*Hader,* Khawaja. Will do."

"Oh, and yes, here is a tip for you on the side . . . You do not need to mention it to your boss," said Khawaja Michael as he handed Subhi fifty piastres. Though it was more than Subhi made in a day, Subhi was disappointed as he took it.

He so wanted to inquire about the promised suit but couldn't bring himself to do it.

"Thank you, Khawaja," Subhi replied, then he took his toolbox and walked beside Khawaja Michael in the direction of the main gate.

"M'allem Marwan, why don't you give Subhi a ride to town?"

"*Hader*, Khawaja," replied M'allem Marwan and reached for the car keys in his pocket.

What about the suit? Subhi kept thinking to himself, but again he was too intimidated to remind Khawaja Michael.

Disheartened, Subhi walked along the canals, which were by now filled with water rushing to rejuvenate the orange trees in the same way it had rejuvenated the owner as well as the workers of the *bayyara*. Suddenly he heard Khawaja Michael yell, "Oh God, what happened to my brain?"

"Goodness, how did I forget!" Subhi was thrilled that Khawaja had remembered the promise on his own, without Subhi's needing to embarrass himself.

"I completely forgot that I have a meeting at the chamber of commerce, so I will give you a ride myself, if not all the way to il Manshiyyeh, at least close enough for you to walk back to the garage."

Subhi kept quiet for most of the ride in hopes that Khawaja Michael would remember Subhi's suit the way he'd remembered his meeting at the chamber of commerce. Subhi was too proud to remind him. *After all, I am a good mechanic, not a beggar,* he consoled himself.

Once again he enjoyed driving along the narrow dirt roads in the midst of the largest orange groves in Jaffa. He was happy to learn the names of the richest orange merchants. "This *bayyara* is owned by the Abu il Jabeen brothers, and this one belongs to Abdelghani il Nabulsi and is by far the largest in town, about one thousand dunams," explained Khawaja Michael, using a unit of measure equal to 1,000 square meters, or about a quarter of an acre. Subhi could not imagine an orange grove bigger than Khawaja Michael's. "And this *bayyara* belongs to the Abu Laban family, and this one on the

left belongs to Ahmad il Muhtadi from the village of Salameh."
Subhi's heart jumped out of his chest when he heard the name of
Shams's village coming from Khawaja Michael's lips.

"Did you say Salameh?" Subhi wanted to hear the word again
and again.

"Yes. You know, it is just around the corner from here."

"Around the corner from where? Which corner?" Subhi asked,
even though he knew quite well where Salameh was.

"I meant to say that the orange fields of Salameh and those of
Jaffa are next to one another. Most of the workers on my *bayyara*
come from Salameh."

The mention of Shams's village, and also of its being next to
Jaffa, cheered Subhi up, but it also made him think again of the one
thing he was trying hard to forget. Once they got to the crossing of
Jerusalem Road, Khawaja Michael turned left while pointing in the
opposite direction.

"You see? If you take a right, you'll end up in Salameh." Oh
how Subhi wished they would turn right rather than left. That was
the road he wished to take soon, if only Khawaja Michael would
remember his promise, or if he, Subhi, could summon the courage
to remind him.

Something about the two domed structures of the Abu Nabbout
water spring, which they had just passed, reminded Subhi of his
grandmother Farida and her telepathy technique: "If you concentrate on something or someone, that thing or that person will ultimately read your mind."

And that was what Subhi did for the rest of the ride.

It took a while before Subhi realized that they were stuck in a
traffic jam caused by yet another demonstration against British policies. From a distance, Subhi could not only hear the chanting of the

demonstrators but could also read some of the huge banners they were holding.

"Stop Jewish immigration to Arab Palestine right now!"

"No to Partition!"

"Promise them a homeland in 'Great' Britain, not in tiny Palestine!"

"Stop grabbing Arab land!"

"No to Zionism!"

Though there were many banners, the one that caught Khawaja Michael's eyes was the one that read "A call for an open strike."

"God help us, I truly hope this does not turn into another open-ended revolt like that of 1936," complained Khawaja Michael as he waited for the policeman to direct him to an alternate route while a group of British soldiers brutally dispersed the demonstrators.

Subhi was taken aback by Khawaja Michael's comments on not only today's demonstration but also the 1936 Revolt, especially since he himself had been taking part in the Friday demonstrations that often started from the Great Jaffa Mosque and gathered at the Clock Tower Plaza, also called il Shuhada Square, or Martyrs' Square. True, Subhi had been only three years old during the 1936 Revolt, but he had heard many stories from his father and grandfather about the heroic freedom fighters who opposed the Balfour Declaration and the British policies that favored the Zionist Movement, trained some of its militias and allowed them to smuggle people and arms into Palestine.

SUBHI HAD HEARD from his grandfather Ali about the day Ali's house, along with many others, was blown up by the British Royal Engineers: "I don't know what was 'royal' about them! I recall the day as if it were yesterday. It was the twenty-ninth of

June, and from the air, the British forces dropped leaflets giving us a day to evacuate our houses. Before we knew it, all hell had broken loose. Like ants, thousands and thousands—thousands, not hundreds—of British soldiers filled the streets and the narrow alleys of the Old City where we lived, and in no time they sealed off the whole area and started blowing the houses up. One after another, like cards, they fell. The British soldiers started from the east and kept dynamiting until they reached the sea. They made a wide road in the middle of the Old City; gone was the *casaba*, gone were the beautiful houses, gone was the mosque, gone were the holy shrines and the *ʒawaya*, the schools, and gone were the alleys, the shops, the people. And that was when we came to live in il Manshiyyeh. The British soldiers came back later to cut another swath so as to control the Palestinian fighters of the Old City. And since then, gone is the glamour of Jaffa's Old City. Only cats, dogs, and poor people and troublemakers live there now. And Farida, my mother-in-law, of course," Subhi's grandfather added, then chuckled.

"We called it a massacre, while the British claimed it was a 'face-lift' and the municipal architect called it a 'Roman city' with two perpendicular streets: one called Decumanus Maximus and the other Cardo Maximus. Don't ask your poor grandfather what these *manus* and *imus* are!"

"I TELL YOU, young man, neither the people nor the economy can afford another six-month strike like the one that started in 1936 and ended with World War Two. People who call for a general strike have no clue what it means for the Arab economy; they have no clue what it means to lose this year's orange crop." Khawaja Michael was still at it.

It was only when Khawaja Michael stopped his car close to the municipal building, shook Subhi's hand, thanked him for his excellent service, and reminded him to convey to M'allem Mustafa that he would come by to settle the account tomorrow that Subhi decided to say something. He opened the door on the passenger side, and got one of his long legs out of the car as he finally worked up his courage.

"But what about the English suit, Khawaja Michael?" Subhi asked as he blushed and broke out in a sweat.

"Oh God . . . of course, the suit!" Khawaja Michael said, then added, "Apologies, my son. I totally forgot about the suit. Get in the car, get in the car."

It was one of those situations when action was faster than words. Like in a rewound scene in a movie, Subhi's leg was pulled back into the car, the door was shut, and the car sped onward.

"So tell me, *ya ibni*, my son, which tailor has your measurements?" inquired Khawaja Michael.

Subhi did not want to admit that no tailor in town had his measurements as he had never had a suit or even dreamed of having one before today.

"No one," confessed Subhi, hoping he might end up at Khawaja Michael's tailor in the richer neighborhood of il 'Ajami or il Jabaliyyeh.

"What do you mean, no one?"

Realizing that Khawaja was in a hurry to attend the meeting at the chamber of commerce, which he headed, Subhi did not want to take any further risks. Quickly he came up with the name of a tailor in his neighborhood.

"How about Abu il Jabeen, the tailor on il Manshiyyeh Street?"

"I was not aware of a tailor by the name of Abu il Jabeen! Is he related to the Abu il Jabeen brothers?"

Zuhdi and Mahmoud Abu il Jabeen were among the richest merchants in Jaffa. Subhi hoped they were not rivals of Khawaja Michael's. Silence prevailed as Subhi concentrated on the road. He was afraid to give the wrong directions. But luckily, the tailor's shop with a big red sign that read "Makhyatet Hassan Abu il Jabeen" was right in front of them.

5

Sugar Daddy

"COME IN, please come in," said the friendly tailor as Subhi and Khawaja Michael stepped into his shop. His welcoming tone, typical of Jaffa, caused Subhi to release some of the tension from his exhausted body and soul. It was this hospitality toward the unknown visitors that gave the city its well-deserved nickname of *Um il ghareeb,* Mother of Strangers. The overfriendliness was perhaps due to the unexpected appearance of such a rich and elegant man in Hassan's modest shop.

"At your service, sir. May I be of service?" asked the tailor, addressing Khawaja Michael.

"I would like you to make this young man a suit in exchange for his excellent service."

"An *English* suit," Subhi felt the need to specify. "I meant to say," he added hastily, "do you happen to have English textiles?"

"I have the best Manchester textiles right here," replied Hassan drily. He was starting to wonder about the peculiar relationship between an older rich man and a fit younger worker. Trying to avoid letting his imagination run wild, the tailor asked, "Which one do you like most, young man?"

"Can I have a closer look at that one, please?"

"This one?"

"No, no, the one right next to it, the dark gray one with the thin red stripe."

"Oh, I see. You have expensive taste, young man." It was not quite clear if he was alluding to the boy's choice of fabric or to Khawaja Michael. Something about the way he said it made Subhi feel uncomfortable. He sensed that the tailor was somehow making fun of him.

Nonetheless, the tailor was now pulling out one bolt of fabric after another, displaying them on the heavy wooden table where Khawaja Michael and Subhi stood. With much tenderness, Subhi placed his rough palm on the soft English wool as if he were caressing his beloved Shams on their wedding night.

"Do you like it? Is that what you want, Subhi?" asked Khawaja Michael, signaling that he was in a hurry to leave.

"Yes, Khawaja, I like it very much. It feels soft. Thank you."

"How much does the fabric and tailoring of the suit come to, Mr. Abu il Jabeen?" asked Khawaja Michael.

"Eight pounds, sir. Your young man surely has extremely fine taste," replied the tailor.

"Indeed he does," Khawaja Michael said with a smile. "Well, he certainly deserves it after all that he did for me today. I can't tell you what a great job he did."

Not wanting to get into the details of the "job," tailor Hassan kept quiet while his wild imagination was still at work.

"OK, then," said Khawaja Michael as he reached for his wallet and pulled out the eight pounds, a gesture Subhi would remember for the rest of his long life. Eight pounds in four notes, to be exact: one red and three green.

"Excuse me, gentlemen, I need to rush to my meeting. I am running late," Khawaja Michael said. As if in a dream, Subhi accompanied him out of the tailor's shop, walked him to his car, and waited until his black Packard had disappeared before he dashed back to the tailor's shop and collapsed in an armchair in the corner of the shop.

"God, what a long and exhausting job that was . . . but I am truly happy about what I'm getting in return for my services."

Not knowing what to think or say, the tailor let an awkward long minute pass before he said, "Let me know when you're ready for me to take your measurements."

"I hope you do not mind, Mr. Hassan, if I rest here for just a few more minutes."

"Please take your time, no hurry whatsoever, son," replied Hassan as he went back to sit behind his Singer sewing machine. Thinking of the hanky-panky between this boy (whom he addressed as his son) and his sugar daddy, the tailor prayed that his own son would not indulge in such affairs.

"I'm ready," announced Subhi as he stood tall and proud in front of the mirror.

"Stand still, turn around . . . bend your arm . . . raise both of your arms up . . . and bring them down. OK, we're done. Your suit should be ready in five days, son," said Hassan.

"Wednesday, Thursday, Friday, Saturday, Sunday. Great, I'll be back early Monday morning, then."

"Not too early, though. I don't open before ten a.m."

"Ten a.m.?" Subhi asked in surprise, and then added, "Sorry, sir, I didn't mean to interfere in your business. See you at ten a.m. sharp."

"I stay late in the evening as most of my customers come after work."

"I fully understand. Some of us work early in the morning and others work late at night, but we all love our jobs," replied Subhi and gave the tailor a big friendly smile. Counting the days until he would be back, Subhi left the tailor's shop, closing the door behind him.

6

Three Green Notes and One Red
(July 1947)

S UBHI COULD NOT SLEEP the night before he went to pick up his English suit. The five days of waiting had felt as slow and painful as the days leading up to the Festival of il Nabi Rubin. For that was the only time of year when he could not only see but also be with Shams.

What worried Subhi most were the persistent calls for a general strike against the Partition Plan. While the Palestinian Arab Party and most of the unions (including the one he belonged to) were in favor of an open-ended strike, the two moderate parties, il Difa' and il Najjadeh, were for limiting the strike to three days.

"What idiocy!" objected Subhi's boss, M'allem Mustafa. "I don't understand how going on strike and hurting our own economy will stop the Partition Plan or, for that matter, more Jews from pouring into our land!"

Most shops owners, not only those in the industrial zone but also those in other parts of town, shared these sentiments. Such calls for an open strike inevitably triggered fear and bad memories of the

1936 Revolt. Though Subhi often disagreed with his boss, this time he was praying to have his suit in hand before any strike took place. Only now did Subhi understand how one's interests dictated one's political positions. He couldn't imagine that he, who had participated in every Friday demonstration, would take a position against the strike this time. But Subhi feared that the escalations of attacks between Arabs and Jews would hinder all possibilities of seeing or being with Shams. Especially because there were strong rumors that Jaffa's municipality might cancel this year's festival in il Nabi Rubin out of fear of Zionist attacks on Palestinian civilian gatherings. And if this turned out to be true, Subhi would be deprived of the one and only venue where he and Shams could meet freely.

FOR FIVE CONSECUTIVE DAYS, Subhi obsessed about the eight pounds paid by Khawaja Michael. He kept recalling the scene in which Khawaja had pulled a fine leather wallet out of his pocket and with no hesitation removed one red note and three green ones. With his sharp, youthful mind, Subhi recalled the shape and the colors of the notes as much as he recalled the color and texture of his suit. The red note read, in capital letters, "FIVE PALESTINIAN POUNDS," while the green notes read "ONE PALESTINIAN POUND." At the top of each note were the words (also in capital letters) "PALESTINE CURRENCY BOARD." Staring at the notes as Khawaja put them in the tailor's hand, Subhi noticed that the one-pound notes had the Dome of the Rock on the lower side, while the five-pound note had a drawing of a tower he did not recognize. Being the clever boy he was, especially with math, he even tried to memorize the numbers on the notes: Y637758, Y627759, and Y637760 on the green ones and A877125 on the red five-pounder.

Because of his salary, Subhi was accustomed to the three 100-mil coins paid to him by his boss, the 5 or 10 piastres he paid for his coffees, and the one or two shillings he spent in the coffee shop where he and his pals spent most evenings playing cards and arguing about politics. The shillings were also spent on items he was starting to buy in secret behind his father's back: cigarettes for himself and gifts for Shams. He was hiding those in his drawer.

As he walked the three kilometers that separated his home from the tailor's shop, for the first time ever Subhi paid attention to what other men on the streets wore. Men's clothing was the last thing that had ever interested Subhi, but now he noticed that only older men wore suits. He counted the number of men his age wearing them on one hand: there were five. The majority of men wore what his father and grandfather wore: the traditional *qumbaz*, a robe that is open in the front. Some wore it with a dark jacket, others without. He also noticed the traditional Egyptian *jallabiyyeh*, the long cotton coat belted around the waist worn by many workers. No one came close to looking as sharp and as elegant as Khawaja Michael, or as Subhi himself soon would look in his suit.

Subhi had to pace in front of the tailor's shop for a few long minutes before Hassan arrived.

"I see someone didn't sleep last night," said the tailor, who by now had either accepted the idea of the sugar daddy and the youngster or, more likely, had heard, like many in town, how clever and deserving the young mechanic was.

"Is my suit ready?" asked Subhi apprehensively.

"Of course it is," he was assured by Hassan, who added, "A date is a date; one should never be late for one's customers."

Subhi couldn't agree more on the principle of never being late for a customer. He always got to the garage not only earlier than his boss but also way before any customers appeared. However, realizing the importance of this occasion, Subhi had taken the day off in order to give his suit the attention it deserved. He wanted to try it on at the tailor's shop; he knew from his mother it might need alterations: "Tailors often need one or two trials." And in case it was ready, he would need to carry it home and show it to his mother and grandmother before hanging it in the closet. Being the conscientious worker that he was, he had alerted his boss to his need to take a day off, but he had not revealed why.

"I can tell you've taken a bath today," Hassan commented, as if reminding Subhi how stinky and sweaty he had been the day he came in with Khawaja Michael. Anxious to try on his new suit, Subhi decided to swallow the insult and refrained from responding. He did not want to get into a long story by telling Hassan that in preparation for trying on his suit, he had gotten up early that day, had a haircut, and taken an elaborate bath in *il hammam*, the public bathhouse. Rather than having his uncle Habeeb cut his hair, he had been to a proper barbershop and had given very specific instructions to the barber: "I want you to give me the most fashionable haircut." Seeing what a terrible cut young Subhi had, the barber had replied in a dismissive way, "OK, OK, sit down."

Far from being fashionable, the barber's crew cut made Subhi look like a British soldier rather than the bridegroom he wanted to look that day. Still, the crew cut was far better than the haircut given to him by his drunken uncle.

After the haircut, it was time for Subhi to attend to the rest of his body. From the barbershop, he proceeded to the Turkish baths located right next to his grandmother's house in the Old City. Though some men went to the *hammam* on a regular basis, most, like Subhi, went only on special occasions such as the "small" and "big" holidays: 'Eid il Fitr and 'Eid il Adha. But many men who were only a few years older than Subhi also went in preparation for their wedding night.

"Give me one more round of rubbing," Subhi pleaded to the half-naked middle-aged man who gave Subhi a rub with a rough black cloth and two rounds of Nabulsi olive oil soap.

"Don't you have Aleppo *ghar*, laurel oil soap?" asked Subhi.

"For that you have to pay an extra piastre."

"Do it, and I will pay you the extra piastre. I want to have the laurel scent. Today is a special day."

"Meeting your sweetheart, right?"

"Not really . . . but in a way, yes."

Having mentioned his sweetheart while having his back rubbed with warm water and laurel soup aroused Subhi and gave him an erection, about which he was rather embarrassed.

"Don't be shy; most men get one when I rub their backs or the inner parts of their thighs. The important thing, though, is not to come after me," said the fat man before he burst into laughter that echoed across the foggy domed rooms of the Turkish bath.

"Don't worry, I am not one of those," Subhi giggled.

"But I am," replied the man, bursting into another round of loud laughter that went all the way up to the blue and round skylights that allowed romantic light into the baths.

Now, at the tailor's shop, Subhi watched Hassan as he went to take his suit from a rack with a few others. Subhi's heart and face lit up when he spotted the gray suit with the red pinstripe.

"You certainly made an excellent choice. This fabric is soft and easy to handle, like dough."

Like dough?! Subhi did not like the comparison of his expensive English suit to mundane dough. But again he refrained from commenting as Hassan carefully placed the suit flat on the wide table in front of him. Subhi wiped his huge palms on his trousers before he tenderly caressed the front of the jacket a few times, then smiled.

"See how beautiful it is?" asked Hassan.

"Yes."

"OK, leave the jacket on the table, take the trousers to the fitting room over there, put them on, and come back. I need to check them out."

Subhi followed the tailor's instructions and in no time had changed and emerged from the fitting room. He walked toward Hassan while looking down, admiring his new trousers and touching his protruding backside with his two big palms.

"Come closer and turn around." Again Subhi followed the tailor's instructions. "Perfect . . . perfect. See, when the customer is thin and tall, it's easy for the tailor to get it right on the first try." Hassan's words pleased Subhi, who was now touching his trousers on the upper parts of his thighs.

"OK, let's try the jacket," said Hassan, helping Subhi put it on.

"Perfect. Turn around and let's see how the shoulders fit in the back."

Standing in front of the mirror, Subhi turned his body while he looked in the mirror.

"No, not that way . . . turn your body as well as your head and stand still. I need to see how it falls in the back."

"Falls! Where?" Subhi asked in a panic, which made the tailor giggle.

" 'Falls' in tailorspeak means 'fits well,' with no bends or curves."

"First it's like dough and now it falls! What kinds of expressions are these?" Now that the suit was almost ready, Subhi felt less anxious and began to engage more in the conversation.

"I must say, it fits you perfectly, young man. OK, turn and look at me now."

Hassan inspected every part of the suit, asking Subhi to bend his elbows, raise his arms, sit down, stand up, and bend forward, all the while asking Subhi if it felt comfortable.

Having inspected Subhi as well as the suit, Hassan was starting to see why Khawaja Michael was attracted to Subhi. However, Subhi's mind was elsewhere.

Standing in front of the mirror, he was stunned not only by how elegant the suit was but also by how different he looked. For the first time, he noticed that he was indeed a handsome boy, as his mother often said: "He is the most beautiful of all my kids, girls and boys." He noticed how wide his shoulders were. Wide enough to have Shams rest her head and spread her long curls on. In the mirror in front of him, Subhi saw Shams standing right next to him in her white dress, only to be jolted back to reality by the tailor's words.

"OK, young man, since the suit needs no alterations, take it off and let me finish it for you. I need to sew the edges, press it a little bit, and place it on a hanger. Come back in an hour or so; it should be ready by then."

"Can I wait for it here?" Subhi asked.

"You want to wait for it?" responded the tailor, surprised, then added, "Of course you can."

But realizing how uncomfortable it felt to pace back and forth in front of the tailor, Subhi soon stepped outside and strode along il Mahatta Street. Having spent the longest half hour ever, Subhi poked his head through a partly open door and was thrilled to hear the tailor enthusiastically say, *"Mabruk,* congratulations. I am very happy to have made you your first suit. I will keep your measurements for your second and third suits, and with God's help for your wedding suit in a few years. How old are you?"

"Fifteen, turning sixteen soon."

"Still young . . . we've got plenty of time."

Little did Subhi and the tailor realize that the dim future awaiting their city would make it impossible for them to meet again.

7

The Grand Suit Tour

O NCE AGAIN stepping out of the tailor's shop onto the busy street, Subhi wondered what to do or where to go next. This was a special day, and he must treat it as such.

Holding his suit on a hanger high above the ground, Subhi moved it from one hand to the other. *How should I celebrate this unique day?* Subhi asked himself as he passed the train station with trains that could've carried him from Jaffa to Jerusalem, a trip he'd always wanted to make but never had.

Had circumstances been different—meaning had he not feared his family's objection to his marrying a peasant girl, or had Shams been his age: fifteen turning sixteen—he would've married her right away. However, since Shams was only thirteen, Subhi had to wait three more years before the law would allow it to happen. Had there not been all these complications, he would have simply hopped on the bus that went from the heart of Jaffa to Salameh. He would have been thrilled to visit Shams's house, or her school, to show her his wedding suit.

Walking along il Mahatta Street, he contemplated another scenario: had the rich and poor neighborhoods of Jaffa not been so segregated, it would've made sense to venture into il Jabaliyyeh neighborhood where Khawaja Michael lived, and show him the fabulous eight-pound suit. But since showing his suit to both Shams and Khawaja Michael proved to be unattainable scenarios, Subhi opted to simply go home. There he would put his suit on, walk around the house like a model, show it to his loving mother, Khadijeh, and his paternal grandmother, Subhiyyeh, then hang it in his closet, give up the idea of taking a whole day off to celebrate his new suit, and proceed to fix more water pumps in the garage where he worked, though that was the very last thing Subhi wanted to do that day.

On his way home, Subhi passed by the Jewish Market, Suq il Yahud, one of the most popular and crowded fruit and vegetable markets in Jaffa, where his family and their neighbors shopped. Subhi's face lit up when he remembered how he had told Uncle Habeeb why it was called the Jewish Market: "My teacher told us that the market, which was built in 1928 between Jaffa and Tel Aviv, acquired such a name because Jews owned many of its shops. Or because many of its customers were Jewish since the *suq* was adjacent to Neve Tzedek," he'd said, naming the Jewish neighborhood to the east of il Manshiyyeh.

"What kind of school do you go to?!" yelled Uncle Habeeb. "And what kind of stupid teacher tells you such nonsense! Come with me and I'll show you what's Jewish about it: tell your dumb teacher it is called Suq il Yahud because it has Jewish prostitutes and not because it has Jewish merchants."

Subhi blushed as he contemplated the idea of accompanying his uncle to see the prostitutes in that market. Again, this was something Subhi wanted to do but did not dare do *yet*.

"One day I would like to go see them in your company, Uncle,"

Subhi added; too shy to utter the word "prostitutes," he opted to use the word "them."

"In my company, you *do* them, you do not *see* them. No one goes there to *see* a prostitute. What's wrong with you, Subhi?"

"My father would kill me if I went there."

"Your father would slaughter us both if I were to take my fifteen-year-old nephew to see, or do, the prostitutes. Hopefully in a year or two you'll have the courage and the urge to venture there on your own or with a friend your age. In any case, I'll tell you where to find the best one or two: go to the eastern section of the suq, the area closer to Neve Tzedek behind Yaakov's shop, and ask for Lea or Shoshanna. Either one of them will teach you all about life and pleasure. All I can tell you, my dear nephew, is that streets and bordellos are the real schools in life, not that stupid school you waste your time in. It is with the gangsters, the *ʒu'ran,* that you learn how to fight and how to protect your country. And it is with the prostitutes that you learn how to make love and peace with your enemy. Learn that from an early age: it is women who bring peace and pleasure to life."

Unlike most of his family members, especially his father, Subhi had a soft spot for Uncle Habeeb, partly because it was he who had stood by Subhi's side defending his decision to quit school in order to follow his passion as a mechanic. Subhi also hoped it would be Uncle Habeeb who would defend his choice to follow his heart and marry a young peasant girl. Though his uncle was often tipsy or drunk, Subhi appreciated his uncle's free spirit in not abiding by any rules, not beating around the bush, and saying things as they were right to people's faces. This of course upset many around Habeeb, especially his eldest brother, Ismael.

"I can't believe how an angel like my mother carried a devil like you for nine whole months. If she had known you would turn into a bum, she could've aborted you."

"Bite your tongue, Ismael. What a horrible thing to say," Subhi's grandmother Subhiyyeh would shout out, as she too had a soft spot for her son Habeeb. "A mother loves her children equally. Habeeb's only problem is his drinking; otherwise he has a heart of gold, pure gold."

"The drinking, and the smoking, and the whores, and the smuggling, and getting in trouble and endless fights, not to mention the rifle the British soldiers discovered under his bed, and God knows what else. And, yes, the hanky-panky, the *gala gala* with his Jewish and British 'friends' and . . . and . . . and . . ." Whenever Subhi's father, Ismael, got carried away, Habeeb, who was sixteen years his junior, left the scene, while their mother, Subhiyyeh, tried her best to either defend Habeeb or stop the argument all together.

WHATEVER THE RIGHT or wrong explanation was for its name, passing through Suq il Yahud made Subhi reflect on the increasing tensions, skirmishes, and fighting between Arabs and Jews in the last few months. Ever since the British had declared their intentions to end their mandate for Palestine and withdraw their forces within the year, most Jewish militant groups—Haganah, Etzel, and Lehi—had increased their attacks on places where Palestinians gathered: cafés, cinemas, and Arab neighborhoods bordering on Jewish settlements, such as Sakanet Abu Kbir in the north and Sakanet Darwish and Tell il Reish in the south, but also in the northeast parts of il Manshiyyeh neighborhood where Subhi's family lived.

Walking along il Mahatta Street, right next to the police station,

Subhi passed by the Islamic Sports Club, where he played football on Fridays. That was also where he had been given instructions on how to use a rifle. Subhi thought of the uneven British policy toward Jewish and Arab militias, which resulted in the superiority of the Zionist militias over those of the Arabs. While the British had allowed Zionist militants to join the Allied forces during World War II and had turned a blind eye to their smuggling weapons into Palestine, Palestinians got a two-year prison sentence if caught with a bullet, let alone a rifle or a hand grenade. This obviously deterred, but also demoralized, young men like Subhi. Nonetheless, Subhi, his brother Jamal, and many of his friends had joined the neighborhood militias organized by il Najjadeh Party. However, due to the scarcity of weapons and ammunitions, they got very little training.

Subhi had no clue as to why his mind had gone to such a dark place on such a happy occasion. He must have feared that the deteriorating political situation would be yet another obstacle delaying his marriage to Shams. How he wished to marry Shams right there and then.

Happy to have arrived home so as to distract himself from all that, in an upbeat voice Subhi called out to the two family members he expected to be home at midday: "Yamma . . . Sitti . . . Mom . . . Grandma, are you home?"

Instead, he got a husky voice: "Subhi, what has brought you home at this early hour of the day? Anything wrong?" asked Grandfather Ali, who often slept during the day and went fishing at night.

"Nothing wrong, Grandpa. I came to show Mother my new suit."

"What did you say?" *Khhhh . . . khhhh.* Loud snores were all that Subhi got in return from his half-deaf grandfather.

"Oh, I see you came back with your new suit. Didn't it need any alterations? How wonderful . . . try it on, try it on, let me see it on you," said Subhi's mother, Khadijeh, stepping out of the kitchen into the living room while holding the sheep intestine she was stuffing with minced meat and rice to make *karshat*.

"Ooh my favorite dish! Are you expecting guests?"

"What guests? We're celebrating your English suit . . . Go, Yamma, go and change. I can't wait to see you in that suit. If you were a few years older, I would find you an *'arous*, a bride. I already have one in mind for you."

Not wanting to engage in futile talk about the bride his mother had in mind, Subhi dashed into his bedroom and came back proud and tall but sweating. Only then did he realize that his English woolen suit was not exactly appropriate for Jaffa's heat and humidity during the summer months. However, for Shams's sake but also for the show-off tour he was planning around town, Subhi was prepared to suffer. Thinking of Shams made him sweat even more.

"*Habibi*, sweetheart. God bless you, son. You look like a bridegroom, like an *'arees*. Grow up and get married or lend your suit to your older brother, Jamal, who is getting married next summer."

"No way. This is my wedding suit."

"I hope so, son. Give yourself a few years. I have the most beautiful Jaffan bride for you." His mother was at it again.

"Why must she be from Jaffa?" Subhi was trying to insinuate to his mother that he might end up marrying a non-Jaffan woman.

"From where else, *habibi*? From Damascus or Beirut?"

"No, somewhere much closer."

"You're so handsome, near or far, old or young, women would die to marry you, son." Subhi's mother came up to him and kissed him between the eyes, then said, "OK, *habibi*, why don't you take your gorgeous suit off now and hide it somewhere? I bet you anything all your brothers and cousins, but also your father, will want to borrow it from you on special occasions."

"Over my dead body. I am not lending it to anyone, and I am not taking it off either. I am keeping it on for the rest of the day."

"For the whole day?" his mother asked as she and the tripe disappeared into the kitchen. "Don't be late. As you know, there has been much trouble and lots of shooting and explosions at night lately. People say that the British might re-impose curfews on Jaffa."

"For your sake but also for the *karshat,* I will be back for dinner by early evening."

"*Ya 'ars,* it's the *karshat,* not me, that will bring you home early!" his mother yelled back from her kitchen.

8

English Pride

SOMETHING ABOUT the English suit boosted Subhi's self-esteem as well as his confidence in a way he had never experienced before, not that he lacked either.

Is this how rich people like Khawaja Michael feel wearing their elegant suits: smart and sure of themselves? Subhi wondered as he once again recalled the way in which Khawaja Michael had pulled the shiny leather wallet out of his pocket and paid the eight pounds. *True, I am missing the wallet with the green and red notes, but with such an English suit, I am sure people will assume I have a wallet filled with colored notes.*

Feeling like an English gentleman, tall and proud, Subhi now understood why the British acted the way they did: arrogant and self-righteous. Subhi recalled the "political lecture" Uncle Habeeb gave whenever he got drunk, which happened more often than anyone would have liked. "Fuck the British, who gave Palestine to the Zionists. Had they, the British, not colonized the world and applied the *farreq tasud*, the separate and rule policy, the world would be a better place today. Trust me, the *Inglese* have no hearts. You think the people who sold millions of Africans to the two Americas would not sell us and our land to the devil? They already did. But it's us stupid Arabs that betrayed the Ottomans in favor of the *Inglese*. And what did we get in return? The Balfour Declaration! And who the fuck is that self-important nobody Lord Balfour to give away our country to new Jewish immigrants who arrived yesterday? I tell you, the British treat the world as a big bordello: they fuck us during the day and fuck the whores at night. I see them in Arab and Jewish bordellos all the time."

"Don't brag about your sins; you're worse than all of them put together." Ismael always had something nasty to say to his younger brother Habeeb. The last thing Subhi wanted that day was to obsess about the deteriorating political situation, or to talk politics, for that matter. It was the English suit and feeling confident that had stirred up all these emotions.

Subhi's head had finally cleared up. The only thing he wished to do was to enjoy his new look. So he decided to get on with his grand show-off tour around the city.

Subhi thought of places he knew, but also of places he did not know. He thought of all the upscale places on King George and in the new Nuzha neighborhood, which intimidated him and which he'd never had the courage to venture into. On his fingers he counted such places: the chic Café Venezia; the lobby of the InterContinental Hotel, where he hoped to encounter one of the many Arab celebrities—singers, actors, writers, and poets—who came to be interviewed by the Near East Broadcasting Station, il Sharq il Adna; and the prestigious il Hamra Cinema, all three located on King George Boulevard. He also thought about visiting the Orthodox Club, the football rival of his Islamic Sports Club, where poor Muslim boys like himself were not welcome or allowed in. Subhi wanted to go window-shopping along the glamorous Iskandar Awad Street and imagine his Shams in a white wedding dress. He also contemplated taking a stroll along the elegant streets of il 'Ajami and il Jabaliyyeh neighborhoods. True, as a mechanic, he had been to many of the fancy villas to fix all sorts of water pumps and engines, but always with greasy hands, dangling trousers, and a toolbox. Finally, if time permitted, he wanted to end his grand tour in the new Istiqlal Bookshop next to the new municipal building also on King George Boulevard. As much as he liked books, Subhi could never afford to buy them. Hence he often spent an hour reading them in or borrowing them from il Mahmoudiyyeh Library, where he went after Friday prayers or after Friday demonstrations. Though he'd quit school at an early age to become a mechanic, books were Subhi's companion and a third obsession (after Shams and machines).

For Subhi, the English suit felt more like a British passport that allowed him into forbidden places in his own city: places he saw from afar but never dared venture into. To enjoy his show-off tour to the fullest, Subhi needed to borrow a few pounds to add to the half pound given to him by Khawaja Michael. The first two people who came to mind were M'allem Mustafa and Uncle Habeeb. Subhi felt confident that his boss would lend him the money, partly because he liked him, but mostly because Subhi's skillfulness had gained him a good reputation as well as rich customers. "I'll be very sad if you leave me and go to work for someone else. Don't you do it, Subhi." M'allem Mustafa always praised Subhi to his face, and also raised his salary whenever he could—or as much as the unstable political situation and the war economy permitted.

Subhi was also sure that his uncle Habeeb would go out of his way and do the impossible to help him: "*Walawo ya zalameh*, of course, man. Even if I didn't have it, I'd lend it to you. If need be, I'd borrow it from the prostitutes. How much money do you need?"

Habeeb's response echoed in Subhi's ears even before he went to the port to find him at Cafe il Madfa', the Canon Café, where he spent early afternoons, way before alcohol and women took him to Tel Aviv for most of the night. Subhi's father, Ismael, had spread rumors that his brother Habeeb spent all his money on Rachel, a Jewish woman—"the whore," according to Ismael—for whom Habeeb rented an apartment in the Abu Khadra Building on the Jaffa–Tel Aviv Road. In spite of these rumors, nothing stopped Habeeb from lending a hand to family members and friends.

Having planned all this in his head, Subhi finally embarked on the grand city tour. He started it by walking along the narrow alley connecting his neighborhood, North Manshiyyeh, to Hassan Bek Street. Conscious of the way he looked, Subhi greeted not only everyone he knew but also everyone who stared at him trying to figure who he was.

"Is that *you*, gorgeous Subhi? God, what elegance! What's going on? Don't tell me you're getting married to someone else?" Um Zahra (Zahra's mother) yelled from her balcony on the first floor. She paused for a while in order to take in Subhi's aura, then added, "Oh, how I wish Zahra were out of school to see how stunning you look. Goodness, Subhi, why don't you come up and show your aunt your splendid suit?" Um Zahra stood on the edge of the balcony full of blooming bougainvillea, geraniums, and red roses. Though she had stopped pulling the laundry line hanging across the narrow alley, her body was still bent over the metal railing, causing her to almost lose her balance.

"Morning, Um Zahra," replied Subhi and walked away as fast as he could, avoiding any eye contact with his widowed neighbor.

As long as he lived, Subhi would never forgot how, only a few months earlier, Zahra's mother had taken him by the arm, pushed him against the kitchen wall, pressed her body against his, given him a French kiss, then touched his private parts. Shocked, but also aroused, Subhi went running out of her apartment with an erection, which he tried to cover with his hand and hide under his loose shirt. He ran down the stairs and out of the building to the street. Subhi did not sleep that night as he masturbated again and again until his older brother, Jamal, with whom he shared the bed, yelled at him, "Wake up, Subhi! Whom are you dreaming of?" Though Jamal knew it was not a dream, he didn't want to embarrass his younger brother.

Whenever Um Zahra visited Subhi's mother, she expressed her wish to have Subhi marry her daughter, Zahra, "*Inshallah*, God willing," Subhi's mother would respond. She pitied her neighbor, whose husband had been executed by British soldiers during the 1936 Revolt, leaving her with one-year-old Zahra. However, both Zahra's and Subhi's hearts were elsewhere.

Though very few cars passed through their narrow alley, Subhi heard one behind him. Allowing the car to pass, he stood against the wall, making sure his suit did not touch it. He waited for the car to pass, but somehow it did not. Subhi heard his friend Hani's flirtatious whistle before he saw his head come out of the driver's window.

"Goodness, is that you, Subhi? What the hell is going on? I saw you from a distance and wondered, What was such a stylish young man doing in our neighborhood? What is the occasion for such elegance? Don't tell me you're getting married at midday?"

"No, I'm not getting married at midday, or anytime soon. I was on my way to work. Might you give me a ride?"

"You mean to the garage in this suit? Or have you changed jobs lately? Come on, tell me the truth, Subhi. In any case, you're dash-ingly attractive. Get in the car and explain what is going on."

Subhi went around the car, pulled down his jacket, and slipped into the passenger's seat. He made sure to sit up straight so as not to wrinkle the suit.

"What a disappointment. I thought I had gotten lucky today," Hani said.

"Lucky?" responded Subhi, not knowing what "getting lucky" meant.

"What's wrong with you? *Ya ʒalameh,* come on, man. Do I have to explain everything to you?" There was a bit of silence before Hani lamented, "I truly hoped it was a *khawal,* a gay man, who had purposely gotten lost in our neighborhood. You know, many rich gay men desire poor boys like us. What a pity. It would've been a good catch."

"A good catch! What do you mean by a good catch?"

"*Khalas . . . Khalas . . .* Stop it . . . Stop it. I don't want to discuss it any further. You're either stupid or too innocent. I'd better take you to your garage to fix more engines and smear your suit with grease. That's all that interests you in life. I've known that was your only passion since you dismantled my bike into fifty-three pieces." Engines were indeed Subhi's passion, but certainly not the only one, at least not today.

As they were driving along il Mahatta Street, Subhi spotted Sabunjian Photo Studio. Since he did not expect to see Shams before mid-August when Mawsim il Nabi Rubin started, Subhi thought of an alternative: *Why don't I step into Sabunjian Studio, have my photo taken in my English suit, and send it to Shams?* How and with whom to send the photo, he would have to figure out later.

"Actually, can you drop me off at Sabunjian Studio? I want to have my photo taken."

"Now we're talking. That makes more sense than taking you to the garage in such a splendid suit."

"Thank you so much, Hani." As he got out of the car, Subhi recalled how Hani had been called a *bannouteh*, effeminate, by all around him since he was a little kid. A bit hesitant, Subhi stuck his head into the car window and said, "Get lucky, Hani."

"You too, Subhi." And they both giggled as they parted.

Walking toward the photo studio, Subhi wondered whether his suit would arouse in Shams the same desires it had so far aroused in a widowed woman and a gay man.

9

A Suit Etched on Paper

ENTHUSIASTICALLY, Subhi stepped into the photo studio and greeted Mr. Rafi Sabunjian, the Armenian photographer, who addressed Subhi by the wrong gender as all Armenians did when they spoke Arabic. This made Subhi smile but also reminded him how insulted he'd been the first time an Armenian customer had addressed him using *inti*, the feminine version of "you" in Arabic, rather than *inta*, the masculine version.

"Do I look like a girl to you? Have you ever seen a woman working as a mechanic in a garage?" After the customer apologized to Subhi and also explained how the Armenian language makes no gender distinction, they became friends and began joking about it. Subhi started addressing his male Armenian customers with the feminine pronoun *inti*. Now, to break the ice, Subhi had addressed Mr. Sabunjian using *inti*, which upset the photographer since he thought Subhi was making fun of his accent. Once more addressing Subhi as "she," Rafi objected, "When you speak Armenian the way I speak Arabic, then you can make fun of my Arabic accent."

"I am truly sorry, Mr. Sabunjian. I did not mean to upset you."

"OK, then let's get down to business. Tell me what you want."

"I want you to kindly take my photo." Subhi was trying to be overly polite to improve the tense atmosphere resulting from his bad joke.

"How many poses and how many copies of each? Also, do you want them in black-and-white or hand colored?"

"One black-and-white copy," Subhi said, fearing the price. Then he changed his mind. "Actually, can I have two hand-colored copies of the same pose?" One for Shams, and one for himself to remember this memorable day.

"That will be a total of thirty piastres." Though thirty piastres was what Subhi made for a whole day's work, he agreed right away.

"OK, fine. Let's do it, then."

"There is a mirror and a comb in the back room. Go get yourself ready." Not familiar with these pre-photo preparations, Subhi thought there must be something wrong with the haircut he'd had that very morning.

"OK, I'll go back and fix my hair, but when will my photo be ready?"

"Tomorrow afternoon."

Subhi was happy to have a long mirror in which he could try to see what it was about his appearance that had aroused both Um Zahra and Hani.

"What kind of a background do you want?" asked the photographer. "Here we have a sea view, Versailles Palace, Istanbul, and London's Big Ben."

Though Subhi had not visited any one of these places, he chose Istanbul.

"Standing up or sitting on a chair, or in an armchair?"

"Standing up, of course," Subhi replied, with no hesitation.

"As you like, though most people prefer to be seated, especially families."

"I promise to come back with my future wife and my kids, hopefully soon."

"Are you engaged?"

"Sort of!"

"What does that mean?"

While Subhi searched for the right response, Rafi disappeared under a dark blanket.

"Stand still. Don't move. Smile," came Rafi's instructions from under the blanket before he blinded Subhi by pressing the flash twice.

Subhi came out of the studio feeling quite pleased. The pleasure of having his English suit immortalized in a photograph made him reconsider the idea of looking for Khawaja Michael to thank him for his generosity. And also to show him how different he, Subhi, looked in the suit. Short of appearing on the doorstep of Villa Michael in the rich Jabaliyyeh neighborhood, Subhi considered passing by Café il Inshirah on il Mahatta Street, where many of Jaffa's *khawajat,* political figures, and intellectuals gathered, or Café Dawoud, located farther down the street in il Salahi Market, where most of the orange merchants gathered for their morning coffee and business dealings. But he should probably wait until he secured a few more pounds to pay for the delicious patisserie and ice cream he often saw but couldn't afford in the upscale coffee shops he intended to visit in the afternoon. He also needed the extra pounds for the Egyptian movie he planned to see in the luxurious il Hamra Cinema on King George Boulevard, instead of going to the modest Nabil Cinema where he often went with his friends.

Having considered the pros and cons, Subhi made up his mind:

he would borrow the extra pounds from Uncle Habeeb instead of M'allem Mustafa. He'd rather be indebted to a family member than to his employer. The truth of the matter was that Subhi was not sure how his boss would react to his having accepted such a gift from a client. The last thing Subhi wanted was to take the risk of spoiling the day with jealousy, an unnecessary guilt trip, or even worse: a lesson in morality.

Subhi looked at his watch before proceeding to the port, specifically to the sailors' café, Café il Madfa', where he expected to find Uncle Habeeb. A smile came to Subhi's face when he recalled the way in which his father described the whereabouts of his younger brother whenever asked: "Oh yes, my 'pious' brother, who observes the five prayers: with morning prayers, *salat il fajr*, he's back from Tel Aviv's bars and nightclubs, then he's fast asleep until midday prayers, *salat il dohor*. With afternoon prayers, *salat il 'aser*, you'll find him on the port gambling with the sailors and fishermen at Café il Madfa', while with sunset prayers, *salat il maghreb*, you'll find him getting drunk at Café Lawrence on the Jaffa–Tel Aviv Road. Between evening prayers, *salat il isha*, and midnight, you'll find him in the arms of a slut or a whore on Chelouche Street. That's where you'll find my pious brother." Since it was early afternoon, Subhi expected to find his uncle at Café il Madfa' or somewhere around the port.

Subhi was intrigued by the way in which his father, Ismael, criticized his brother's daily activities by setting them between prayer times. Ismael not only expressed disapproval of Habeeb's way of life but also stressed how pious he was himself. Subhi was also intrigued by the cool way in which Uncle Habeeb responded to his brother's frequent insults and accusations: "Sultan Abdul Hamid II is turning in his grave realizing how backward you still are, using the five prayers rather than the huge clock tower he installed for you in the very center of town. He did that not only in Jaffa but also in Jerusalem, Acre, Nablus, Beirut, and Damascus. Poor Ottoman sultan, he tried his best to modernize people like you, but *'al fadhi,* in vain."

The one thing Subhi's father purposely failed to mention was that Habeeb often went to the port to work. He worked as a laborer on the small boats that transported oranges from the port to the big ships anchored a kilometer or two away. The big ships could not dock in Jaffa's port due to its shallow and rocky nature. Like his father, Ali, Habeeb was a good fisherman. He often ventured into the sea and more often than not came back with all sorts of fish— sea bass, sea bream, red mullet, *mushut, bouri, maleeten*—which he shared not only with family members but also with his friends at the port. Unlike Subhi's father, Habeeb loved and identified with the sea, with the fishermen and the sailors, rather than with the land and the orange groves. Like many of Jaffa's sailors, Habeeb took pride in the fact that it was the sailors' union rather than the Orange Merchant Council that had sponsored Umm Kulthum's trip to Palestine and her concerts not only in Jaffa but also in other cities in Palestine.

As Subhi walked along the elegant Bustrus Street, he reflected on how different his father and his uncle were in every aspect of their lives and characters. While his father was serious, grumpy, and conservative, Uncle Habeeb was a fun-loving, vivacious guy. The two brothers also differed in their politics. Like most merchants, especially rich orange merchants, Subhi's father supported the moderate il Difa' Party (the opposition) headed by the Jerusalem-based Nashashibi family, who allied themselves with King Abdullah of Jordan. Meanwhile, Habeeb and other fishermen supported the Majlisioun, or the Palestinian Arab Party of Haj Amin Al Husseini, who adopted a more confrontational policy against both the Zionist militias and the British army. And accordingly, Habeeb also supported il Jihad il Muqaddas, the holy struggle organization headed by Abdel Qader il Husseini, which was the militant arm of the Palestinian Arab Party headed by Jamal Husseini. The conflict between the il Difa' Party and the Palestinian Arab Party or between the two Jerusalemite families—the Nashashibies and the Husseinis—exemplified their positions concerning the 1936 Revolt and the general strike that lasted for six months. While the Nashashibi Difa' Party called for the end of the strike, Haj Amin Al Husseini supported the open strike. In order not to take sides, Subhi, like many young members of the Islamic Sports Club, joined the Jaffa-based il Najjadeh organization, headed by Mohammad Nimer il Hawwari. Under the pretext of its sports activities, the Islamic Sports Club, or il Najjadeh, began to secretly train youngsters like Subhi on using weapons in order to protect or defend their neighborhoods, and later their city, from the increasing attacks by the Zionist underground militias, especially Haganah and Lehi.

On his way to the port, Subhi strolled along the fashionable Bustros Street. There he went on a window-shopping spree. Not having the means to buy any of the fancy dresses he saw on display did not stop him from gathering the fanciest of trousseaus for his future bride in his imagination.

10

From the Fools' Café to the Intellectuals' Café and that of the Fishermen

B EFORE HE WENT to borrow the extra pounds from Uncle
Habeeb, and much before he ventured into the upscale cafés
and il Hamra Cinema, Subhi thought he'd get reactions to his suit
from his friends and acquaintances at his café, Café il Tious, known
as the Fools' Café, owned by two identical brothers, Isa and Musa.
Confusing the two brothers was a major source of entertainment for
the café's customers and also the two owners.

"You must've asked my brother," one of the owners said whenever he was late delivering a cup of coffee or an *arghileh*, a hubbly bubbly. Though identical, the brothers had one slight difference
between them: either Isa or Musa was cross-eyed. Whenever he
poured coffee or tea into the small cups—and that was hundreds of
times a day—the customers would scream and jump back, thinking
that it was about to spill on them. No one seemed to know, or care
to know, if the Fools' Café's name was in reference to its identical
owners or to its poor and underprivileged clientele. Whatever the
reason, the name was another source of entertainment for both.

The Fools' Café was where Subhi and his *shilleh*, his clique, met after work or later in the evenings. For hours on end, they played cards or backgammon while engulfed by *arghileh* smoke. Being one of the cheapest and most modest cafés in town, the Fools' Café was also where Egyptian migrants from il 'Arish, Syrian laborers from Hawran, and Palestinian workers from Gaza and the nearby villages gathered. Echoing the ethnic divisions of most old cities, the Fools' Café was divided into four areas, one for each ethnic group, each distinguished by its accents and traditional garb.

The minute Subhi approached the sidewalk outside the café, where day workers sat on low chairs smoking *araghil,* Subhi heard the voice of the Egyptian diva Umm Kulthum coming out of the brass gramophone placed on a heavy wooden table next to the entrance. Next to the gramophone were a number of dusty LPs of other Egyptian singers, like il Sayed Darwish, Mohammed Abdel Wahab, Laila Mourad, and the Syrian singer Asmahan, and the Lebanese singer Sabah. Since most of the LPs were scratched, it was enough to run one LP for the whole day. And since there were more Egyptian workers than Hawranis, Gazans, or Palestinian villagers, Egyptian voices prevailed not only in the Fools' Café but in Jaffa's poor neighborhoods as well. This had been the case since 1832, when Ibrahim Pasha of Egypt conquered Palestine. Though he was defeated and escaped back to Egypt in 1841, many of his soldiers stayed behind and built residential areas outside the city walls. Some of these neighborhoods included il Rashidiyyeh, il Manshiyyeh, and Sakanet Abu Kbir to the north, and also some smaller housing areas such as Sakanet Darwish to the east, all of which were named after the Egyptian workers' hometowns. Such impoverished neighborhoods sprung up mostly on the outskirts of the city. And although most residents worked as day laborers in citrus-related industries, some worked in construction and services.

"Come on in, come on in, Khawaja," one of the twin brothers excitedly welcomed Subhi, who he thought was a rich new customer.

"And who are you? Musa or Isa?" inquired Subhi playfully as he always did whenever he arrived at his café. Subhi's joke made one of the twin owners stare closely at Subhi, let out a high-pitched laugh, then yell, "Goddamn, is that you, Subhi? What on earth is going on? I swear to God I didn't recognize you."

"Neither did I recognize you; are you Musa or Isa?" Subhi repeated, giggling.

"You almost fooled me. I thought it was a real *khawaja* who by mistake came to our café rather than to Café il Inshirah."

Musa's remark thrilled Subhi and made him think he might be mistaken for a real *khawaja* after all. Subhi was still worried that he would stand out among the intellectuals and rich merchants who frequented Café il Inshirah.

"That's where I'll be going next, Musa," Subhi told the owner, but also all the other customers who were by now following the conversation.

"First of all, I am Isa and not Musa, and second, only fools pay four piastres for a cup of coffee when they can pay one piastre in my café."

"But it's your café that is called the Fools' Café, not il Inshirah," Subhi teased him.

"We're called the Fools' Café only because of customers like you, Subhi. By the way, I am Musa and not Isa," responded one of the twin brothers as he burst into loud laughter and then asked, "Do you still like your Turkish coffee sweet or have your tastes changed along with your looks?"

"Yes, sweet, very sweet. True, I have acquired an English suit, but I have not acquired the taste of an English lord *yet*. Only real *khawajat* like their coffee bitter."

"Four piastres for a cup of coffee with no sugar, what a shame!" commented Musa or Isa and disappeared into the kitchen to make "Khawaja Subhi" his sweet cup of coffee.

Though it did not take long for Isa or Musa to appear with a round brass tray with a matching coffeepot, a glass of water, and a small white porcelain cup, he had to force his way through a crowd of workers who had gathered around Subhi to express their admiration for his English suit. Having been touched more times than he would have liked, and also fearing that the men's rough and dirty hands might stain his suit, Subhi decided to perform a fashion show. He stood up from his chair and, like a model, walked a few steps and then spun around.

"*Ya 'ein, ya 'ein,* wow, look at that!" yelled the crowd in awe and amazement.

While Subhi's new looks made him stand out among the fools at his café, the last thing he wanted was to stand out at Café il Inshirah, where he was heading next and where he hoped to find Khawaja Michael. In the hopes of encountering Khawaja Michael, Subhi also contemplated walking past Café Dawoud, known as the Orange Merchants Café, located farther down the road on il Salahi Street. Or if need be, he might even venture up Iskandar Awad Street in the direction of Ehmaid Café on the posh 'Ajami Road just before the Government Hospital. These two cafés stood at opposite ends of the spectrum of social groupings, and reflected the deep socioeconomic divisions in Jaffa's society.

Café il Inshirah

The Intellectuals' Café

I F THERE WAS one place in Jaffa that intimidated Subhi, it was
Café il Inshirah. That was where most of Jaffa's intellectuals,
well-to-do merchants, and politicians, including members of the
municipal council, gathered.

Subhi was keen on meeting, in person, some of the journalists
who wrote for the numerous daily papers published in Jaffa, especially *il Falastin* and *il Difa'*, the two he often read. Subhi was also
keen to encounter some of Jaffa's political figures. He wanted to
hear firsthand what those men predicted for the future of their city,
and what that might mean for his future with Shams.

Now that the British government had declared its intention to
end its mandate for Palestine in a few months, Subhi, like many,
feared that the Jaffans would be left to hold their ground against
the highly equipped Zionist militias in Tel Aviv and the surrounding Jewish settlements. But also like many, Subhi objected to the
Partition Plan proposed by the British to the UN Council. It meant
giving half of Palestine to the Jewish immigrants, a plan that he,

his father, and his grandfather had been trying to stop, without success. Though Jaffa—the richest and largest Arab city in Palestine, with a population of a hundred thousand—was designated part of the Arab State, the Jaffans still feared for their future. The arguments about how to safeguard and protect Jaffa from the increasing skirmishes and vicious attacks varied. Some argued that the Zionist forces would concentrate their attacks on Palestinian towns and villages in areas designated as a Jewish State. Others argued that one should never trust the intentions of the expansionist Zionist movement: "*Il sahayyneh* will take what is designated for them and go after what is designated for us Palestinians," Subhi's grandfather Ali often said.

As Subhi was recalling his grandfather's words, he came face-to-face with one of Café il Inshirah's waiters. While the Fools' Café had identical owners who served their customers, Café il Inshirah had many waiters, all dressed in white shirts and black trousers. And by the time Subhi had settled in at one of the small round tables made of Italian white Carrara marble, a tall and elegant waiter had appeared next to him with a menu. Wondering why the waiter had handed him a book with a brown leather jacket, Subhi opened it, and read the list of incredible choices and outrageous prices. The words of Musa or Isa played in his head—"Only fools pay four piastres for a cup of coffee when they can pay one piastre in my café"—as he looked at the price that was in fact double that. Eight piastres was the minimum that Subhi must spend in order to wait for Khawaja Michael to appear, assuming that he would.

Having passed as one of many who wore elegant suits, Subhi was instantly drawn into the heated discussions around him.

"The mayor of Jaffa should simply meet with the mayor of Tel Aviv and sign the Non-Aggression Pact."

"Trust me, escalating our attacks on Jewish settlements and neighborhoods would be the biggest mistake; we're not up to their military superiority."

"The British not only helped them smuggle in the most sophisticated weapons but also allowed them to join the Allied forces."

"The Jewish military pressure is increasing by the day. They're going to attack Jaffa before the British army withdraws, mark my words."

"Not only that, they're going to blow up Jaffa and drive us all out."

"Stop it, men. It's rumors like these that are demoralizing the inhabitants of Jaffa. Every single day, I meet people who, out of fear from such rumors, want to leave the city."

"Fear of what? Believe me, the Jews are cowards and stand no chance of conquering Jaffa."

"Nonetheless, we should be ready to defend ourselves. We must purchase more arms. We should also call on the Arab State to send its armies before it's too late."

"Like it or not, there is no way out of this: we must go on an open strike against the Partition Plan."

Not again, Subhi thought, since he'd grown up hearing the two arguments at home. His father was utterly against the open strike, and Uncle Habeeb was for it. The two men disagreed not only about history and the pros and cons of the six-month strike in 1936 but also about the present one, both of which had been called for by il Mufti Haj Amin Al Husseini and his Palestinian Arab Party.

"Whom are we striking against and whom are we hurting? Whose economy is being hurt: theirs or ours? No doubt, our economy is suffering, while the Zionists' economy is booming."

"For God's sake, what have we achieved by striking except destroying the exports and imports from Jaffa Port? Don't you all recall our stupid decision to forbid the Jews from using Jaffa Port, which made the British approve the construction of a Jewish port in Tel Aviv? They ended up taking all the business from us."

"Did you expect the Jewish merchants to wait for three years until your strike ended? Of course they went ahead and built their own port and stole the show from us."

"What do you want us to do? Stand still and watch the Jewish immigrants land in our port and settle our land? We have no choice but to confront them."

"Confront them in an intelligent way, not in a way that harms us."

"You tell me how. We say an open strike, you say no. We say resist with arms, you say no. We say attack them, you say no. How on earth are we to stop them from taking our country?"

"All I can tell you is that Haj Amin Al Husseini's call for an open strike ended up destroying our economy eleven years ago and it will destroy our economy now. It was wrong then, and it is wrong today: we should not escalate with the Jews. On the contrary, we should listen to Mayor Haikal and Mohammad Nimer il Hawwari and go meet with the mayor of Tel Aviv and sign the Non-Aggression Pact."

"Even if we sign that damn agreement, and even if Jaffa is designated as part of the Arab State, trust me, the Jews will not leave us alone. It is no secret that Menachem Begin, the head of the Haganah forces, wants to get rid of what they call 'the Arab enclave.' We are in a sea of Jews, in case you haven't noticed."

"It is *they* who came and settled around us and not *us* who came and settled among them. We have no option but to fight back."

"Fight back with what? With our bare hands?"

"That's why we should buy weapons."

"Buy weapons from where? Excuse me, but you talk like an idiot."

Listening to the heated discussions and different points of view, Subhi noted that the comments were coming from two opposite corners of the café. While his café was spatially divided among four different ethnic groups, this café was divided along party lines. Those who supported the Grand Mufti of Jerusalem Haj Amin Al Husseini and his Palestinian Arab Party were sitting to his right, while those who supported Mayor Haikal and the Difa' Party, the Nashashibi Opposition Party, and il Najjadeh of Mohammad Nimer il Hawwari were sitting to his left.

"Here is your coffee, young man," said the waiter as he placed a white porcelain cup with a gold rim, two biscuits on a matching plate, and a bill for eight piastres on Subhi's table.

"Excuse me, sir, do you happen to know Khawaja Michael? Is he by any chance one of your customers? Do you know where I might find him?"

"*Walawo!* Of course! Who doesn't know Khawaja Michael? But since he is a rich orange merchant, you'll probably find him at Café Dawoud in il Salahi Market. You know where that is, don't you?"

"Of course I do. I've never been to Café Dawoud, but I'll find it."

"I've never seen you here before, sir. Are you visiting the city?"

Flattered to be addressed as "sir," Subhi responded with a smile, "Yes, it's my first time here."

Having sipped his coffee slowly and nibbled on the biscuit, he placed his most precious eight piastres on the table and left the scene. "This for sure will become my café if I ever become rich, not only in appearance but also for real—soon, I hope," mumbled Subhi to himself.

Having spent eight piastres, Subhi knew he had to pass by his uncle's café on the port before venturing into even more expensive places such as Café Dawoud in search of Khawaja Michael. He also wondered how wealthy these people must be to be able to afford spending hours on end drinking and eating in such places.

Contrary to what Subhi thought, in spite of its late-nineteenth-century boom in the orange industry and because of its interrupted history, Jaffa had never had a feudal aristocracy. In reality, many of Jaffa's wealthy families had come from other cities such as Beirut, Damascus, Aleppo, Nablus, and Jerusalem. The largest orange grove in Jaffa, with an area of one thousand dunams, belonged to Haj Abdelghani il Nabulsi, who, as his name indicated, came from the city of Nablus. The same was true of the rich Bustros and 'Araqtinji families who arrived from Beirut. Jaffa also had small Armenian, Italian, and Greek communities, as well as a native Jewish community in the Old City and northern parts of il Manshiyyeh.

By the time Subhi arrived at the Clock Tower Square, he noticed that he had become accustomed to wearing a suit. Having been accepted in the prestigious Café il Inshirah gave Subhi the confidence he needed to carry on with his grand tour of his city.

12

From Boyhood to Manhood

I T WAS UNCLE HABEEB who first spotted the handsome young man in a suit. Excited, he dropped his cards on the table, stood up, and whistled as he realized that the man was his nephew.

"What on earth is going on, Subhi? Are you getting married behind our backs?"

The eyes of the sailors and fishermen were fixed on Subhi first, then went back and forth between him and his uncle.

"With your blessing and help, perhaps I could marry soon, Uncle."

"Seriously, what is up, Subhi? Sit down, let's talk." Habeeb pulled up a chair for Subhi while the other three card players paused in their game.

"Come on, let me offer you a cup of coffee. M'allem Atta, get Khawaja Subhi the sweetest cup of coffee." Thrilled to be addressed as "Khawaja" for the second time on his tour, Subhi broke into a big smile. He pulled his chair closer to Uncle Habeeb and whispered, "Uncle, I'll tell you all about the suit once we're home, but first I need to borrow some money from you—"

Before he had finished explaining, Uncle Habeeb responded, "Sure, how much?" He stood up from his chair and pulled some green notes and coins out of his pocket.

"Two or three pounds if possible," Subhi answered hesitantly.

"Here are four, but first I need to know what you are up to, Subhi."

"Can't you see? I am celebrating my new English suit. I am going on a ground tour to enjoy the city and do all I have not done in my life so far. I want to go to Café Venezia and the Hotel InterContinental and see a film at il Hamra Cinema."

"And you call this enjoying the city! Come with me to Chelouche Street in Tel Aviv and I'll show you what enjoying the city means."

"Why take him all the way to Tel Aviv? Take him to Nijmeh in the Old City," said one of the fishermen with a laugh.

"Jews are better and more skillful in everything they do, including *il sharmatah,* prostitution," replied Habeeb at the top of his voice, bursting into louder laughter. Subhi blushed listening to the conversation between his uncle and the other men as they bragged about their adventures.

"Take him to Abu Shalhoub. He has not only the best *sharameet* in town but also the best prices."

"I've tried them all . . . no one is as good as Shoshanna. The Abu Shalhoub *sharameet* just want to get it over with: no playing around, no foreplay, no fun. Tick . . . tock . . . and they're done."

"It is you, Habeeb, who is ticktock and done, not the poor women!"

"Come on, man, you know what I mean. They are in a hurry for another *zboun,* client. It feels like you're standing in a production line. Shoshanna takes her time and gives you everything you need to enjoy yourself."

"I agree with Habeeb. The Abu Shalhoub girls do it as if they are on duty or have homework to finish. They don't take their time to please you."

"Man, I tell you, every sin and evil was brought to us by the fucking *Inglese* and il Yahud, including *il sharameet*."

"You must be kidding. You obviously don't know your history, or worse, the history of your city. Prostitution has been here since eternity, before the Jews and before the Philistines arrived in this land."

"The kingdom of prostitution was the first kingdom in Palestine."

"You mean the *empire* of prostitution."

"Yes, an empire that preceded the Roman Empire."

"Ask your father and he'll tell you that the first licensed brothels were established in the Old City of Jaffa and later in il Manshiyyeh. It was only during the British Mandate that they were moved north to the Jaffa–Tel Aviv Road, to Neve Shalom and other Jewish neighborhoods."

A chubby middle-aged fisherman drew close to Subhi and took him by the hand. "Listen to me, my son. I am the oldest of them all, and I know better. The cheapest whore in town is *'arous il lail*, the night's bride. Ask your grandfather Ali. He knows. Just walk in the narrow alleys of the Old City late at night and one of the *'arusat il lail* will appear before you from one corner or another. You pick and choose for nothing."

"For nothing! Stop that nonsense. *'Arous il lail* will give him syphilis!" yelled Habeeb at the top of his voice.

"*'Arous il lail?* What on earth is *'arous il lail*, Uncle?" Subhi inquired, totally confused.

"*'Arous il lail* are beautiful young women dressed in white garments who appear late at night. They grab men by the arm, flirt with them, and try to seduce them in the hopes of marrying them. However, if a man resists their temptation, they will build stone walls to prevent his escape. They then kidnap him and keep him for hours before releasing him. Arriving home late, men in Jaffa always had a good excuse, for even their wives were aware of the existence and the bad behavior of *'arous il lail*."

"Goodness, Uncle, do you always talk so openly with your friends?"

"Yes, *habibi*, we're fishermen and sailors, not orange growers or nuns! You'll soon learn that playing with prostitutes is the best part of living in Jaffa and Tel Aviv. Wait until you see and do Shoshanna. She will teach you all you need to know about sex and much more."

"Yes . . . and the 'much more' is the best hashish in town," joked one of the three card players around the table, who was smoking hash himself.

"Really?" asked Subhi. With his dropped jaw, Subhi sat there listening to everything the sailors and fishermen had to say on the subject.

Realizing how innocent and sheltered his young nephew was, Habeeb put his arm around Subhi's shoulder and said, "Come on, nephew. Let's go for a walk on the port and discuss life matters in privacy." Subhi wondered how much more private one could be after all that Habeeb and the fishermen had said. Nonetheless, Habeeb's request pleased him. He found in it a chance to tell his uncle all about Shams in hopes Habeeb could help him convince his father and the elderly men and women of his family to approve his marriage to her. After all he had just heard about the nightlife in the city, Subhi wanted to inquire what it meant to go to a brothel for release when he was in love with Shams.

"Nephew, God created brothels not only for release—this you

can do on your own—but to learn how to enjoy sex for the sake of sex, with no responsibility, no emotional attachment, no fear of getting a woman pregnant, nothing but pure sex: no love and no nonsense. Not only to enter a woman, pump her a few times, and ejaculate in five minutes but to take your time to play around, to experiment with all sorts of positions. Don't be shocked if she, Shoshanna, gets on top of you and not the other way around. You and she will take turns. You can ride her once, then she will ride you. But to do this, nephew, you'll have to drink a beer or two to loosen up and get rid of your shyness."

"But what about Shams?"

"Who is Shams? And what about her?"

"Shams is the love of my life. She is a gorgeous girl from Salameh."

"Shoshanna will teach you not only how to enjoy sex but also how to please your future wife."

"Really?"

"Trust me, Shoshanna is going to teach you how to please that peasant girl. You know villagers are timid, and you need to learn how to make them lose their frigidity."

Not knowing what "frigidity" meant, Subhi decided to leave it at that as he felt he had heard more about sex today than he could handle.

"One last question, Uncle."

"What is it?"

Embarrassed, but also hesitant to share his thoughts with his uncle, Subhi kept quiet but smiled.

"Come on, ask me."

"Why are fishermen and sailors called *ashawes,* heroes, when all they do is fuck or talk about prostitutes?"

"Trust me, nephew, it takes more courage to fuck a prostitute than to face a Jewish militant or a British soldier. Look at you trembling about the idea of going to a whorehouse. Anyway, it was Al Mufti Haj Amin Al Husseini, not us, who called the fishermen of Jaffa *il ashawes*. We are heroes because we were the ones who discovered that many of the ships that brought Jewish immigrants to settle in our land smuggled weapons for the Zionist militia. It is also because all of Jaffa's revolts have started from this port, then spread out to other parts of Palestine. It is from this very port that all demonstrations against the British and the Zionists began." Though his uncle was a fun-loving man, Subhi was not surprised that Habeeb was one of these *ashawes*.

Leaving the port and the sea behind him, Subhi understood for the first time how different sea culture was from inland culture. He finally understood that if he wanted to be one of the *ashawes*, he must go and face Shoshanna.

"OK, Subhi. I have a round of cards to finish. Go enjoy the town your way for an hour or two, but then meet me at Café Lawrence on the Jaffa–Tel Aviv road for a couple of beers before I take you to Shoshanna, who will show you what enjoyment and pleasure mean."

Reflecting on all he had heard and learned that day, Subhi felt as if the English suit was transforming him from a boy to a man.

13

At the Brothel

S UBHI'S LEGS TREMBLED and his heart skipped a beat as he followed Uncle Habeeb up the narrow stairs. For some reason, he had a flashback to his first day of school some ten years before, when his father took him by the hand and left him with Miss Amira, whom he would adore for the rest of his life. Uncle Habeeb's knock at the brothel door brought Subhi back to the present moment.

In no time, a striking Neapolitan-looking woman appeared at the door. Everything about her was abundant: her hips, her thighs, her black hair pulled back into a chignon, her big eyes accentuated by thick lines of kohl, and her voluptuous lips highlighted by red lipstick. She welcomed Habeeb as if he were a long-lost cousin, addressing him in a deep, sensuous voice. *"Akhlan wa sakhlan,* welcome *khabibi Khabeeb,* you are most welcome, dear Khabeeb. Come in, come in."

Despite his feelings of panic, Subhi could not help but smile as he heard her pronounce the four h's in those words with a *kh* sound, the way most Ashkenazi Jews do when they speak Arabic.

Subhi worriedly examined her size, thinking she was the legendary Shoshanna. But to his relief, he soon figured out that she was the brothel's *qahramaneh,* or madam. Five younger women sat behind her. One in particular drew Subhi's attention: a blonde who had turned her wooden chair around and sat on it with her legs open and her arms on its back.

"Lea, this is my nephew Subhi. It's his first time in a brothel, so tell Shoshanna to take care of him but also take it easy on him."

"What about you, Habeeb?"

"I'll come back later tonight. I want my nephew to feel at home without me around."

"First time, ha. I can take care of him," said the young blond woman, who had noticed the spellbound glance Subhi had cast at her when he first came in.

"Mind your own business, Rochelle," replied Lea. "Sit down, young man. Shoshanna will be with you in a moment."

Like a good student, Subhi sat on a chair and waited for what seemed like the longest and most awkward moment of his life.

"There she is," said Lea as a tall, thin, olive-complexioned woman appeared. The décolleté of her purple dress accentuated an ample bosom.

"Shoshanna, this handsome boy is Habeeb's nephew. Habeeb wants you to teach him a few things."

"That shouldn't be difficult. Come with me, young man," said Shoshanna, extending her hand to Subhi, who was too shy to take it but followed her meekly through the narrow corridor to her room.

"So I hear it's your first time in a brothel," she said as she closed the door behind her.

"Yes."

"Still a virgin, I presume?"

"Yes," Subhi replied, though he had not realized that the word or concept of "virgin" applied to boys as well as girls.

"Are you scared?" she asked, almost whispering in his ear.

"A bit."

"Come closer and tell me what is it that scares you." By now she had taken off her purple dress and was standing next to her king-size bed.

"Don't know," he said, blushing.

"How does that feel?" Shoshanna asked Subhi as she placed her hand on his private parts, rubbing them softly while pressing her protruding bosom against his chest. She grasped his penis firmly, and suddenly her lips were on Subhi's.

"See, there is nothing to fear or feel shy about. Here, feel my breasts, squeeze them." She got them out of her bra and placed Subhi's palms on them. "That feels good, doesn't it?"

Absolutely, thought Subhi. By that time, his dick was pushing against his trousers.

"Let's free that nice bird from its prison before it breaks," Shoshanna joked as she went down on her knees.

Is she going to help me unzip my trousers? Subhi wondered. He reached out and unzipped them himself.

"Come on, sweetheart. Let's get rid of those."

Though totally aroused, Subhi didn't want to wrinkle his suit by dropping his trousers on the floor.

"Take off your trousers and your underwear."

He dropped both.

"Relax, take your time, enjoy, and hold on. Do not ejaculate quickly. The longer it lasts, the more satisfying and fun it'll be. That's what women like: men who can hold themselves. You understand?" Shoshanna instructed Subhi before she grabbed his member and stuck it in her mouth.

Lost in lust, Subhi moaned and moaned before he had an orgasm.

Up off her knees, Shoshanna laid on the bed on her back.

"Strip naked and come lie down next to Shoshanna."

Subhi threw his jacket recklessly on the floor and followed her instructions.

"Come closer." She gave him a French kiss that totally took his breath away but got him going again, and the next thing he knew, she was on top of him.

"If you want a third round, you can now come on top of me."

He did.

It was after the third round that Subhi realized that one can actually feel "full of sex" to a point where one does not ask for more.

"Next time you come to me, we'll play other games."

Worried about the cost of such great pleasures, Subhi reached for his wallet and asked, "How much?"

"Your uncle has already paid for you. Hope you liked our services. Come back soon."

"I for sure will," Subhi replied, reflecting on the word "services."

14

Mawsim il Nabi Rubin

(August–September 1947)

S UBHI COULD NOT SLEEP that night. Like a broken record, or rather a scratched one, the famous Jaffa saying *Ya bit Rubini ya bittaliqni*—You either take me to the festival of il Nabi Rubin or you divorce me—echoed in his head. Though this was the one proverb that Subhi, like many children in Jaffa, grew up hearing around this time of the year, this was the first time he had sympathized with his mother, who jokingly (or not so jokingly) threatened his father with divorce.

After looking forward to being with Shams for a whole month, Subhi understood the urge to make such a threats. "I would kill to be with Shams again," Subhi mumbled to himself as he jumped out of bed and got ready for il Nabi Rubin's flag celebrations, the official opening of the festival. Each of the three cities had its own *bairaq*, or flag, celebration on three consecutive days: Monday in il Lyd, Tuesday in il Ramleh, and Wednesday in Jaffa.

Ever since he was a little boy, Subhi had put on his best clothes and joined other youngsters in his neighborhood to go to the Grand

Mosque located off Clock Tower Plaza and celebrate Jaffa's flag ceremony. In and around the Grand Mosque gathered the high-ranking officials of the city: the heads of the Muslim Awqaf (the Muslim Endowment, which is the guardian of Muslim holy places but also helps the poor and the needy), the mayor of Jaffa and all the members of his municipal council, heads of political parties, merchants, and union leaders. They were joined by religious figures—sheiks, darwish, and Sufis of different *turuq*, or sects—half the population of Jaffa, and of course Subhi and his gang.

Carrying the yellow flag of il Nabi Rubin, the crowd came out of the mosque into the city port. From the gate of the Grand Mosque, Subhi and other youngsters ran to see how the fishermen and the sailors, including Subhi's grandfather Ali and uncle Habeeb, demonstrated their political clout and power by carrying their own flags and by joining in big numbers, which doubled the size of the procession.

Excited, Subhi had always joined the crowds of boys who dotted the two sides of the narrow alleys. In most cases, they climbed trees or high walls to see the official procession that toured the narrow alleys and the markets of the Old City with bands and performing horsemen. From the Old City of Jaffa, the procession would proceed up 'Ajami Road, make the rounds, and come back to the Grand Mosque again.

Now that the official announcement had been declared, as always, on a full-moon Friday, the whole city was moonstruck. It was getting ready to desert the suffocating heat of the city and leave behind the hard work of the orange season and go out to enjoy a four-week vacation by the sea.

In no time, a tent city was constructed on the site of il Nabi Rubin, located fourteen kilometers south of Jaffa between the Mediterranean shore and the Rubin River, all under the pretext of venerating the domed shrine where the Prophet Rubin was buried.

"But who is Rubin?" Subhi once asked his grandfather Ali.

"Bite your tongue, little boy. He is a prophet, so he is called il Nabi Rubin, not Rubin."

"Sorry, Grandpa, but still, who is he?"

"He is the son of Jacob."

"Is he Jewish?"

"No, he is not Jewish, he is Muslim."

"How can the son of Jacob, the patriarch of the Israelites, be Muslim?" More confused with his grandfather's explanations, Subhi tried to make sense of it all.

"*Ya Subhi, ya ibni,* my grandson, don't you know that Muslims venerate all prophets who came before them even if they were Jews or Christians? Musa, Isa, Joseph, Isaac, Ismael, all of them. Many holy shrines are venerated by the three religions or two, such as il Ibrahimi Mosque in Hebron, Rachel's Tomb in Bethlehem, Maqam il Khader in the village of il Khader, just to mention a few. Oh yes, I forgot to mention Joseph's Tomb near Nablus."

"But I never saw a Yahudi at il Nabi Rubin festival."

"In my day, when Arabs and Jews lived peacefully together, way before the British bastards arrived in Palestine, and way before the Zionists arrived in our country, and way before the *shawasher,* troubles, between the Arabs and the Jews began, many Jews came to il Nabi Rubin. However, since the 1936 Revolt, they have stopped coming. And I fear that if the present *shawasher* keep escalating, we might not be able to celebrate *il mawsim,* the festival, ourselves."

"How I would've liked to have lived in your day, Grandpa," Subhi replied, even though his heart skipped a beat thinking that one day soon he and Shams might be deprived of the one place where they could spend summer vacation close to each other, if not totally together.

"Is it true that he, I mean il Nabi Rubin, was buried in three different places? How can that be?" Subhi carried on with his inquiries.

"Yes: there is one tomb in Muqattam Mountain in Cairo, another in Kabul, and a third in—"

"In Kabul, Afghanistan?"

"No, not in Afghanistan, in Kabul here, in the Galilee, in Palestine. But of course the real tomb is the one we have here in Jaffa. That is why the real *hajj* is here. But as you see, the *hajj* has turned into a Luna Park in the last few years."

Since he only knew it as Luna Park, Subhi was rather surprised to hear his grandfather refer to Mawsim il Nabi Rubin as "*hajj.*" Subhi could not help but recall his father's comment about Uncle Habeeb: "Even if you take him to the real *hajj* in Mecca, Habeeb will discover places of sins." This was Ismael's comment when the security men gave their strict instructions to all coffee shops in the tent city: "No gambling, no alcohol, and no drugs."

"They did not say 'no prostitution,' did they?" replied Habeeb jokingly.

15

A Temporary Tent City

LIKE MANY IN HIS CITY, Subhi woke up early on the first day of il Nabi Rubin, eager to take part in the communal journey from Jaffa to the site of the festival.

The site was owned and administered by the Muslim Awqaf, which had worked very closely with city leaders to construct the temporary tent city that would house some forty to fifty thousand people for the next month. Jaffa's civic societies, sports clubs, and cultural organizations; the chamber of commerce; and the influential Sailors and Fishermen Union had also pitched in. The Sailors and Fishermen Union, together with the Muslim Awqaf, ran a soup kitchen that provided a free hot meal for tens of thousands of participants for twenty days consecutively. The tent city of il Nabi Rubin was divided into five hierarchical camps, or, as it were, five different living quarters: the best location was obviously allocated to the Jaffans, who also had the largest and fanciest tents; the second best was assigned to the inhabitants of il Ramleh, the third best to il Lyd, the fourth best to il Majdal, and the remaining one to the villages.

The four or five commercial streets, which ran parallel to one another and had numerous shops and cafés, were located in the very center of the tent city, hence bringing the inhabitants of the different city-based neighborhoods together, as did the many events that ran through the whole month. Most popular of all were movies at the open-air cinema, shows in the two or three theaters, concerts, puppet shows, horse races, wedding parties, and circumcision ceremonies, as well as Sufi and darwish chanting and performance dance circles.

Subhi could not believe what his father had just told him: "This year, neither I nor Khalil have the time to make arrangements for the festival. There is still a load of work to be done at the *bayyara*. So why don't you meet up with Mohammad and go to Abu Zuluf's Rent-a-Camel Khan and get two medium-sized tents and four camels: two for our family and two for Khalil's."

Ismael's out-of-the-blue comment, but more so, the normality of asking him to meet Shams's brother, made Subhi hope that the two families could one day become close in-laws. Wanting to make sure what he'd just heard was right, Subhi asked, "Which Mohammad is that?"

"What's wrong with you, Subhi? Mohammad, Khalil's eldest and only son."

"Oh, that Mohammad. OK. Take it easy on me, *Yaba;* most males around here are called Mohammad," Subhi joked, then added, "Should I go fetch him from his house in Salameh?" Though he was about to be around Shams for a whole month in il Nabi Rubin, Subhi obviously needed an excuse to go to Salameh to show Shams his English suit.

"No need to go to Salameh. Meet him at Abu Zuluf's Rent-a-Camel Khan. He is probably there already."

Excited about seeing Shams ride a camel (with other women, girls, and children in her family), Subhi asked, "Should I rent decorated camels or non-adorned ones?"

"Have you lost your mind? Have you any idea how much decorated camels cost? What for? We're not carrying a bride or a circumcised boy to il Nabi Rubin, are we?"

How much Subhi wanted to say, *Yes, Father, we are indeed carrying a potential bride,* but he kept quiet.

"Do you think carrying my *karkubeh,* old, mother in-law, or your mother, merits paying for a decorated camel?" Ismael giggled, then added, "We're only carrying house stuff, old women, and children of our family and that of Khalil."

"Would you rent my bride a decorated camel if I marry next year?" Subhi asked, testing the waters.

"Of course, my beloved son: your wedding camel will be decorated from head to tail. However, you have to wait your turn: first your brother Jamal, then you."

Not exactly pleased with his father's response, Subhi asked another question: "Will our tent and Khalil's be close to each other?"

"Jaffa tents are erected on a hill close to the sea, while Salameh's and other villages' tents are erected inland, close to the Rubin River."

"Close to il makhassa, the shallow area where we swim?"

"Exactly. Now stop asking questions and go meet Mohammad."

As he ran to Abu Zuluf's Rent-a-Camel Khan, all Subhi could think about was cultivating a strategic friendship with Shams's brother, who was one year her junior. Soon the two boys were chatting as they waited among huge crowds. Talking with Mohammad, Subhi learned of the boy's fascination with kites, and also with bows and arrows. It did not take long for Subhi to make a promise: "Once we're in il Nabi Rubin, I will make you the biggest and most colorful kite. I will also teach you how to make the best bows and arrows."

"Really?!" Mohammad's sparkling eyes and big smile assured Subhi that he had just gained an ally. When their turn finally came, each of them gave his family's name and address and paid the fee for a medium-sized tent and two camels.

To build on this burgeoning calculated friendship with Shams's brother, Subhi suggested, "Come on, let's go buy colored paper, bamboo sticks, and some thread for the kites, but also some sticks for the bow and arrows."

"But I have no money on me. I will——"

Before Mohammad had a chance to finish his sentence, Subhi interrupted, "Don't worry about money. It is my present to you."

After he had bought Mohammad all the materials for the kite and the bow and arrows, Subhi said, "Now let me treat you to some sweets at Abu Ata's. Do you prefer *knafeh* or *mtabbaq*?" But before Mohammad had a chance to answer, Subhi added, "Why don't I get you both?"

As the Arabic saying goes: "Feeding the mouth shies the eyes."

16

The Kisweh Celebrations
from Jaffa to il Nabi Rubin

L IKE THOUSANDS of men and young boys, Subhi helped his
mother, grandmother, and two sisters load the two camels
standing in front of their home with floor mats, mattresses, cush-
ions, blankets, cooking utensils, clothing, and all that was needed
for their one-month vacation in il Nabi Rubin.

Taking advantage of the chaos as family members ran from one
corner of the house to another, Subhi snuck into his bedroom, took
his English suit out of the closet, and placed it in a bag he had bought
the day before especially for this purpose.

Since the tent city was like a summer camp on sandy dunes, with
the intense heat and humidity of August, most men wore modest
light clothes such as the traditional cotton *quftan* or *jallabiyyeh* during the month of the festival. Hardly anyone, especially boys of
Subhi's age or background, wore a suit. Which would have made it
difficult, even rather ridiculous, for Subhi to go around wearing his
English suit. However, the numerous events that took place every

night gave Subhi hope that he might have an opportunity to wear it. Subhi was determined to find the right occasion to show it to Shams.

Having packed his English suit neatly, Subhi ran out to the street to help the women get on the backs of the two camels that would carry them from Jaffa to il Nabi Rubin. He handed his mother and his sisters white umbrellas to protect them from the hot August sun. Once they had balanced the women and girls on the backs of the camels (led by two young men sent by Abu Zuluf Rent-a-Camel), men often used other means to get to the festival site. While young men like Subhi and Mohammad went on foot, others rode horses and donkeys or got on one of the many buses that ran between Jaffa and il Nabi Rubin. In 1937, the Bamieh Bus Company ran the line in order to move businessmen who had to commute between Jaffa and the tent city.

Subhi and Shams's brother, Mohammad, were among the tens of thousands who, en route to il Nabi Rubin, took part in il Kisweh, the religious celebration of the covering of the prophet's tomb in the Holy Shrine with a large green velvet cloth embroidered in gold. The three cities of Jaffa, il Lyd, and il Ramleh took turns providing the cover each year. To get the blessings of il Nabi Rubin, Subhi and Mohammad joined the women and children who passed under the open *kisweh*, which was carried by eight strong men. How Subhi wished he were under the holy *kisweh* with Shams rather than with her brother.

BY LATE MORNING FRIDAY, some forty thousand festival participants had gathered around the Grand Mosque and the adjacent domed structure of Maqam, the Holy Shrine of il Nabi Rubin. Exhausted from the fourteen-kilometer walk, Subhi and Mohammad, like many, collapsed under a eucalyptus tree and watched the grand opening ceremony from afar.

While government officials, religious men, and members of the municipal council carried their flags, various boy scout bands played their instruments and darwish and Sufi *turuq* chanted their songs, declaring the official opening of *il mawsim*. While men stood in rows in and around the big mosque to take part in the communal Friday prayers, *salat il jum'a*, women and girls gathered in and around the holy shrine not only to pray but also to ask the holy prophet for specific favors: to help them get pregnant or have a baby boy, or to cure a sick person. Once the religious ceremony was over, Subhi and Mohammad joined the thousands of people who had gathered in front of the soup kitchen run by the Muslim Awqaf to receive the first of the free lunches that would be served every day for the next twenty days. After lunch, it was time for Subhi and Mohammad to part ways and proceed with the crowds to their respective encampments and tents.

"When and where should we meet?" Mohammad asked. He was keen to fly a kite.

Thrilled that his strategy had worked, Subhi replied, "Let's get some rest now. Why don't you come by my family's tent around five p.m. tomorrow?"

"Where is your family's tent? I don't know how to get there."

"Ask your father; he'll tell you."

"OK."

"Goodbye, then."

"Goodbye."

After a long siesta, empty streets, shops, and cafés began to fill up with customers. Dressed in their comfortable summer clothing or their cotton *jallabiyyeh*, most men gathered to play cards or smoke *arghileh* in the dozens of coffee shops, while women went off to the vegetable and fruit markets or to the "Women's Market," where men were not allowed. There they found clothing, costume jewelry, makeup, and all sorts of trinkets. Sweets shops were the destination for most children.

Since the festival started on a full moon night, thousands of people spent their first evening—or even their first night—on the beach or along the banks of the Rubin River. They cooked, barbequed, ate, played music, and sang as children ran around trying to locate old friends or make new ones. That evening Subhi looked for his Shams in vain, but knowing he was to see her brother the next day, he slept well that night.

Since everyone in the tent city was up and about way after midnight, it was not until late morning that daily life resumed. People sat in front of their tents having coffee with family members or friends in neighboring tents. Men and young boys were sent out to buy breakfast: hummus, falafel, and the famous sweet pie *temriyyeh*. Women moved in and out of their tents attending to the needs of numerous family members. By noon, children were running around the narrow streets in search of a magic box, a *krakouz* puppet show, or a music box. Older boys and young men Subhi's age were on their way to have a swim. But since the Mediterranean Sea could be rough and dangerous, swimming was restricted to the Rubin River. On both sides of the river, families would picnic under the huge eucalyptus trees. For those who did not need or care for an afternoon siesta, the festival offered many options, such as horseback riding, boxing, football, and bird hunting, as well as flying kites on the open and windy seashores.

Evenings were the best part of the festival. By late evening, whole families could be seen strolling together along the alleys trying to figure out what the festival committee had brought them this season. Il Nabi Rubin was by now one of the biggest and most renowned cultural events not only in Palestine but also in the neighboring Arab countries. People could watch the latest Egyptian movies in the open-air cinema, see new productions of Lebanese and Syrian plays, listen to an Aleppo music group, or join the celebrations of a real or "fake" wedding. Youngsters were particularly enchanted by the fake weddings, where men dressed as women and belly danced. Many families opted to join Sufi and darwish circles in which religious hymns were chanted and religious dancing such as *il mayla-weiyyeh*, the spinning dance, was performed, until late at night or until the spinners fell exhausted on the soft sand dunes and slept, waking up the next day. Many, like Uncle Habeeb, went to naughty "coffee shops" to gamble, drink, and smoke hash. Some opted to simply entertain family members and friends by barbequing in front of their tents, on the beach, or on the riverbanks. Il Nabi Rubin was also where business deals and marriage proposals were made, and love stories such as that of Subhi and Shams thrived.

Bearing in mind not only the city-based encampments of the tent city but also some of the gender-based activities, Subhi had to be Machiavellian about seeing, meeting, or, if he was lucky, being with Shams. In the midst of all the festival activities, Subhi was strategic about his moves, careful not to arouse any brotherly suspicions or family objections. Though men and women had separate domains, at fifteen and thirteen, Subhi and Shams were still considered "children," who had access to both. Little girls and boys were often seen running with no inhibition in and out of cafés, in the streets, and in the women-only market. Having made friends with Mohammad, Subhi now had an excuse to be around Shams.

17

The Kite Maker

I T WAS NOT clear who was more excited about the afternoon kite appointment on the beach, Subhi or Mohammad. As had been agreed the night before, Mohammad carried all the materials Subhi had bought him the day before and went to meet him at his family tent. Walking along the sandy alleys, Mohammad was stunned how much fancier the Jaffa encampment was compared to that of Salameh.

"Their tents are palaces. Each is erected in the middle of a huge lot surrounded by walls!" Mohammad told his mother that night.

"You don't mean walls, though, right? You mean partitions made out of palm reeds or fabric?"

"Yes, that's what I mean."

"Well my son, *il nas maqamat,* people are of different standings and have different social status: they are Jaffans, and we are Salamites. They are city people, and we are peasants."

"They're obviously better than us."

"No, *habibi* Mohammad, no one is better than you, my son, and you'd better remember that, sweetheart," she said and hugged him tightly.

Subhi was standing outside his family's tent when he spotted Mohammad struggling with the bulky supplies he was carrying.

"That's a lot of stuff, Mohammad! Why don't I teach you how to make a kite today and we'll leave the bow and arrows for tomorrow or another day?" Subhi suggested.

"Fine with me." Mohammad was happy to lighten his load. He handed Subhi a bundle of sticks, a knife, and two balls of thread to deposit in his family tent until the next day.

"Here, I'll carry the kite paper too because it tears easily," Subhi said, taking the colored paper from Mohammad's hand.

"OK," responded Mohammad as he happily jumped up and down on the sandy path leading them to the beach.

"Look at those kites and tell me which one you like most," Subhi said to Mohammad, pointing to the six kites that were flying high in the sky, held by a few kids who had come to the beach earlier that day.

"I like the red and orange with a diamond shape," Mohammad replied, admiring the one that flew the highest. "And I also like the green one with the long tail."

"I will make you the longest tail possible, and we will call the kite 'Mohammad the Monkey.'"

"I like that," Mohammad giggled.

On the beach, Subhi spread out a blanket delineating his "workshop" and said to Mohammad, "OK, why don't you give me the best two bamboo sticks? One should be longer than the other by fifteen to twenty centimeters." Not that he knew how long fifteen centimeters was, but Mohammad nonetheless examined the quality of the sticks and handed two to Subhi, who used the knife to make an indentation at each end of each stick and two more indentations where the sticks crossed each other.

"These notches will give the thread a good grip," Subhi explained as he knotted the two sticks in a cross shape. He then stretched the thread into the indentations at the ends of the bamboo sticks.

"See, now we have the diamond shape you like. Now let's spread the paper on the blanket, cut it, then glue it to the sticks," Subhi said as he unfolded the red paper on the blanket and put the diamond-shaped kite on top of the paper. "What we do now is cut the paper one or two centimeters bigger than the bamboo structure"—which Subhi did—"and fold the paper like this around the thread. Here, press it a bit until the glue dries." Mohammad did exactly as he was told.

"OK, it's time to make the monkey tail. What color tail do you want?"

"Orange," Mohammad responded.

"May I suggest a multicolored tail? Here, why don't we add green, blue, and red to the orange?"

"Can we? Yes, I like that," Mohammad happily agreed.

"Now take the small scissors and cut these sheets of paper into little strips like this and glue them to the kite's tail."

Mohammad took the scissors, sat on his knees next to Subhi, and started cutting the different colored paper as instructed. Meanwhile, Subhi made a fishbone-shaped tail by knotting short pieces of thread to the long thread tail and gave it to Mohammad.

"On each branch of your tail, you glue a different colored paper. Once you're done, we can stick the tail onto the kite and you'll be all set. In the meantime, I will tie the kite-flying thread to a short stick; this way, it will be easy to maneuver the kite. You don't want to get your flying thread all entangled and bring your kite down on its head."

By the time Subhi and Mohammad were done with their tasks, dozens of kids had gathered around them. Some stood around the blanket, while others took the liberty of sitting right next to Subhi.

"Can you make me one?"

"Me too. How much is it?"

"Here, I'll pay you right now," said a redheaded boy as he enthusiastically pulled a few piastres out of his pocket and offered them to Subhi.

"Take this and make me a diamond kite with a long tail."

"Wait, wait, I first need to finish this one, then I'll teach you all how to make your own kites."

"Really?! You are going to teach us how to make kites?"

"Can you fix mine? The wind tore it apart," asked another boy.

"The bamboo stick broke on mine."

"Hey hey hey, move aside, boys. You're about to step on Mohammad's new kite. I'll only make a kite for those who stand off the blanket. You hear me? Step back, otherwise no kites." Like soldiers in a well-trained army, to Subhi's utter surprise, they all rolled off the blanket and stood next to it.

"Now, listen to me carefully. Do not touch a thing and follow me. I first want to show Mohammad how to fly his monkey-tail kite, then I'll teach you."

Subhi led the way as Mohammad and an army of excited little boys came running after him.

"Here, Mohammad, hold the kite and run against the wind. Once the kite takes off, keep running and give it more slack. But keep the tension in the thread. You're lucky there is a nice breeze. Go for it, Mohammad, go!"

With his kite in his hand and the long tail dragging behind, Mohammad ran as fast as he could as he followed Subhi's instructions carefully.

In no time, Mohammad's diamond kite was high up in the sky.

"OK, those who want to learn how to make a kite, follow me. I don't sell kites, but I will teach you how to make one."

In the midst of a growing crowd of children, Subhi made a second, a third, and a fourth kite. And just as he raised his head to give the fourth kite to one of the kids, his eyes spotted Shams's head in the crowd. His heart almost stopped as he fixated on the orange spots on her white dress. Once he gained control of his emotions, he took a deep breath and stared into Shams's hazel eyes and smiled. She smiled back. Not knowing what to do next, Subhi yelled at the top of his lungs, "OK, boys, we're done for today! As you can see, I have run out of materials. Those of you who want to learn how to make kites, ask your father to give you five piastres and meet me tomorrow at Abu Hani's bookshop. I'll be there after lunch, say around three p.m."

Noticing Subhi's flirtations with his sister, Mohammad innocently, or not so innocently, came running up and said, "But I thought you were going to teach me how to make a bow and arrows tomorrow."

"I showed you how to make a kite today, but tomorrow you're going to make one yourself."

"OK," Mohammad giggled and ran after his kite again.

Left alone, Subhi and Shams had a chance to exchange another smile and a few words of admiration.

"Thank you for the photo you sent me. You looked smart in that suit. Am I going to see it for real?"

"You seem to be more excited about seeing the suit than about seeing me."

Not knowing what to say, Shams blushed and kept quiet. To smooth over the awkwardness created by his flirtatious remark, Subhi quickly added, *"Akeed,* for sure, that is why I brought it with me. I am waiting for an occasion to wear it. Look around: no one wears a suit in this heat."

"But I want to see *you* in it." Shams chose her words carefully this time.

"Don't worry, I'll find a way. I hope you realize I went to the trouble of making this whole kite festival just for you."

"For me?" Shams blushed again, then added, "Is that right? Thank you."

"How could I see you freely if it weren't for the kite show?" Subhi smiled.

In order not to arouse family suspicions that could result in restrictions on Shams's movements for the coming weeks of the festival, both Subhi and Shams kept a low profile and gave no hint of their mutual admiration and his burning love. Something about Shams's curls, melancholic eyes, and shy smile continued to drive Subhi out of his mind. Every time he got close to her, or even stared at her from a distance, his heart melted, while other parts of his body hardened.

FOR THE NEXT FEW DAYS, Subhi ran workshops on kite making for dozens of kids, but this time with Shams by his side. As an expression of his love for her, the skies were soon filled with kites of all shapes, sizes, and colors. Some had geometrical shapes: triangles, squares, and diamonds; others took the shapes of animals—birds, snails, octopus, jellyfish—or plants or flowers. The ones the kids liked most were kites on which Subhi drew faces (supposedly theirs but also Shams's): a smiley face, a face with a winking eye, one with a Pinocchio nose, one with golden curls. Every day brought new shapes, new colors, and new techniques. Every afternoon revealed a new spectacular show: a riot of colors filled the sky. Subhi's "kite show" had by then become a visual treat for onlookers. While they were struck by the colorful skies full of Subhi's kites, Subhi was struck by his love for Shams. However, Shams was perhaps still too young and innocent to understand Subhi's burning lust and adoration for her.

18

The Love of My Life

Now that his kite bond with Mohammad was starting to pay off, Subhi pushed his luck a bit: "Tell me, Mohammad, do you like Ismail Yassine and Farid il Atrash?" he asked, knowing that all children Mohammad's age adored the Egyptian comedian Ismail Yassine but not necessarily the Lebanese singer Farid il Atrash. However, to Subhi's surprise, Mohammad expressed interest in the singer.

"I adore Farid il Atrash, and I know most of his songs by heart."

"Come on, really? I won't believe you until I hear you sing one of his songs."

It did not take much to prompt Mohammad to perform. He stood up straight, imitating Farid il Atrash, and started singing one of Farid's famous songs: *Ya waili min hubbuh, ya waili min 'aẓabi fi nahari u laili*, I am scared of his love, which gives me pains day and night. Once done with that song, without being asked, Mohammad sang another, *Yabu Dhuhka Jnan*, you with the divine smile.

As Subhi wondered about Mohammad's provocative choice of songs, Mohammad was about to sing yet a third song when Subhi intervened: "OK, OK, Mohammad. I believe you." Careful not to hurt Mohammad's feelings, he added, "What a beautiful voice you have."

Indeed he did.

"Why don't you bring your older brother and come see Ismail Yassine's film at the open-air cinema tonight?" suggested Subhi, knowing full well that Mohammad had no older or younger brothers.

"I don't have an older brother, but I have an older sister."

"How old is your sister? I only ask because the festival doesn't allow kids your age to enter on their own."

"But you saw my sister; she is thirteen."

"OK, good. Why don't you bring her and meet me at the entrance?" Subhi feared that Mohammad would say *But you're a grown-up and I could enter with you*, but he did not. "And what is your sister's name?"

"Shams. But I thought you had talked to her."

Subhi ignored Mohammad's comment and said, "Shams, that's a nice name. OK, see you and your sister Shams at eight o'clock tonight."

"OK. I will tell Shams and perhaps bring my younger sisters as well, but you have to promise to make me the biggest kite and teach me how to make a bow and arrows tomorrow."

"Of course I will." Subhi was taken aback that Mohammad was indeed making "a deal" with him.

Knowing he was going to see Shams that night, Subhi contemplated wearing his suit. However, in order not to be ridiculed by his family for overdressing, Subhi gave up on the idea. But he still had to look elegant and smart for his first official outing with Shams. Subhi would wear his second best.

While Subhi's father and brothers went to play cards and smoke *arghileh* in the different cafés, Uncle Habeeb joined the gamblers and the drinkers, and his mother and sisters spent their evenings either attending one of the events or in the Women's Market, which stayed open until midnight. Just before his film rendezvous, Subhi ran into the now empty tent, took off his *qumbaz*, and put on his best trousers and a new light blue shirt. Not having a mirror, Subhi prayed that Shams would love his look. And just before he stepped out of his family's tent, he reached for his uncle Habeeb's cologne, poured half the bottle on his big hands, and rubbed his face and neck.

Subhi whizzed through his section of the Jaffa encampment to the open-air cinema in the middle of the tent city, with sand dusting his shiny shoes and elegant trousers. Subhi sighed and thought his heart would explode the second he spotted Shams in her white and orange dress. Standing next to her were Mohammad and her two younger sisters, Nazira and little Nawal. Subhi's hand trembled as he extended it to shake hands with Shams. He held Shams's cold palm for a bit and then squeezed it. She blushed and pulled it away.

"That is a beautiful dress, Shams."

"Really?" She acted surprised, then placed her hands on the lower part of her dress and said, "Glad you like it."

Now that his dream of being with Shams was finally coming true, Subhi was not going to miss the chance to sit next to his sweetheart for the duration of the film. True, this open-air cinema—half under a tent and half under a full-moon sky—was not as dark as Jaffa's movie theaters, but Subhi still saw great possibilities for expressing his love for Shams.

"Come on, let's go sit over there." Subhi strategically chose five seats.

Subhi made sure to have Mohammad, Nazira, and Nawal sit to his left, and to have Shams alone on his right in the hope that none of Shams's siblings would be aware of what Subhi's right hand intended to do. Thanks to the hilariousness of Ismail Yassine, the singing of Farid il Atrash, and the belly dancing of Samia Gamal, Shams's younger siblings were totally absorbed by the film, *The Love of My Life*.

Sitting on a low stool half sunken into the sandy ground, Subhi got as close as he could to Shams, and with every dark scene in the film, he made his thigh touch hers. Once reassured of her reciprocity, he placed his hand on hers, again pleased when she didn't pull her hand or body away. Thus encouraged, halfway through the film, Subhi placed his hand on Shams's arm and slid it over to touch her small, firm breasts. But that was when she pulled herself away from him. Not knowing what to do, Subhi sat still for a while before he took Shams's hand in his once more. She let her hand be and sat still. Not knowing what to do next, Subhi waited for them both to calm down.

They were the last ones to leave the cinema after the movie. "Good night" was all that they said to each other as their eyes met, and a warm smile came to Shams's face when Mohammad broke the delicate silence and asked, "Are you making us more kites tomorrow?"

"Yes, of course I am. I will first make kites for the boys, then dollhouses for the girls."

"Really? Will you make me a dollhouse?" asked seven-year-old Nawal enthusiastically.

"Definitely. Why don't you all meet me at Abu Hani's bookshop to buy the necessary materials, then we can proceed to the seashore together to make you the nicest dollhouse." Subhi looked at Nawal this time.

"I can also make us a big dollhouse," Subhi then said to Shams. Once more she blushed and smiled.

And just like the kite festival had been for the boys, the dollhouse workshop turned out to be a little girls' paradise. Subhi's mechanical skills, which had earned him the infamous English suit, also garnered him admiration from and popularity with the children of the tent city. Subhi's splendid "kite show" as well as his "dollhouse exhibit" became two of the most well-attended events of il Nabi Rubin that year.

Having plotted all sorts of ways to be with or around Shams during the monthlong festival, Subhi now needed to plan a memorable finale for him and Shams: a memory to sustain him until they saw each another again. To do so, Subhi tossed and turned all night recalling all the love scenes he had seen or experienced in his life: love scenes from the different films he had watched at the Nabil Cinema; the love, or rather lust, scene he had been caught in by his widowed neighbor Um Zahra; and last but certainly not least, the sex scenes from his encounter with Shoshanna.

Though he had promised himself not to think of Shoshanna when he was with Shams, or vice versa, the sensations, the emotions, and the excitement of Shoshanna's French kiss were indeed memorable. And that was, of course, the only possible or acceptable scene for him and Shams. However, this time he would be the one in control by playing the lead role of the confident Shoshanna with inexperienced and innocent Shams. Having spent the whole night thinking about his and Shams's first kiss, Subhi felt confident when, the next day, he said to Shams, "Why don't you come by this evening when everyone is out? I want to show you my suit for our wedding."

"Our wedding!" Shams gasped and giggled, then said, "What

if someone sees me in your family's tent alone with you? My father would kill me."

"No one will see you, but more important, no one would dare lay a hand on you when I am around, not even your own father."

Not knowing what to think of such a strong statement, Shams replied, "We're peasants, not Jaffans."

THAT EVENING, Subhi's heart jumped when he spotted Shams at a distance coming to his tent. He buttoned his jacket, straightened his trousers, and stood right in front of the tent. Luckily, the front alley was empty except for two boys who were busy chasing their ball.

Subhi stepped into the tent the minute he made sure Shams had seen him. In spite of his macho statement that morning, the last thing he wanted was to get Shams in trouble.

When the two stood face-to-face, he asked, "How do you like my wedding suit?"

"You and the suit are the most beautiful things in this world," Shams replied.

"Soon I'll have the money to buy your white wedding dress."

"White! Why white? In Salameh, *thub il malak*, the embroidered wedding dress, is very colorful," she said.

Not wanting to spend the time discussing the differences in dress codes between the peasants and the Jaffans, Subhi let her comment go.

He moved closer to her and looked into her eyes until that shy smile appeared on her gorgeous face. He then pulled her blond curly hair back, pressed his body against hers, and kissed her on the mouth. Once he felt her body pressing against his, he went for more: he held her even tighter and gave her one of Shoshanna's

French kisses. He kept at it until she ran out of breath. Both blushed. Excited, she took a deep breath, sighed, then whispered, "Let me get out of here before someone sees us."

She pulled away from him, gave him a smile that would capture his imagination for the rest of his life, and said goodbye. With a heavy heart and stiffened private parts, Subhi said goodbye to his beloved, who ran out of the tent and hurriedly walked away.

Subhi stood in the alley and watched Shams's silhouette vanish in the dusk.

"All good things come to an end except for my love for Shams. Now that I've gotten used to being with her every single day, how will I survive a whole year before I can be with her again?" Subhi mumbled to himself.

The next morning, he contemplated revealing his love for Shams to his mom. But she was busy gathering the family's belongings from the tent and loading them onto the back of the two camels that were about to carry them back to Jaffa. Subhi felt the same urge to reveal his love for Shams to his father, as he helped his father and brothers pull down the tent and fold it away. Fearing that his father would spoil it all with disapproving words, however, Subhi said nothing.

Once all was dismantled and packed, Subhi looked around the site and wondered, *How could the tent city that nourished our love disappear just like that?*

In less than forty-eight hours, the site had gone back to being empty sand dunes, in the middle of which stood the shrine and the mosque. The holy site of Prophet Rubin felt empty and abandoned, just like Subhi.

Part II

Back to Jaffa

಼ೲ಼

19

Post-Vacation Blues

(Jaffa, September 1947)

I T TOOK a few weeks before the inhabitants of Jaffa got back to their daily routines. Subhi wondered about his post-vacation mood: *Why do I feel blue when I should be joyful about having spent a whole month with or around Shams?*

He missed her like never before.

Where, when, and how will I see her again? he asked himself and then sighed.

And just when the city was regaining its vivacious tempo as well as its economic and cultural vibrancy, it was struck by a rumor that had by now become a reality: the British government had officially announced its intention to end its mandate for Palestine by midnight May 14, 1948, and withdraw its forces. The British had no intention of enforcing the UN Partition Plan, which the UN General Assembly would vote on on the evening of November 29, 1947.

Two months were left for the Palestinians and the Jews to figure out their strategies, to show their strength and flex their muscles (in the case of the Palestinians, they were lacking all three). While the different political parties argued about the pros and cons of ending the British Mandate, apprehension, fear, and confusion took hold of the city. Realizing the military superiority of the Jewish militia, the Palestinians felt uncertain about the future of their city. Subhi recalled his grandfather's words a few months earlier: "I fear that if the present *shawasher* keep escalating, the way they've been lately, we might not be able to celebrate the festival."

God! What if that is true?

Where and when would I see Shams again?

Walking along il Mahatta Street on his way to work, Subhi could feel the tension in the air. Passersby as well as merchants expressed anxiety and fear about the withdrawal of the British forces: "This will create a political and a military vacuum that can only be filled by Zionist forces. The British bastards will withdraw and leave us at the mercy of a well-trained and well-equipped Jewish militia." By the time Subhi got to the garage, concerns had shifted to the Palestinian economy: "Goddamn . . . Who's going to pay the salaries of the thousands of civil servants: policemen, schoolteachers, and government officials? I cannot believe the British are simply going to pack up and leave, just like that."

Subhi overheard the conversation between his boss, M'allem Mustafa, and the Palestinian police officer who had come to have an electrical generator fixed. What perplexed Subhi most was the love-hate relationship Palestinians had with their British occupiers.

"We've been complaining about the British bias all along, and now that they're ending their mandate, we're acting like orphans! What's wrong with us?" Subhi complained to his boss once the police officer had left.

"No, it's not that . . . fuck the *Inglese*. The real problem is that since they arrived in Palestine in 1917, they've allowed Jews to immigrate to our land, allowed them to smuggle in weapons and get the best military training, and now they leave us at the mercy of the bastards. I tell you, son, we stand no chance whatsoever." It was the first time Subhi had heard his boss curse and speak so heatedly. M'allem Mustafa took a deep breath, then added, "Well, I guess it might be time for me to take my wife and kids to Beirut."

"Take them to Beirut! Why? What for?"

Realizing how alarmed Subhi was by his words, M'allem Mustafa backpedaled: "No, no, don't worry, Subhi. If I take my family to Beirut, I will for sure come back right away."

Of all the concerns and fears that Subhi had heard over the last few days, this was the one statement that panicked him most. If M'allem Mustafa left Jaffa, Subhi feared he would be left with no job to sustain himself and marry Shams. Feeling depressed by his boss's comment, Subhi plugged a broken engine into the electricity, and in no time, he was absorbed by his work.

LIKE WILDFIRE, fear, apprehension, and confusion spread through not only Jaffa but all of Palestine. The uncertainty about the future of the city was of great concern to all. Some argued that there was no reason to fear, since Jaffa was part of the area designated as an Arab state, while others argued that the Zionists would take what was allocated as theirs and go after what was designated as others'. A small minority called for accepting the UN Partition Plan, while the great majority of Palestinians stood against it. So did the Jewish parties of Lehi and the Irgun.

Some called for escalation with the enemy, while others advocated for a nonaggression agreement.

Some called for a three-day strike, while others argued for an open-ended one.

Some asked for more arms, while others warned against further armament.

Whatever people thought, on the evening of November 29, the UN General Assembly voted on Resolution 181, which called for the partitioning of Mandatory Palestine into two states: an Arab state and a Jewish one. It delineated the borders of each. And as expected, Jaffa was part of the Arab state. UN Resolution 181 also gave Jerusalem special status: "Corpus Separatum" under a permanent international regime.

Thirty-three countries voted in favor, thirteen voted against, and ten abstained.

Sitting at home listening to the radio with family members, friends, and neighbors, Subhi could not tell if the shots they heard right after the declaration of a Jewish state in Palestine were bullets of protest from the bleeding heart of old Jaffa or bullets of celebration from the youthful heart of Tel Aviv.

Indeed, while the newly born nation cheered and danced in the streets of the White City, Tel Aviv, the heart of an old nation bled as its eyes brimmed with tears. They feared the worse was still to come.

Happy or sad, no one slept the night of November 29, 1947. The next day, fear struck. One hostile act led to another. Cars and buses on both sides were attacked. In no time, there was an unprecedented escalation of hostilities. A cycle of violence reigned over Jaffa and Tel Aviv. Bordering Arab and Jewish neighborhoods became zones of friction. While the head of il Najjadeh Party, Mohammad Nimer il Hawwari, called for the evacuation of most outlying areas, Haj

Amin Al Husseini of the Arab Party called for citizens' steadfastness. Violent incidents took place inside the Carmel Market: Arab and Jewish shops were set on fire, forcing shop owners and peddlers to escape the scene. Jewish families living in Jaffa also fled. Soon all forms of cooperation between Arabs and Jews broke down, then ceased, affecting the construction sector and orange export business.

Although shootings and explosions were heard all through the night, the life-loving Jaffans, including Subhi and members of his family, carried on with their daily routines. This was the case until daytime attacks struck three of Jaffa's packed cafés. On December 12, four Yemeni Jews set Café Sambu on fire. One was seen running away with the café's radio. On December 30, a truck stopped right next to il Hamra Cinema, dropped a barrel with explosives in the middle of King George Boulevard, and drove away. It took a few seconds before the barrel rolled a few meters down the road and exploded right next to the upscale Café Venezia. Twenty-seven of the café's customers were killed.

On that same day, December 30, death came too close to home for Subhi: fear had struck the fearless hearts of the brave *ashawes*, the sailors and fishermen of Café il Madfa' on the port. "A small boat from Tel Aviv came close to Café il Madfa' and started shooting at us. We fired back at them, and they ran away, as did most of the people on Jaffa's port," reported Uncle Habeeb, who was visibly shaken.

With such attacks on civilians, fear reigned over public life. Political leaders urged people not to gather in cafés and public squares. Jaffa's buzzing streets started to empty by early evening. In order to prevent hostilities between the two communities, and also to control the increasing incidents of looting and robberies in the different parts of the city, the British forces imposed curfews, especially on peripheral neighborhoods.

Gone was the nightlife of Jaffa.

Gone was the courage of men like Uncle Habeeb to venture into Tel Aviv shops, cafés, and bars.

20

Death Oranges

(Sunday, January 4, 1948)

S UNDAY, JANUARY 4, 1948, was a crisp and sunny day.
Nothing about the tranquility of the day, the serenity of the
Mediterranean Sea, or the daily scene of a truck carrying heaps of
oranges, in the "City of Oranges" raised any suspicions.

Why should it?

Just as he always did, Subhi woke up at five a.m. With sleepy eyes,
he stepped out onto the balcony, sat on a chair, and stared at the sea
as he waited for his mother to hand him a glass of goat milk and a
sweet cup of Turkish coffee. In no time, he was walking along il
Manshiyyeh Road on his way to the garage. And as on any other day,
once there, Subhi looked at the photo of a bride hung on the wall
above his toolbox, thought of his beloved, smiled, and got to work.

He was bent over one of his broken engines when two sequential
explosions shook the garage and threw him off balance.

"*Ya sater ya sater ya sater ya rub*, goodness, what on earth is going
on?!" yelled Subhi at the top of his lungs as he was knocked over.
Instinctively, he wrapped both arms around his head as he fell on

the ground. Quickly he was back on his feet, only to find M'allem Mustafa and two of their customers crouching under a table. Shaken to the core, Subhi turned in circles, believing that something had struck the back of the garage. In a state of terror and puzzlement, he exited the workshop onto the main street, which had turned into a madhouse.

Some people were running toward the city center, where the explosions had struck.

Others ran away from it.

Panic-stricken, some deserted their cars.

Others froze in their cars, not knowing what to do or where to go. Stuck in chaotic traffic, people feared the worse.

Some pedestrians took refuge inside buildings.

Others dashed out of the same buildings.

Terrified mothers and children whirled around in total panic.

Others froze.

Some fled north.

Others fled south.

Some ran to the sea.

Others fled inland.

While clouds of dust from building rubble filled the sky, dooms-day scenarios filled the hearts and minds of the confused crowds.

"The Jews exploded the mosque."

"They exploded the clock tower."

"They booby-trapped the Ottoman saraya."

"A truck full of oranges detonated the municipal building and brought it down."

"All members of the Arab Higher Committee have been blown up."

"A series of explosions brought down all the banks: the British Barclays, the Ottoman, and the Arab Bank."

"Money is flying everywhere; let's go collect some."

"Are you out of your mind? Don't go there. Haven't you learned their dreadful pattern? One explosion goes off, people gather, and a second and more deadly one follows."

"They want us all dead. As they say, 'The only good Arab is a dead Arab.'"

In spite of all the rumors that spread like wildfire around the city, no one had, so far, heard the heartbreaking news that the main victims of the ground-shaking explosions were children: orphans who were having lunch at the soup kitchen run by the Social Affairs Department located on the second floor of the Saraya Building.

Like many others—civilians, along with members of the Palestinian police force and the British army—Subhi ran to the scene. In front of him stood a mound of rubble filled with parts of or whole bodies and corpses. Low- and high-pitched cries could be heard from beneath the rubble. Except for the four Roman columns of the main facade, which were still standing, the three-story building had collapsed, bringing down with it the innocent boys and girls in need of a hot meal.

The screams and moans of those trapped under the rubble made Subhi sob. Helping to pull the dead and the wounded from under the rubble was a nightmare that would deprive Subhi of sleep for years to come.

Once people knew that the Saraya Building was the target of the terrorist attack, the speculation about the number of victims and who was behind the attack began.

"Most of the victims were children who had lost their lives in exchange for a bowl of soup, which they probably did not finish that day."

"Some twenty children have been killed."

"Had it not been Sunday, the number of victims would've been triple."

"I bet you anything it was the British forces that did it."

"Only Arab collaborators and informants are in a position to plant explosives inside the Saraya Building."

"Come on, it must've been the Jewish underground that did it."

"What's so underground about them when they carry out their attacks in daylight?"

It would be revealed only years later that the two men who drove the booby-trapped orange truck with a half-ton of explosives from the heart of Tel Aviv to the heart of Jaffa were members of the Jewish group Lehi. It was not until the day after that Subhi discovered that his neighbor and friend Hani (who had given him a ride to the photo studio the day he got his English suit) was among the victims. He happened to be passing by the Saraya Building at that very moment.

February 6 was funeral day. In silence, and in tears, Subhi marched with thousands of mourners from the City Hospital to the Christian and Muslim cemeteries. "*Miskeen*, poor Hani, what luck, he was so kind and peaceful," Subhi kept repeating as he helped Hani's father bury the amputated body of his eldest son.

With red eyes and a splitting headache, Subhi sat on a low stool next to his grandfather Ali that evening and asked, "But why would the Jewish militia target an orphanage soup kitchen when they must've known that the Arab National Committee had moved out of the Saraya Building a few months ago?"

"Fear, my son, fear. They want to fill our hearts and minds with fear. That's what they want, and that's what they have achieved," Subhi's grandfather said. He took a long and deep drag on his cigarette, then blew smoke rings as he exhaled.

Fear had indeed struck Subhi's heart as he thought of Shams and wondered when and where he would see her again.

21

A Train Robbery

(end of March 1948)

WALKING ALONG il Manshiyyeh Street on his way to work, Subhi heard the alarming but also exciting news about a train robbery. Since most shopkeepers and café owners on both sides of the street had tuned their radios to the Near East Broadcasting Station transmitting from downtown Jaffa, it was easy for him to follow the details of the story without needing to stop, pause, or even slow down. He also heard the comments of shopkeepers, customers, and passersby like himself.

On its way from the Sarafand military camp to Haifa, a train carrying British ammunitions was robbed as it was passing through il Khdaira Station. A group of armed men got on the train, arrested its guards, and forced it to stop. The armed men unloaded all the ammunitions and weapons aboard and ran off. British forces and police are investigating the incident in order to identify the robbers.

Listening to the news, at first Subhi thought it was an advertisement for the 1941 Western movie *The Great Train Robbery*, featuring

Bob Steele and Claire Carleton, which he and his friends had seen at Nabil Cinema two years earlier.

"Investigating! What for? The plot is clearer than the sun. It is all a *masrahiyyeh*, a play, a performance. It is obviously an agreement or an understanding between the withdrawing British forces and the Zionist militia. Since the British government declared its intention to end its mandate for Palestine and withdraw its forces on May 14, 1948, it has continued to play tricks on us. It is obvious that the British want to give all their weapons and ammunition to the Zionists. The British want to make sure that the Jews have the upper hand and will continue to kick us in the ass in the same way the Brits did since they arrived in this land," Subhi heard one merchant comment.

Another responded in a slow and calm manner: "Wait . . . Wait . . . Don't jump to conclusions. You never know. It could very well be the Arab Futtuwweh who robbed the train," he said, referring to the militant arm of the Palestinian Arab Party led by Haj Amin Al Husseini.

"Why il Futtuwweh and not il Najjadeh?"

Since the confrontations between Arabs and Jews had escalated after the declaration of the Partition Plan on November 29, 1947, Subhi, like many young men, had joined the neighborhood night guard, trained by il Najjadeh party headed by Mohammad Nimer il Hawwari.

"Whoever they were, we only hope it was the Arab militia that robbed the train, as we need those weapons to defend ourselves against the vicious Zionist forces."

"Rumor has it that it was il Jihad il Muqaddas, the military arm of the Palestinian Arab Party headed by Abdel Qader il Husseini, that robbed the train."

"What rumors, man? We just heard the news on the radio. You're the one who is spreading the rumors. I love how rumors are fabricated and spread even before the event takes place! We are a nation of rumors, that is what we are," objected the owner of Café il Inshirah as he was getting his coffee ready for his first customers.

"None of the Arab militant groups have the skills to rob a train full of British ammunition. Come on. Arabs are only capable of fighting one another. That's what we're good at," said the chubby cynical barber, who was hanging his towels along the sidewalk.

Like many, Subhi knew how few weapons the Arab militia had and how heavy-handed British punishment was for those who were caught with a bullet, let alone a rifle.

He recalled the words of Abu Jamal, the neighborhood trainer, the day he joined the il Manshiyyeh neighborhood night guards: "Young men, be careful and don't brag. You'll get a few years imprisonment for bullets, and a life sentence if caught with a rifle." As much as he wished it had been il Najjadeh that had robbed the train, Subhi knew full well that they had neither the military training nor the skills for such an operation.

"All I can say is, get ready for more days under curfew, more home searches, and more arrests. Mark my words, the Jews get the weapons, and we get the punishment. This has been British policy for the last thirty years, and it is not going to change during the last two weeks of their mandate."

"If it turns out to be the Haganah, or even worse the Irgun or Etzel, who robbed the train and got hold of the weapons, Jaffa is doomed."

"For God's sake, don't be so self-defeating. The Partition Plan is clear: Jaffa was designated part of the Arab State, hence they are not going to attack Jaffa or occupy it. Get it out of your head."

"This is pure nonsense. The Haganah wants to occupy il Manshiyyeh," added Abu Sami, the owner of the best bakery in town. Every time Subhi smelled the freshly baked bread and pastries, he thought of the delicious peasant *taboun* bread, which he hoped Shams would bake for him once they got married and had a home of their own.

"Mark my words, they want to occupy not only il Manshiyyeh neighborhood but the whole city. Jaffa is like a thorn in their throat, and they will not allow it to stay part of the Arab State."

But as it turned out, the real two horsemen behind the Khdaira Station "Western Cowboy film" robbery were neither Bob Steele nor Claire Carleston but rather with Menachem Begin, leader of the Jewish group Irgun, and Yosef Nachmias, a Jewish military expert from Jerusalem. The robbery provided Begin's Irgun militia with some twenty thousand mortar shells that, in a few weeks, would land in the very heart of Jaffa, determining its fate and the fate of all the villages around it.

22

Jerusalem's Macabre Parade
(April 8, 1948)

A S THEY SAY, bad things come in threes.
However, in Palestine,they came in fours.

On April 8, 1948, the whole of Palestine and the Arab world woke up to shocking news: Abdel Qader il Husseini, the head of il Jihad il Muqaddas, the military arm of the Palestinian Arab Party, had been killed in the Battle of il Qastal near Jerusalem. Only years later would it be revealed that Husseini, the son of the mayor of Jerusalem, was first injured in the battle. He pleaded with his adversary for a drop of water. He got a bullet in the head instead.

Early in the morning of April 9, not far from il Qastal village, the Irgun, Lehi, and Haganah forces attacked the village of Deir Yassin. In cold blood, they hunted down 250 Palestinian civilians as they ran for their lives. Those who survived the massacre were loaded into trucks and paraded through the streets in the Arab neighborhoods of Jerusalem.

As intended, the macabre parade through Jerusalem sent waves of horror across Palestine. The news about the monstrosities against civilians resulted in the evacuation of civilians, especially women and children, away from war zones. And all the Jaffans talked about for the coming weeks was escape:

"Why don't I drive your mother and sisters to stay with our relatives in Beirut?"

"It may be a good idea to send my wife and children to Damascus, where they can stay with my aunt for a month or two until things settle down."

"Why don't we go to Alexandria for an early vacation this year until the situation improves?"

"Maybe we should rent a place in Ramallah or Nablus and move there until the end of the summer."

This was the talk of the town, especially in areas close to Tel Aviv in the north and Bat Yam in the south. But also in villages close to Jaffa such as Salameh. It was such talk that irritated and scared Subhi the most. However, like most families in Jaffa, Subhi's family argued about what to do and where to go:

"Why don't you take my parents, our daughters, and Amir and go stay with our relatives in Nablus for a few weeks?" Subhi's father instructed his wife, Khadijeh.

"I am not taking anyone to anywhere or any place. We either live together or die together."

"For once, listen to me, Khadijeh. It is not a matter only of life and death. As you know, women and girls were raped in Deir Yassin."

Once the taboo word was uttered, fear prevailed.

Silence prevailed.

Nonetheless, Subhi's mother stood her ground, but not for long. The exchange of fire, the frequency of explosions, and the criminal acts against civilians, including women and girls, made her doubt her steadfastness.

"Did you hear what happened in Salameh this morning?" Ismael asked her, then added, "A group of Jewish settlers tried to kidnap a young woman working in the fields."

"What?" screamed Subhi as he jumped out of his chair and went to his father.

"What's wrong with you, son?" Ismael asked Subhi, then added, "Thank God she screamed, kicked, and fought back until her father and her brothers came running and saved her." Knowing that Shams had only one younger brother, Subhi's worries eventually subsided. But as such stories became more common, and as a night's sleep became rare, Subhi's mother eventually gave in: "There is hardly anyone left in the neighborhood. Most neighbors have already left. I think it is time for all of us to either go to Nablus or Amman or take refuge in the orange grove."

"What do you mean, 'all of us'?" Subhi responded. "I'm not going anywhere, and neither is Jamal. We're not leaving the house for the thieves! The two of us will stay with Uncle Habeeb and the neighborhood guards. We need to protect our house and defend the neighborhood."

Subhi could not reveal to his mother that his chances of seeing Shams or at least knowing her whereabouts were much higher if he stayed put in Jaffa rather than fleeing to Nablus or Amman.

"*Habibi* Subhi, you're both too young to stay behind on your own, or God forbid, to fight. Neither of you knows how to use a rifle."

"Yamma, I am not leaving the house. Do you want us to leave the house for the robbers?"

"OK, OK, Subhi. Why don't you and Jamal stay home with Uncle Habeeb, but promise not to carry a rifle or fight. Meanwhile, I'll find a way to take my in-laws and your sisters to our relatives in

Nablus. Ismael, why don't you take Amir to keep you company and help you in the orange grove. The *bayyara* should also be protected from vandalism. What a mess! God damn il *Inglese,* il Yahud, and the fucking Arab regimes. They are all conspiring against us." Khadijeh was becoming hysterical.

"Take it easy, Yamma. I have never heard you curse in this way." Realizing how shaken his mother was, Subhi went to her and hugged her tightly. Overwhelmed by it all, Khadijeh wept.

Though the plan about who would go away and who would stay behind was discussed and altered numerous times, no one left the house that day.

The closer it got to midnight on May 14, 1948, the last night of the British Mandate for Palestine, the more vicious the Jewish attacks on Arab towns and villages became, especially on areas designated as part of the Jewish state. Though the Partition Plan designated Jaffa, the biggest Arab city, as part of the Arab state, Menachem Begin, head of Irgun, thought differently. His plan was to grab as much land as possible before May 15—in other words, before the Arab armies could enter Palestine. And since none of the Egyptian, Iraqi, Syrian, or Jordanian armies could enter before the end of the mandate or before Britain withdrew its military forces, the Jewish militias made up their minds: strategically and tactically, it was easier to occupy Jaffa, or at least the northern parts of the city, specifically il Manshiyyeh neighborhood, before the Arab armies, especially the Egyptian army, arrived.

Sunday, April 25, Monday, April 26, and Tuesday, April 27, were three days from hell.

Since cutting off il Manshiyyeh, "the bottleneck," from the rest of the city was the declared aim of the heavy mortar bombing that arrived from Tel Aviv, Subhi's neighborhood took the lion's share.

Early in the morning on Sunday, April 25, the ammunitions that had been robbed from the train finally reappeared in the skies of Jaffa. A barrage of some twenty thousand shells struck the heart of the city for three days.

And unlike in previous springs when flocks of birds filled the skies of Jaffa, this spring, the last spring for the Arabs of Jaffa, flocks of mortar shells flew over the city, forming dark clouds in its skies. The indiscriminate firing of mortar shells spread fear, horror, and death among the city's inhabitants, ultimately bringing the city and the Jaffans to their knees.

Mortar shells whizzed through Martyrs' Square, adding a few more martyrs to a long list.

Mortar shells landed on hospitals, where the sick got sicker and pregnant women gave birth to premature babies.

Mortar shells fell on holy places, where people prayed this would not be their last day.

A barrage of mortar shells fell on schools, on marketplaces, on shops and shoppers, and on banks.

Panic, horror, and hysteria took hold of the city.

Those who were inside buildings rushed out, and those in the streets frantically hurried into buildings.

The injured and the dead were left lying in the streets.

Run for your life or join the dead.

Everyone was searching for a way out: by car, by bus, on a truck, on a cart, on a bike.

Looting was pervasive.

Robberies were many.

There was no water, no electricity, and no fuel.

No ovens to bake a loaf of bread, or shops to buy food from— or, for that matter, banks from which to withdraw money.

One day from hell and the city had become completely dysfunctional.

Like most in the frenzied city, members of Subhi's family spun around themselves and around the house. Rushing in and out of rooms, they argued about what to take and what to leave behind. They yelled at one another as Subhi's mother and sisters gathered some valuables but also some random odds and ends: a pillow, a blanket, a freshly baked orange cake, a birth certificate, an old carpet, a knife. As the chaos continued, Subhi's father rushed out to the street in search of anything on wheels: a car, a truck, a bicycle, or even a carousel. Considering the lack of fuel in the city, a taxi or private car would be way beyond his means to hire, even if he could have found one. Awaiting the verdict of who was to leave and who was to stay, Subhi's grandparents helplessly sat in a corner away from the madding crowd. Only the kids seemed to have enough presence of mind or a heart to think of their petrified pets.

"Grandma, can I take Sambo with me?" asked Sami, Subhi's four-year-old nephew.

"Grandchild, I don't know if they have a place for me, let alone a place for your pet."

"But you're huge, Grandma, and Sambo is tiny." That certainly brought a smile to Grandma's face.

"No, *habibi*, leave the cat with Subhi. He will bring her with him when he comes to Nablus, or to the farm, or you'll see her when we come back."

"When will we come back?" asked little Sami.

"I don't know, *habibi*. Soon, I hope."

But, as we all know by now, soon never arrived.

In spite of the fact that most roads going inland to Salameh and Jerusalem were blocked and too dangerous to cross, with the help of their neighbor Abu Hani (the father of Subhi's late friend Hani), Khadijeh and her share of the family made it safely to Nablus, and Ismael and Amir made it on foot to their orange grove, while Subhi, Jamal, and Habeeb stayed put at home.

ON MONDAY, APRIL 26, the Jewish forces changed their approach. The frontal urban attacks that had followed the mortar shelling on April 25 were now replaced by what Jewish war experts called "train wagon" tactics. Rather than fighting in the narrow streets and alleys of il Manshiyyeh neighborhood, the Jewish militia moved from one conquered Arab house to another, igniting big openings in the interior walls of the homes as they advanced. As big bangs got closer and closer to his family's house, Subhi—like many other ill-trained young fighters in his alley—realized it was time for him to give up his rifle and flee the scene. He wished he were in a position to inform Uncle Habeeb or his brother Jamal about his escape. However, that would've increased his chances of being killed, because Uncle Habeeb was on the front lines. He was one of the hard-hitting fighters whose mission was to booby-trap the narrow alleys of the neighborhood where they expected the enemy to come from the north and east. Having given up on finding Uncle Habeeb and Jamal, Subhi hoped only to leave his home and reach his grandmother's house in the Old City of Jaffa safely. Seeing the Israeli flag flying on top of Hassan Bek Mosque brought tears to Subhi's eyes. Only then did he realize that his neighborhood had fallen.

Escaping west, he felt as if he had only escaped from one side of hell to the other. The whole city was fleeing to the openness of the sea: like a waterfall made of human bodies, thousands and thousands of people were pouring onto the seashore. Some hundred thousand inhabitants were trying to reach the city's port in search of a raft, a fishing boat, a sailboat, a yacht, or a big ship—anything that would take them to nowhere or to the unknown.

Jaffa's port had become a big suq, a market where bargains were made about human bodies: a whole family or half of one, a quarter of a family or one-third or even one person alone.

"Here, I'll give you all the money I have, just get my mother and children away from here."

"Can't you see the boat is full? It's about to tip over with every-one on board."

"God forbid," the father said, and moved on to bargain with the owner of another small boat: "Just take these two children and their mother. I and my three boys can wait."

"I only have two spaces left. Hurry up and make up your mind."

Hard choices had to be made right on the spot. Families were divided: a mother with two of her children, the rest left behind; a father with his kids, their grandmother left behind; an old or a sick person left behind all alone, as were most housemaids and pets.

The same small boats that had until recently been loading and unloading millions of oranges from the shallow water of Jaffa's port to the big ships docked a kilometer or two away were now loading and unloading the "Lords of Oranges" and their families. The same fleet of British ships called "Liberty" that had until recently brought Jewish immigrants to Palestine was now carrying Palestinians away from their homeland. A new nation was being born as an ancient one was being annihilated.

As has been the case throughout history, familiarity with the Mediterranean Sea and its alluring blue color made people trust it in spite of its deceptive nature. Caught in a storm for three days, some of the escapees ended up at the bottom of the deep blue sea, while others, like the Prophet Jonah, were swallowed by giant fish that vomited them up on the southern and northern shores, away from home where they and their descendants wandered for the rest of their lives.

Part III

New Masters

೧೦

23

The Day After

(Jaffa, May 1948)

S UBHI HAD NOT SLEPT for several nights. The sudden collapse of his world, the disappearance of his city, of his people and his beloved, was beyond his comprehension. *How could my whole existence be shattered in just a few days?* Subhi wondered. In an attempt to cope with his new reality, he kept thinking about the three consecutive attacks: the twenty thousand mortar shells, the train-wagon tactics, and the bombardment of the Jewish militia by the British air force that determined the fate of his city and shifted the course of his life.

The images of the chaotic exodus of a whole town—people fleeing their homes, sleeping on the shores for days on end as they waited for a boat or ships to take them to unknown destinations— kept Subhi awake all night. A strip of nightmarish images had projected themselves on the insides of his eyelids, giving him splitting headaches. Worse were the moans of the elderly, the shrieks of a mother in search of her lost child, the frantic screams of a child in search of his mother. Like a broken record, it all cyclically echoed in his ears in spite of the deadly silence of his long and lonely nights. Though most of the city's inhabitants had disappeared beyond the horizon of the Mediterranean Sea, like ghosts, their souls were still hovering over the abandoned homes and haunted city.

Their absence seemed to have more presence than their presence.

From the balcony of his grandmother's house, all that Subhi could see or hear all day and night was the deserted Palestinian homes being broken into. The new Jewish immigrants, whole families sometimes, were now joining in the organized robberies that had thus far been carried out by the Jewish militia. They were going into houses and taking every piece of furniture, to be either carried away on foot or loaded into trucks: whole living room sets, bedroom sets, dining sets, kitchen cupboards, fridges, ovens, Persian carpets, chandeliers, baby cribs, radios, pianos, books, mahogany tables and chairs, and Chippendale chests of drawers. Nothing was left untouched: hospitals, schools, banks, shops, offices, clinics, markets, factories, fishing boats. In addition to the stealing of books and terrified pets, what saddened Subhi most was the looting of brand-new cars, especially the Mercedes-Benzes, the ones he often stopped to admire at the Gharghour Showroom on his way to and from work.

It was the eerie silence of a ghostly city that also kept Subhi's eyes wide open through the night.

Gone was all he could think, around the clock.

Gone were his family members and his family's house.

Gone were his neighbors and his neighborhood.

Gone were M'allem Mustafa and his garage.

Gone were the engines Subhi had repaired.

Gone were his job and his reputation as the best mechanic in town.

Gone were all his clients who had been classified as rich, poor, or in between, with three different fees.

Gone was the Islamic Sports Club, where he had played football with his friends.

Gone were the neighborhood boys with whom he had swum.

Gone were his friends with whom he had played cards, with whom he had gone to Friday prayers at the Grand Mosque, and with whom he had participated in demonstrations at Clock Tower Plaza.

Gone was the library from which he had borrowed books or torn pages with photos of white wedding dresses for his Shams from magazines.

Gone was Hassan, the tailor of his English suit.

Gone were the city's numerous cafés, cinemas, and bookshops.

Gone were the foreign workers of the Fools' Café.

Gone were the politicians and intellectuals of Café il Inshirah.

Gone were the rich orange merchants.

But most tragically, gone was his Shams.

And what use was his English suit when all hopes of getting married to Shams had vanished?

Gone was his city, which had once been called the "mother of strangers."

For she herself had become the stranger.

Gone was his city, which on May 9 declared itself an "open city."

Subhi could not help but think of rape whenever the expression "open city" was mentioned. Yafa 'Arous il Bahar, Jaffa the Bride of the Sea, was indeed violated and dishonored in every sense of the word.

Gone was the city whose municipal council, or more accurately, its "Emergency Committee," had signed a surrender agreement on May 13, 1948, a day before the end of the British Mandate. In hopes of protecting the little that remained of the city and its inhabitants, they handed the city "peacefully" to the head of the Haganah forces, who promised to safeguard Jaffa and its people. However, before the ink had dried on the agreement, the city was violated, robbed, and the Haganah forces terrorized the few thousand Jaffans who remained.

An English suit, a deaf grandmother, and an obsession with knowing what had happened to his Shams were all that Subhi had the day after.

Trying to grasp all that was gone, but also all that remained, Subhi thought of his eighty-year-old grandmother Farida, who had refused to leave her house in the Old City when her daughter Khadijeh risked her life to reach it, to take her mother to Nablus with the rest of the family.

"Over my dead body!" screamed deaf Farida at the top of her lungs. "I left my house once in my life, but never again."

Farida was referring to World War I, when the Ottoman government evacuated the majority of the inhabitants of Jaffa, especially the Jewish community, for fear that they would cooperate with the Allies.

"I warn you, daughter, one never feels at home away from home." Farida paused and then added, "In your home, you die once and for all; *fi il ghurbeh*, in the diaspora, you die every single day out of humiliation." And since no one anticipated the fall of Jaffa, Khadijeh respected her mother's wishes and left her alone.

Not aware of this incident, Subhi wondered what had made his grandmother stay put in her house when a frenzy of a mass flight struck the whole city. *Is it because she is deaf or because she is a "stubborn old lady," as her sons and daughters, including my mother, often refer to her?* Curious, Subhi came close to Farida and yelled at the top of his voice, "Sitti, weren't you scared of the mortar shells?"

"Of what?" she screamed back at Subhi, who giggled, something he hadn't done in a while.

"Of the mortar shells that struck the city all Sunday and Monday, but also Tuesday. Poor neighborhood, I tell you, nothing was left of it. God knows what happened to our house. I escaped through the window as the Jewish militia exploded the inner walls, making a huge hole in my parents' bedroom!" Subhi yelled. Narrating and re-narrating the same events was Subhi's way of coping with his new reality.

"You mean when the *Inglese* fighter planes bombarded the fuck-ers and made them withdraw to Tel Aviv? Oh, that day I celebrated by eating a whole chocolate cake all by myself."

"You ate the whole thing all by yourself? What about your diabetes?"

"What about it?" Farida asked in denial and then added, "Of course I gave some to the neighbors' kids."

Farida was referring to the day, Tuesday, April 27, when the Brit-ish bombarded the Jewish militia, forcing them to withdraw from il Manshiyyeh. Unhappy with the militia's violation of the agree-ment in occupying Jaffa, the British forces eventually intervened. In their cool conspiratorial manner, the British eventually gave a warning and then an ultimatum to the Jewish militia asking them to withdraw from il Manshiyyeh; otherwise, they would use their air forces. Having been bombarded on that Tuesday, the Jewish militia was forced to withdraw from Jaffa, leaving behind a neighborhood in ruins whose population had by now taken refuge on the open shores.

"I tell you, Sitti," screamed Subhi, "the British should've intervened from day one. Not after the two days of shelling the city and dynamiting the whole of il Manshiyyeh neighborhood. If you had seen the Israeli flag flying over the minaret of Hassan Bek Mosque and the Palestinian police station, you would've cried just as I did."

"I'm happy not to have seen it and happier not to have cried. However, my beloved grandson, try to save your tears as much as you can for now. Trust your old grandma, you'll need them in the future."

Whatever the reasons Farida had remained in Jaffa, Subhi was grateful to have a place to stay and an old wise soul to talk to.

24

New Masters

A NEW NATION WAS BORN while an old one was eradicated. Or to quote the words of Israel Zangwill (a close associate of Father of Zionism Theodor Herzl's) written in 1901 for the *New Liberal Review:* "Palestine is a country without a people; the Jews are a people without a country." This was a lie that had been shrewdly branded, marketed, and bought by the "free world." It resonated with the free world only because it reminded them of their own history. Whatever the reasons were for such sympathy for the newly born state, a crime that had been praised refused to halt.

"*Bang . . . bang . . . bang . . .* Open the door before I ignite you with it!"

Subhi jumped out of bed in his underwear expecting the worse. *Who could it be at this early hour of the day?* he wondered, hoping that the banging and yelling would not wake up his grandmother. Was it the Jewish militia that had been terrorizing the two thousand Palestinians who had stayed behind, or was it one of the many gangs of robbers that had thrived and taken control of a lawless city?

With shaking hands, he pulled back the iron latch on the entry door, and before he knew it, a dozen militiamen had poured into the living room.

"Hands up! Face to the wall!" they yelled, but before he could follow their instructions, four of them knocked him down on the floor facedown, twisted his arms behind his back, and handcuffed him.

"Who else is in the house?"

"My eighty-year-old grandmother, who is deaf."

"Who else is here? Any other male terrorists in this house?"

"No, my father and brothers are all gone."

"Gone where?"

"I don't know."

"*Kazzab kbeer*, big liar. You don't know where your family is?"

"They're all gone."

"Gone where?"

"My mother, my two sisters, and my grandparents went to our relatives in Nablus or maybe Damascus; my father and my younger brother, Amir, went to our orange grove; and I have no idea where my brother Jamal and my uncle Habeeb are." This was the very first time that Subhi had considered the benefits of being beyond the reach of the new masters. The last thing he wished for his father, uncle Habeeb, and two brothers was to be humiliated the way he was now. Perhaps he should've boarded one of those crammed boats.

While the commander continued to interrogate Subhi, six militiamen roamed around the house with their heavy machine guns. The way they pointed their rifles, pushed doors wide open, and jumped from one angle to another made it feel as if they were in a major battle. The only enemy they found after a long search was Subhi's snoring grandma Farida.

"Stand up and stay put," said the commander as two fighters

came forward, ordered Subhi to spread his legs, and looked in his underwear. What disturbed Subhi most, in addition to the inspection of his testicles, was the presence of two Palestinians whom he knew well. While Fawwaz 'Asfour had a chicken shop on il Salahi Street, Salim 'Arbeed was a guard for the municipality of Jaffa. *Am I hallucinating or is this for real?* Subhi asked himself.

"Fawwaz, Salim, what on earth are you doing here?" he blurted out, though he had by then figured out the tragedy: the two Palestinian men were collaborators.

"Shut up, young man. It is us who conduct the interrogation here, not you," responded the Jewish commander, then added, "Tell us what you've stolen in the last few days before we turn the house inside out."

"Me! Stolen! I have not stolen anything. I haven't even been out of the house for the last five days."

"Liar, like all of you *Aghabs*, Arabs."

Totally offended by the accusation, Subhi mumbled, "I have never stolen a thing in my whole life, not in the past, not now, and not in the future."

"*Harami u kazzab*, a thief and a liar." This seemed to be the one phrase that the Jewish commander had memorized by heart because he kept repeating it. "Go around the house and see if there are any stolen items," said the commander in Hebrew to his men, but also in Arabic to Fawwaz and Salim, the two Palestinian collaborators, who went to search the bedrooms.

"But how can your men tell whether an item has been stolen or not if you don't know what we have in the first place?" Subhi couldn't help but ask.

"Don't argue with me. Stay where you are and don't move!" yelled the Jewish commander as he went around the living room inspecting every item on the coffee table and every book on the bookshelves that covered the whole wall.

"Whose books are these?"

"Ours. I mean, my grandfather's." Subhi did not understand the interest in his grandfather's library.

"I was told you were a mechanic." Subhi was more disturbed by the use of the past tense—"you were a mechanic"—than by the insinuation that mechanics don't read.

"From which public library or private houses have you stolen these books?" the commander asked, then made a hand gesture to his militiamen, indicating that they should go ahead and empty the shelves of all the books. They seemed to be prepared for such a mission as carry bags appeared on the spot.

"But sir . . ."

"Shut up, or I'll have them take you to the stairwell and shoot you like a dog."

Tears, which Subhi thought had dried up after all he had seen in the last few weeks, brimmed in his eyes as he watched the bookshelves being emptied of his grandfather's law books. Though circumstances had not yet allowed for it, Subhi, who had a great passion for books, still hoped that he, or his younger brother, Amir, would study Islamic law at il Azhar University in Cairo just like their maternal grandfather. In spite of the fact that Subhi had left school at an early age to follow his passion, books meant the world to him. Subhi's Friday routine was predictable: an early bath and a late breakfast of hummus, *foul,* and falafel, followed by the communal Friday prayers in the Grand Mosque of Jaffa, an anti–British policy demonstration in Clock Tower Plaza, and a visit to the Islamic Library to borrow a book or two. There was rarely a Friday that Subhi missed going to the Islamic Library.

Unable to wipe his tears with his cuffed hands but wanting to hide them, Subhi closed his eyes, then took a deep breath. He reopened his eyes only when Fawwaz walked out of Subhi's bedroom carrying the English suit on a wooden hanger.

"From whose house have you stolen this expensive suit, Subhi?" inquired Fawwaz in an authoritative voice with a cynical smile and an air of victory.

"That is my suit. Leave it alone." Tears ran down Subhi's cheeks freely now.

"See, you're all worked up, which proves you stole it."

"You son of a bitch, leave my suit alone. . . . I did not steal it. It is mine."

"Yes, sure, you did not steal it! How could a young mechanic like yourself afford an expensive English suit like this one?"

"Shut up, you two. I don't want to hear one more word. Arrest the thief and take him to the *qishleh,* the police station, right away."

"I'll show you, *bawarjeek,*" were the last words that Subhi said to Fawwaz before he was forced out of the house, down the stairs, and into the street, where two military jeeps were waiting for him. And just before he was pushed into one of the jeeps, Subhi looked up and saw his grandmother watching him from her balcony. Still in his underwear, he was taken to the police station.

Only while in prison did Subhi realize how the circumstances of the last five and a half months had prevented him from reflecting on his love for Shams. Subhi recalled the one saying his mother often repeated, "Far from the eye, far from the heart." "No, far from it," he mumbled to himself. There was hardly a day—or more accurately, a night—that passed that he didn't think of Shams. Being in prison for two full days gave Subhi the uninterrupted time to relive the precious moments he and Shams had had together: the first time he saw her in il Nabi Rubin wearing the orange and white dress he liked, the time he stared at her for too long and got his first erection, the time he was kicked out of the holy shrine in Salameh, the excitement he felt the minute his eyes fell on her every time he took the bus from Jaffa to Salameh and back. But what he treasured most was the kiss they had shared.

TWO LONG DAYS WERE spent in rooms of *il qishleh* before Subhi was brought to stand in front of an investigation committee headed by a Yemeni captain by the name of Obadiah.

"Young man, make it short: yes or no, did you steal this suit?"

"No, I did not."

"Do you have any idea how much such a suit is worth?"

"Yes, Captain Obadiah, three green notes and one red note. I mean, it is worth eight pounds."

"And how much does a mechanic like yourself earn a day? Is it twenty or thirty piastres?"

"Thirty."

"Thirty piastres!"

"Yes, Captain." Not used to addressing Jewish militants, Subhi alternated between captain, general, and sir.

"And how does a mechanic who earns thirty piastres afford a fine suit like this one? Can you explain this to me?"

"I did not pay for it, sir."

"See, you stole it."

"No, I did not steal it. It wasn't I who paid for it, it was Khawaja Michael."

"*The* Khawaja Michael?" asked Captain Obadiah, who seemed to recognize the name.

"Yes, sir, *the* Khawaja Michael, Amin Michael, Abu Salim."
Subhi gave all of Khawaja Michael's names so as to convince the
interrogator that he knew one of the most influential men in town,
and knew him well.

"Yes, of course we know who Khawaja Michael is, but how do
you know him?" The committee head looked at other men in the
room, then added, "You're in big trouble, young man. As the Arabic
saying goes, *habel il kizeb qaseer,* your lie will soon be revealed, as
Khawaja Michael is one of the few businessmen who did not leave
the city."

"You mean you have not yet thrown him out of his home?"

"We threw no one out of their houses, young man. It was your
leaders who asked you to leave."

Exhausted and defeated on all levels, Subhi was not in a position
to argue with the victors about the defeat of his city. He had lived
it all, witnessed it all, and experienced it firsthand. Nonetheless, he
decided to be strategic and concentrate on getting his suit.

"I am delighted to know that Khawaja Michael is still in town so
he can be a witness to my innocence."

"OK, take him away and lock him up until we summon Khawaja
Michael tomorrow or the day after."

No news could have brought more hope to Subhi's aching heart.
Not only because Khawaja Michael was the perfect witness to his
innocence, but also because he might know something about the fate
of Salameh, and by extension, the fate of Shams. Subhi had heard
that Salameh's women and girls had been evacuated weeks before
the town fell on April 29, but he wanted to know more. "Things
happen for a reason," Subhi recalled his mother's saying. The only
reason he had been unjustly accused and brought to prison was to
see Khawaja Michael.

Not that he needed an additional reason not to sleep that night: collapsing on the floor of the prison room, his head against the wall, Subhi recalled the intimate details of his encounter with Shams on their last day of Mawsim il Nabi Rubin. Thinking of Shams often warmed his broken heart and elevated his spirit.

Subhi also recalled the number of times he had gotten on the Jaffa–il Lyd bus in Salameh in the hope of seeing his beloved as she got out of school and walked along the road where the bus stopped. Thrilled to see her smile at him, he would stay on the same bus that took him to il Lyd and back to Jaffa via Salameh again. Both he and Shams had memorized this bus schedule by heart.

With fondness, he also recalled the day he had accompanied his mother and grandmother to Salameh for their annual visit to the holy shrine of il-Sheikh Salameh (after which the village was named). He remembered the exact date: it was the fourth of the Hijri month Sh'aban, hence the name of this celebration, il Sh'abawieh. He smiled remembering the words of the shrine caretaker, who kicked him out, saying that only small boys could accompany their mothers and that he, Subhi, was a *jahsh,* a big ass, and needed to leave the premises right away. In spite of it all, the desires of "*il jahsh*" were fulfilled. From a distance, he spotted Shams among the crowds of women and young girls. He gave her a big smile and a wink, and she responded with that shy smile that made his heart melt. Short as it was, the encounter filled Subhi's heart with enough passion that it sustained him until he engineered another encounter.

With the fall of Jaffa, the fall of Salameh, and the disappearance of Palestine, there was hardly any hope for him to see Shams ever again. In spite of the bleakness of it all, thinking of the warmth of Shams's body on his allowed him to sleep for a few hours that night.

25

The "Disputed" Suit Interrogations

"S UBKHII, *meen* Subkhii. Who is Subkhii?" yelled a guard as he cracked open the heavy metal door of the prison hall.

"*Ana,* I am." Half asleep, Subhi jumped to his feet.

"Come with me." Drowsily, Subhi followed the guard along endless corridors before he was instructed to wait in a room jammed with other Palestinian men. Subhi looked around in search of Khawaja Michael but could not find him. He came forward when his name was called and followed the same guard, who brought him to the same room where he had first been interrogated two days earlier.

In the "courtroom," Obadiah sat behind a metal desk. Right behind him stood the two militiamen who had searched Subhi's house. To their right was Fawwaz, one of the two Arab collaborators. Subhi's heart fell when he noticed the absence of his suit. He looked around, inspecting the room in vain. Like all Arab properties in Occupied Palestine, everything (land, orange groves, houses, villas, buildings, shops, schools, hospitals, cars, boats, factories, banks, even books and furniture) belonged to the newly established state until proven otherwise. While Subhi's suit had become "a disputed" suit whose ownership had to be proven, Subhi himself had become "a criminal," a "thief," until proven otherwise.

Preoccupied with the disappearance of his suit from the courtroom, Subhi didn't notice right away that the shabby-looking man who was bent over in his chair in the corner was Khawaja Michael. He could not believe his own eyes: the most elegant man in the whole city of Jaffa was in his pajamas and robe. Tears rolled down Subhi's pale cheeks, and his lips quivered. As painful as it was, he could not turn his eyes away from the unshaved man who had obviously been dragged to this farce of a courtroom against his will. Subhi recalled the first time he saw Khawaja Michael at the entrance of the garage where he worked: the light behind him had made him look like a deity, an English lord, or a knight.

Nothing had ever impressed Subhi more than Khawaja Michael's elegance, with his cashmere suit and his fedora. Nothing had ever given Subhi more joy and hope for his future, and that of Shams, than the suit given to him in appreciation of his ingenious work. More tears brimmed in Subhi's tired eyes as he thought of what had become of one of Jaffa's richest and most influential men. Like his city, which until recently had been vivacious, elegant, affluent, proud, and open, Khawaja Michael was broken, shattered, a ghost of his former self.

In the meantime, Subhi had forgotten that he himself had been in his underwear since they had dragged him to prison two days earlier.

Awakening from the initial shock, Subhi yelled, "Goodness, is that you, Khawaja?" He took a few steps in the direction of Khawaja Michael.

"Shut up and go back to your place!" yelled Captain Obadiah as two armed men grabbed Subhi by the arms and pushed him back.

"You're forbidden to talk to the witness or look in his direction, *mafkhoum*, understood?" said Captain Obadiah.

Witness? Witness?! Is that what has become of Khawaja Michael, a "witness"? First you strip him of his rank as a khawaja, *then you refer to him by his first name, and now he has become a mere witness. A witness to what? To your crimes? To your cruelty? We've all become witnesses to the biggest robbery in the history of mankind. You steal our land, our cities, our oranges, our orchids, our homes, our shops, our garages, our fishing boats, our cars and buses, our livestock, our furniture, our books, our lives, and our souls. You steal a whole country, a fully furnished country, then have the chutzpah to accuse me of stealing my own suit!*

Having argued the case in his head, Subhi looked at Khawaja Michael expecting him to say something, but the khawaja stayed silent. Like a statue, he was frozen in his chair; his glazed eyes and expressionless face made Subhi suspect that he might've had a stroke.

He might as well have been dead.

"What's your name?" asked Captain Obadiah from behind his desk while staring at Subhi.

"You brought me and my suit to the *qishleh* and kept me here for two nights not knowing my name?"

"Shut up and give me your full name!" yelled Obadiah.

"Subhi Ismael Abu Shehadeh."

"First witness, can you tell me your name?" yelled Obadiah, addressing Khawaja Michael, who kept quiet.

As no response came from Khawaja Michael, it was Subhi who replied: "But captain, you know Khawaja Michael's name; you're the ones who brought him here."

"Keep quiet. I did not ask you. I am asking the witness."

"Amin Michael," whispered one of the two Jewish militiamen

who knew the terrible condition Khawaja Michael was in before forcing him into a military jeep that carried him to the *qishleh*. "Amin Michael, do you happen to know this man?"

Sill frozen in his chair, Khawaja Michael did not reply. He took a deep breath, which reassured Subhi that his only witness was still alive.

"Amin Michael, the thief standing in front of you claims that you paid for the expensive English suit we found in his bedroom. Can you testify to that?" Khawaja Michael gazed at the ceiling, took another deep breath, and kept quiet.

Obadiah reformulated his question: "If that is true, can you make a head gesture indicating yes or no?" To everyone's utter surprise, Khawaja Michael slowly nodded. A smile came to Subhi's face before Obadiah asked another question.

"First witness, can you describe the suit? Can you tell us what color it is?" Only at this point did Subhi understand why the suit had disappeared from the investigation room. A long silence prevailed before Khawaja Michael uttered the few crucial words that set Subhi and his suit free: "Gray with a thin red silk line."

This time it was Captain Obadiah, his three militiamen, and the two Arab informers who gazed at one another, then froze. Subhi's smile grew as he looked in the direction of his suit-savior only to find Khawaja Michael lost in a daze once again.

"Take the witness back to his house," said interrogator Obadiah in a disappointed voice as he stood from behind his desk, turned his back, and exited the room. Subhi's heart bled when he saw the two militiamen raise Khawaja Michael, who could hardly walk, from his chair and escort him out of the courtroom.

"Here is the suit," said informant Fawwaz as he reappeared in the empty interrogation room with Subhi's suit. Subhi took note of the fact that Fawwaz, like his false accuser masters, avoided saying "your" suit.

Still thinking of shattered Khawaja Michael, Subhi stretched out his arm and snatched the suit from Fawwaz's hand. Something felt wrong, very wrong. The hanger felt much lighter than it should be. To his utter dismay, Subhi saw that his trousers were missing.

"What happened to my trousers?" Subhi yelled.

"I don't know," replied Fawwaz in a coolly vindictive manner.

"What do you mean, you don't know?"

"I don't know means I don't know."

"*Yabnel kalb,* son of a bitch, where are my trousers?"

"I just told you I don't know."

"Motherfucker, give them back to me."

"I don't know where they are. You should be grateful you got the jacket back."

Having run out of words, Subhi took a deep breath, then in a resigned voice, said, "Why am I surprised? What should one expect from a collaborator who helped the enemy steal his own land?"

Eager to get out, Subhi restrained himself from spitting on Fawwaz, but he gave him a long hard look.

With half of his suit in hand while still in his underwear, Subhi exited the *qishleh.*

Angry and in despair, Subhi wandered aimlessly through the streets of Jaffa. He thought not only of the missing half of his suit but also of Shams: the missing half of his dream. He was mostly concerned about the fate of his older brother, Jamal, and his uncle Habeeb. Both were part of the neighborhood militia who had fought against the advancement of the Jewish militia into il Manshiyyeh.

Not knowing where to go or whom to ask about the fate of Jamal and Habeeb, he decided to venture into his neighborhood and, if possible, his house.

However, since the area was surrounded by barbed wired and had been declared a closed "military zone," Subhi did not want to risk going home. Walking around his neighborhood, he found it difficult to believe that all this destruction and devastation had resulted from the three-day battle over his neighborhood. He could see that most of the houses, including his family's home, were being bulldozed in order to prevent him and others from coming back.

26

At Jaffa's Port

To SUBHI'S SURPRISE, it was his young brother, Amir, who opened the door for him when he arrived back at his grandmother's house in the Old City. They had not seen one another for weeks, and Subhi had no idea what made Amir clutch him and sob until their father appeared with the terrible news. Jamal, Subhi's older brother, had been killed in the battle over il Manshiyyeh, while Habeeb had been injured.

"It's all Habeeb's fault. I told him that you and Jamal were too young to join the neighborhood guards. You were also untrained to meet the Zionist monsters. But I am so happy you came out alive, Subhi." Subhi's father hugged him tightly and wept. Devastated by the death of his brother, Subhi collapsed next to his grandmother, placed his head in her lap, and moaned.

Subhi wondered how was it possible that everything in his life had changed forever except for family dynamics. How cruel it was of his father to accuse Uncle Habeeb or make him responsible for the death of Jamal. What bothered Subhi most was the fact that it was his father who had run away and hid in his orange grove and left the three of them behind to defend their home and their neighborhood. It was then that Subhi realized he had not inquired about the rest of the family, including his injured uncle Habeeb.

"Any news from my mother and sisters? And what about Uncle Habeeb?" Subhi asked.

"Yes, they are in Nablus, and I will find a way to smuggle them in soon."

"Smuggle them in? Why smuggle them?"

"Where have you been, son? Don't you know that your city is being ruled by a military administration headed by a Jewish governor who has declared it a closed city? That means we need a special permit to leave or enter."

"And why is that?" Subhi asked, trying to digest all the bad news brought to him by his father.

"So they make sure no one comes back home. Don't you know all of this?" Surprised, Ismael repeated his earlier question: "Where have you been, son?"

"I've been in prison, Father, in *il qishleh*."

"That much I gathered from my mother-in-law. And for what? A stupid suit."

Subhi was hurt by his father's thoughtless comment about his suit. However, considering the tragedy of losing his older brother, and the loss and the separation they were all going through, Subhi decided to let it go.

"Can you get my mother, my sisters, and my grandparents permits to come back?"

"What permits? They don't give these permits to anyone, but I have gotten to know a group of smugglers who bring people back to their cities, or villages, for a fee." The one thing Ismael failed to mention was that he himself had joined this gang.

Considering the total collapse of the economy, the lack of jobs and lack of income, the only option for someone like Ismael was to join a gang of robbers or a gang of smugglers—or both.

"So are you bringing my mother back for a fee?" Subhi joked, trying to make light of the heavy reality.

"I'll have my mother-in-law pay that," replied Ismail, looking at Farida.

"What?" she yelled back.

"My mother-in-law's hearing has always been selective; nothing new about that."

It was his father's joke that made Subhi aware that he himself was also running out of the little money he had. This was the first time he had thought of the urgency of finding a job. How weird the idea of that felt in a shattered city whose employers had disappeared. He wondered how long it would take before they came back. Learning that Jaffa had become a closed city did not give Subhi much hope. It was at critical moments like these that he thought of M'allem Mustafa and Uncle Habeeb, the two men who had come to his aid when he needed it.

"Come on, Amir, let's go back to the *bayyara* before it gets dark," said Ismael, and bent to pick up a bag full of kitchen items and cooking utensils given to him by Farida.

Just before his father and brother exited the house, Subhi gathered his courage and asked, "How serious are Uncle Habeeb's injuries? And what hospital is he in?"

"Hospital? He is not in any hospital, he is where he belongs: in prison. He was taken as a prisoner of war."

"How do you know?"

"I went to the ICRC offices and inquired about him and Jamal."

Realizing how much he had to learn about the new realities of his postwar life, not knowing that the ICRC stood for the International Committee of the Red Cross, Subhi kept quiet.

"I only wish I'd lost a brother, not a son," Ismael said in a quivering voice before he burst out crying.

It was Ismael who cried out loud this time.

27

Disputed

TO AVOID FURTHER ASSAULTS, bullying, and humiliation not only by the Haganah forces but also by the hostile *olim*—the new Jewish immigrants arriving in Jaffa from Bulgaria, Bukhara, and Yemen to settle in Palestinian homes—Subhi tried to stay out of trouble by limiting his trips out of the house to the sheer minimum. The lawlessness and unruliness of the city filled the hearts of Jaffans with fear. A 7:00 p.m. to 6:00 a.m. curfew was imposed on Jaffa, as well as on all other Palestinian cities and villages in Palestine, now known as Israel.

In order to subjugate the remaining two thousand Jaffans, but more important, to appropriate their homes and properties, the newly established state set up a "transfer committee." The objective of such a committee was not only to expel Palestinians from their towns and villages but also to fire at anyone trying to sneak back to their homes. Like il Manshiyyeh, neighboring villages such as Salameh, Yazour, il 'Abbasiyyeh, il Safrieyyeh, and many others had been depopulated and leveled. A "relocation plan" was also set in order to transfer the Palestinians who had stayed in their homes to designated Arab ghettos. The relocation plan also entailed the settling of new Jewish immigrants in Palestinian homes. The relocation of the remaining Palestinians and the settling of new Jewish immigrants in Palestinian homes went hand in hand.

Though il 'Ajami was one of Jaffa's posh neighborhoods, its location away from both Tel Aviv in the north and Bat Yam in the south made it suitable to become Jaffa's Arab ghetto. In addition to hosting the remaining two thousand Jaffans who had been evicted from their homes in the different neighborhoods, il 'Ajami received an additional three thousand Palestinian peasants who had been evacuated from their homes in nearby villages. A total of five thousand Palestinians were now living in an overcrowded neighborhood that had been officially named "Area A." As soon as the Jaffans and peasants from the neighboring villages had been transferred to il 'Ajami, Area A was surrounded by barbed wire, with three guarded entry points.

A few months separated Subhi's first imprisonment over the disputed suit from his second imprisonment. However, the allegations this time were far more serious. Subhi was arrested under the pretext of illegally "occupying an absentee Arab property." And the disputed property happened to be his grandmother's house. Farida's home, where he had been living for a few months now, was all he had as his family's house in il Manshiyyeh had been leveled to the ground.

Since the nerve-wracking life under the "new masters" included their breaking into people's homes, the frequent banging on Farida's door and that of the neighbors was not exactly music, not even to Farida's compromised ears. One morning, Subhi found his grandmother dead in her bed. Devastated by the loss of his grandmother, the only member of his family who had stood her ground and stayed in her home, Subhi collapsed on her bed and sobbed. He gathered his courage and held her freezing palm and stared straight into her face. What perplexed him was the cynical smile on her peaceful face. He could not but interpret it to mean: "I am thrilled to be dead so as not to hear more banging on doors or see more of the unpleasant chapters of this *nakba*, this catastrophe, which will not end for some time. Farewell until we are united in heaven, away from this hell."

A week or two after the death of his grandmother, Subhi was awakened by yet another aggressive banging on his door. "Oh no, not again!" he screamed, thinking it was the Haganah forces that had total control over the city by now. Subhi had no option but to open the door. But before he knew it, four Bulgarian families were fighting one another over their share of his grandmother's house. And he was on his way, once more, to the *qishleh*.

"But—" objected Subhi.

"I know that Farida was your maternal grandmother, but you are not her heir. Do you understand? Her heirs are her children, and those are your mother, Khadijeh; your aunt Abeer; and your three uncles. I can name them for you if you want. But as you know, they are all absentees; hence their property is categorized as an 'absentee property.' "

Confused and defeated by the occupiers' lawlessness like all the residents of the Old City, Subhi was evicted from his grandmother's house. He was now sharing a house with two Palestinian families who had been evicted from the nearby village of Yazour. The five and seven family members were brought to live in one of the deserted Palestinian homes in il 'Ajami. What worried Subhi most was that more displaced families would arrive. He could no longer tolerate sharing his tiny room with yet another family. Needless to say, only a few Jaffans such as Khawaja Michael managed to keep their homes to themselves.

As an escape from the overcrowded house and also the tight scrutiny and surveillance in Area A, the sea had become Subhi's only friend and refuge in spite of its reputation as deceptive, *ghaddar*. Every day, he watched the horizon, beyond which the people of his city had completely disappeared. The tragic images of their flight and their deafening shrieks still resonated in his head. While the deep, rough sea erased all traces of crimes committed in it, crimes on land were much harder to hide. Every time Subhi looked east, meaning inland, into the remains of his city, his eyes filled with tears. Looking east reminded him of Salameh and Shams. Looking east meant staring into a ghost town of broken people, old men and women left behind, a starving horse or meowing cat or fearful stray dog, bombarded or flattened to the ground parts of il Manshiyyeh, empty markets, closed shops, robbed banks, and boarded-up villas whose owners had left them in fear, hoping to come back once the bombing stopped. Looking east reminded him of death. Like the missing trousers of his English suit and his grandmother's house, most aspects of his life had become "disputed." Like sand dunes, everything was shifting under his feet.

To avoid getting in more trouble but also to save himself the pain of seeing more vandalism and mass looting of Arab homes and properties, Subhi often changed his route. On his way to meet Abu Ghaleb, an old family friend who had promised him a job in his repair shop on Jaffa's port, Subhi passed by Villa Bitar, located in Hai il Nuzha, which until recently had been the most elegant and modern neighborhood in Jaffa. Like many in Jaffa who read the daily newspaper *il Falastin*, Subhi knew who the owner, Mr. Abdurrahman il

Bitar, was. But also, he himself had been to this splendid villa once or twice to repair something he could no longer recall.

IN ORDER NOT to raise the suspicions of the Haganah forces that had been supervising the systematic looting of Villa Bitar, Subhi opted to cross the road rather than go back. In spite of his fears, he was too curious about this particular operation. From a distance, he saw six Haganah soldiers supervising two teams of porters. While one team was loading the villa's luxurious furniture into a big truck, the other team was loading Abdurrahman il Bitar's personal library into a smaller one. Because he loved books, but also because of the looting of his grandfather's library and that of the Islamic Library, where he often went, the stealing of books was what infuriated Subhi most. *Why steal our books when most of them are in Arabic? And why steal Arabic books when you detest everything Arab?* Subhi wondered. Listening to the instructions given by the head of the looting gang to the dozens of porters carrying chairs, carpets, chandeliers, radios, and books, Subhi concluded that most if not all of the porters were Palestinians. Or why else would the head of the Haganah give, or rather yell, instructions in broken Arabic? True, until recently, Arabs and Jews had been members of the same gangs. However, since May 13, 1948, when Jaffa officially surrendered to the Haganah forces, looting had become an exclusively Jewish activity. While the state took hold of all Arab real estate, meaning land and buildings, movable property such as house and office furniture, clinic and hospital equipment, trucks, cars, herds, and boats were looted or given to the new Jewish immigrants.

Intrigued by the aspects of this particular robbery, Subhi walked slowly so as to take in the scene. To Subhi's surprise, one of the porters coming out of Villa Bitar's lush garden carrying a box full of books looked like Uncle Habeeb. Subhi rubbed his eyes twice, once to make sure that the bearded man with a limp was truly his uncle, and a second time to figure out why Habeeb, who had never read a book in his whole life and whose interests lay elsewhere, would bother to steal books.

Am I hallucinating or have I gone mad? Subhi asked himself. Meanwhile, his trembling legs involuntarily took him to the other side of the road.

"God . . . is that you, Uncle Habeeb?"

Habeeb came closer to Subhi and hugged him, or rather clung to him in such a way that no amount of yelling or pulling by the Haganah soldiers could tear them apart. United, they shed tears until one of the Jewish militiamen who understood the situation yelled at the top of his voice, "For God's sake, leave them alone!"

It took a few inquiries to know who was who and how the two men were related before the whole picture became clear to everyone, Arabs and Jews alike. As Subhi had learned from his father two months earlier, Uncle Habeeb had been injured in his right leg in the il Manshiyyeh battle and was taken as a POW. And like most Palestinian prisoners of war, he had been put to work doing all kinds of odd jobs, including giving the apparatus of the newly established state a hand in looting Arab properties. Some of the educated Palestinians such as Abu Khaled il Batrawi, the librarian of the Islamic Library, were asked to classify books, while others like Uncle Habeeb were given manual work. Little did Subhi know at the time that it would take a few decades before the classified material of the Zionist archive would reveal that the books of the private Palestinian libraries (not only in Jaffa but in all of Palestine) were organized by the Haganah forces on behalf of the new Israeli National Library

and the Hebrew University Library. They slowly but surely sur-
faced on the shelves of these two libraries.

Exchanging a few sentences with his uncle, Subhi learned that
Habeeb would be released in six weeks. Briefed about the news
of most members of his dispersed family, Uncle Habeeb promised
Subhi to come look him up either in il 'Ajami or at Abu Ghaleb's
repair shop on the port. "Provided they don't throw me across the
border as they've done with many other POWs, I'll find you."

"I am sure you will, since only a few Jaffans are left in this
khirbeh, these ruins."

"I hope Shoshanna is still here as well!" Habeeb joked, and burst
into hysterical laughter.

28

Back to Being the Best Mechanic in No-Town

NOTHING LIKE HAVING a profession in one's hands or an education in one's head. Only these two things have proved to be of use or value. They are the only real passports for the poor Palestinians, *il falastiniyyeh il masakhameen*," said seventy-year-old Abu Ghaleb, who was Subhi's new employer and owned a tiny boat repair shop in Jaffa's port. "Not these," he added, holding his Palestinian passport in one hand and a stack of Palestinian notes in the other. Waiting for a rare customer or a broken engine to appear on the scene, both Subhi and Abu Ghaleb sat on the waterfront opposite the repair shop drinking coffee or cheap *'arak*, depending on the hour of the day. With hardly any work, they gathered at the port to chat the day away with the few fishermen and the many unemployed.

"This has become a useless document that can only be exhibited in a museum. And these have also become collectors' items." With difficulty, Abu Ghaleb rose from the empty wooden orange box he had been sitting on, and supporting his aging body with a black cane, walked to the very edge of the harbor platform. He stood there for a moment, looked at his passport and the few notes he had in hand, and with full force, flung them into the sea. Totally taken aback by his act, people stood up and came running, fearing the worst. They feared that Abu Ghaleb was about to throw himself into the sea.

"Oh no!"

"Are you crazy? Have you lost your mind?"

"What on earth have you done? But why?"

While some objected to Abu Ghaleb's act, some kept quiet, and others wept.

"From now on, you can call me Abu Maghloub and not Abu Ghaleb, the father of the defeated and not the father of the victor, understood?" he said angrily as his eyes filled with tears.

Silence prevailed for a few seconds before an older fisherman said, "Abu Ghaleb is right—"

But before he could finish his thought, Abu Ghaleb interrupted him: "If I am right, why do you then still call me Abu Ghaleb when I told you my name is Abu Maghloub? From now on I will not respond to anyone who calls me by my old name."

"Be patient, Abu Maghlu. Why are you so pessimistic?" asked one fisherman, who had known Abu Ghaleb for decades and could not bring himself to utter the word *maghloub,* "the defeated."

"Listen, men, Abu Maghloub is one hundred percent right. Get ready to turn in your Palestinian IDs and passports and prepare yourselves psychologically to receive Israeli ID cards. I wonder what they will write on that bloody document: 'Mohammad Ali, a Palestinian, a fourth-class citizen,'" said Abu Nasser, one of the Abu Ghaleb's friends.

"*Walawo,* come on! A fourth-class citizen? Just like that? Why not second- or third-class citizen?" responded the same fishermen, while other men started speaking, all at the same time.

"No, those designations are reserved for the Yemeni and Moroccan Jews, which is why we Palestinians will be fourth class."

"If we're lucky. I'm afraid Palestinians have no class. I think from now on we are their slaves."

"*Fasharu*, no way. We're nobody's slaves. These Jews are *lamam*, riffraff, who have been gathered from all over. Look at them. They are a gang of robbers, that's what they are!" yelled a young man.

"And this riffraff, these *lamam*, they beat the hell out of you. Stop talking nonsense; that is exactly what got us to this point. It's people like you who are waiting for the Arab lords and Arab armies to arrive and save Jaffa. Have you seen one Arab soldier show up to defend your city, young man?'

The young man got up from his chair and stood his ground: "What's wrong with you men? Why are you such defeatists? This crisis will pass. Think how many times Jaffa has been defeated or destroyed. Here, I can list the conquerors for you: the Persians, the Romans, the Byzantines, the Crusaders, Napoléon, the Egyptian Ibrahim Pasha. But we always come back and land on our feet stronger than ever before. Come on, don't be such losers. We've got to resist."

With the word "resist" came a chill and utter silence. And with the silence came the suspicion that the muscular young man who had given such an insightful speech was a collaborator. It took a while before someone spoke again.

"Who was it exactly who landed on their feet and became stronger?" asked an older fisherman in a resigned voice reflecting utter desperation and fatigue.

"We, the heroic people of Jaffa," responded the young man in an exuberant tone.

"And where are your 'heroic' people of Jaffa today? Have you asked yourself this simple question?"

"But they'll soon come back," insisted the young man.

"Soon! How soon? And from where? You'd better stop dreaming and face the nightmare we're in." The old man took a deep breath, smiled, then added, "Anyway, young man, I appreciate your enthusiasm. Why don't I offer you a glass of *'arak* and you pay me back when you find a job or when your Palestinian lords come back?"

Not knowing what to conclude from such a remark, they all cracked up into bitter laughter, then ordered their fourth round of *'arak*. It was the first time that Subhi was tipsy enough to engage in a discussion. "We'll all be in seventh heaven only if they lift the night curfew on us or cancel the permits to move in and out of Jaffa. I heard there is work in Tiberias."

"Tiberias of all places? Who told you that?"

"Uncle Habeeb."

"Oh yes, where the hell is your uncle? I haven't seen him in ages. I assumed he had left on one of the boats."

"No, he did not. He was taken as a POW, but he'll soon be released. He's promised to take me with him to Tiberias."

"He must be kidding. What's your name, young man?"

"Subhi."

"Subhi, military rule has been imposed on all Palestinian cities and villages. They'll never lift it. Soon you'll need a special permit to breathe or sleep with your wife. Excuse me, young man." The older man began laughing, and so did Subhi and the rest.

"Did you hear the last joke about the curfew?"

"No, I did not. I didn't even know there *were* jokes about the curfew."

"A Haganah soldier shot an elderly Palestinian twenty minutes before they imposed the curfew. When asked why he shot him, he replied, 'I know where he lives, and I'm certain he wouldn't have made it home in twenty minutes.' "

In spite of the fact that the curfew was to be imposed in forty minutes, they kept at it. "If they're not going to allow the Jaffans to return home, at least they could send the *fallaheen*, the peasants, who've degraded and ruined il 'Ajami neighborhood, back to their villages."

"Hey, hey, stop it, man. This is unacceptable. That is pure racism. You Jaffans are worse than the Jews. Do you think we're happy to live on top of one another: three families in one of your gardenless homes? Yes, I wish they would send us back to our homes and our open fields. But you and I know full well that they're not going to do so as they've already bulldozed our villages to the ground. So you'd better get used to living with us *fallaheen*, you lords of Jaffa."

"I just need to get out of this damn Arab ghetto, that's all I need," commented another.

Subhi didn't know what to think or make of these anti-peasant sentiments. Even though he still missed Shams, only now did he realize that circumstances had prevented him from thinking of her as often as he had in the past. Subhi felt conflicting emotions, for he himself was suffering living in the same house with two displaced peasant families from the village of Yazour. It is because of them that he spent all the non-curfew hours (from 6:00 a.m. to 7:00 p.m.) on the port drinking coffee and cheap 'arak while making new friends and arguing about their new reality.

"Stop it, you two. Isn't it enough what they've done to us? Dividing us into Arabs and Jews, Muslims and Christians, and now you add new categories of *madani* and *fallah,* city dweller and peasant! I am glad we have the same color complexion as the Mizrahi Jews, or they would've added yet another category."

"Believe me, it is all of our own doing. Look at the Jews. Learn from them. They brought people from every corner of this globe, people of different nationalities, different cultures, different colors who do not even speak the same language, and made a nation out of them."

Like everyone else, Subhi was getting tired of the futile discussions and ready to go home when he suddenly spotted someone or something at a distance. Being more than tipsy, Subhi almost did not believe his own eyes. Wanting to make sure he was right about both the person and the trousers, Subhi stood up from his seat. His adrenaline levels shot up, and his face turned pale. Noticing that his new employee was frightened or hysterical about something, Subhi's boss suspected that the Israeli Haganah forces had appeared on the port to arrest someone. He turned his head in the direction where Subhi's eyes were fixed but saw no soldiers, hence he asked, "What's wrong, Subhi?"

"Oh my God . . . It *is* him . . . It *is* him . . . Son of a bitch!"

By the time Subhi had uttered these words, he was certain it was Fawwaz 'Asfour, the Palestinian collaborator who had given Subhi half of his English suit claiming he did not know where the trousers were.

There was Fawwaz wearing Subhi's trousers, pacing along the waterfront.

Having suspected all along that it was Fawwaz who had stolen the lower part of his English suit, Subhi often inquired about Fawwaz's whereabouts. Months after having been interrogated about his suit, Subhi learned that Fawwaz's services had been terminated, that he had been kicked out of the police service and had gone to live (or spy) in Haifa, where he worked in a shop plucking chickens.

"I will pluck this son of a bitch in the same way he plucks those chickens."

Those were the last words that Subhi uttered before he grabbed the wooden orange box on which he had been sitting, lifted it in one of his strong arms, ran in Fawwaz's direction, and attacked him with it. Once the box had bounced off Fawwaz's head and broken into pieces, Subhi went for his trousers. With his arms, he pulled "Fawwaz's" trousers down. Taken completely by surprise, all Fawwaz could do was protect his head with his arms and then reach for his underpants, which went down with the trousers. Totally exposed, Fawwaz pulled his underpants up. Up and down, up and down went the English trousers and the underpants until both were torn to pieces.

"My trousers . . . my trousers . . . my trousers . . ." was all that Subhi yelled until a few men came and pulled Subhi and Fawwaz apart.

Had it not been for the curfew that was about to be imposed on the Arab ghetto in less than twenty minutes, Subhi would've gone home with parts of Fawwaz's flesh rather than with a fragment of his English suit.

Part IV

Shams

ဢ

29

A Surrogate Mother

(il Lyd, May 1948)

WHAT IS YOUR NAME, young lady?"
"Shams."

"Louder . . . louder!" yelled the social worker, who was bewildered in an ocean of lost bodies and souls.

"SHAMS!" she raised her voice, revealing utter exhaustion.

Since mid-April when the Jewish militias had intensified their attacks on Jaffa and its neighboring villages, including Salameh, thousands of refugees had been pouring into il Lyd, a mid-sized town with twenty thousand inhabitants, located twenty kilometers to the east of Jaffa. Like Jaffa, il Lyd was designated part of the Arab State.

In the main square of il Lyd, hundreds of refugees gathered in search of lost members of their families. On a raised platform stood a few employees from the Social Welfare Department and the Muslim Awqaf who looked more exasperated than the refugees they were trying to help.

The scene of the madding crowds surrounding social workers

looked like Judgment Day as described by Apostle John 1,948 years earlier: "I saw a great white throne, and Him sitting on it, from whose face the earth and the heaven fled away. And a place was not found for them. And I saw the dead, the small and the great, stand before God. And the dead were judged the final judgment—the end of human history and the beginning of the eternal state."

Indeed, it was exactly that: "the end of human history and the beginning of the 'eternal state.'" However, in this case, the "great white throne" was a shabby elevated wooden platform, more like a stage, on which stood not the holy "Him" but rather desperate social workers.

Not wanting to miss out on the possibility of finding her mother, her father, and her twelve-year-old brother, Mohammad, Shams screamed at the top of her lungs.

"My name is Shams, and my sisters' names are Nazira and Nawal!" She repeated this loudly more than once as she tightened her grip on her two young sisters, just seven and six years old, who clung to her.

FOR THE LAST FEW WEEKS, or since the day when Jewish militia arrested her father and other men from under the olive trees (where they had been "living," or, more accurately, waiting for their mother and brother to appear)—and took them "to dig mass graves and bury the dead along the roads" but never came back—the three sisters had been glued together. Like kittens, they slept on top of one another in spite of the dreadful June heat. And like triplets with one body and three heads, they moved together. They ate from the same plate, went to the bathroom together, and held hands as they walked around the courtyard of il Dahmash Mosque, where hundreds of refugees gathered.

Since the day she lost her mother among the huge waves of refugees fleeing east, Shams had become a substitute mother who was blindly obeyed by her two sisters. This was not surprising, considering what they had been through since they fled their village of Salameh two months earlier.

In such catastrophic circumstances, time ceased to have meaning for Shams. For what mattered since they fled their home in Salameh was *what* happened rather than *when* it happened. Hence whenever she was asked by social workers or anyone else "When?" she would reply, "A month ago," and when asked "For how long?" she would also reply, "For a month."

"When did you flee Salameh?"

"A month ago."

"How long did you stay in that empty house next to il Lyd's train station when your family fled Salameh?"

"A month."

"When the Jewish soldiers kicked you out of that house, how long did your family stay next to the vegetable farm?"

"A month."

"Were all your family members with you at that point?"

"Yes." She paused, then added, "Yes, my mother, my father, my brother, and my two sisters, as well as our neighbor Fatima and her two daughters."

"Did you lose your mother and brother first or your father?"

"I lost my mother and brother first, then my father."

"And when did the Jewish soldiers arrest your father and other men for slaughtering the cow?"

"A month ago."

"When did you lose your mother and your brother?"

"A month ago, when the soldiers were firing at us and yelling 'Go! Go! Go to Jordan! Go to Abdullah!'"

"And how long did you wait for your mother and brother under the olive trees?"

"A whole month."

"And the second time they arrested your father, in order to dig graves and bury the dead along the road?"

"A month ago."

"And for how long has your father been missing?"

"He has been missing for a month."

"And when did they bring you and your sisters to il Dahmash Mosque in il Lyd?"

"A month ago."

"And how long have you been there?"

"For a month."

Except for losing her sense of time, fortunately—or rather, unfortunately—Shams recalled all these events vividly, even seventy years later.

"Shams, for God's sake, give me your full name so we can help you find the three missing members of your family! I need the name of your village, your father's name, his family name, your mother's name, and the name of your brother."

"My full name is Shams Khalil Abu Ramadan from Salameh!" screamed Shams at the top of her lungs more than once. However, fortunately for Shams, her full name went unrecorded by the social worker, who was grabbed by the hand and swept away by waves of desperate refugees seeking help:

"Have you seen my son Majed?"

"Have you found my husband, Mohammad?"

"Have you come across two young boys by the names of Khaled and Maher?"

"For God's sake, has anyone seen my two daughters Mai and Amal?" a woman screamed like mad, then had a fit and collapsed dead on the ground.

Death was no stranger to the refugees.

"These three girls are from the village of Salameh. They are the daughters of Khalil . . . Khalil who?" asked the official.

"Abu Ramadan," replied Shams.

"Khalil Abu Ramadan from Salameh, are you here? If so, come forward and take your three daughters," announced the social worker and waited for someone to respond, before continuing, "If not their father, is there a relative or a neighbor from Salameh who knows these girls?"

Shams looked around anxiously, hoping that her missing father would come forward to claim them, but in vain. With broken hearts, she and her sisters just stood there.

Unexpectedly, a young woman with a high-pitched voice came forward. "Yes, yes, these are the daughters of my relatives. They are the daughters of my niece Amal, who is married to 'Alaa Nijim from Salameh." Shams's heart skipped a beat as she stared at the fair and plump woman whom she had never seen before.

"These are the three girls of my niece in Salameh. They are the relatives of my in-laws in Salameh."

Shams was at a total loss.

But who is this woman?

Who is her niece Amal?

Which in-laws?

And who is the Nijim family? How are they related to us?

Stunned and not knowing what to make of this peculiar and unexpected development, Shams kept quiet while the woman came up to her and squeezed her hand in a gesture meaning *Keep quiet for now and you will soon understand everything.*

Having gone through so much hardship, and having given up any hope of finding her mother, her father, and her younger brother, Shams simply surrendered to her fate.

Confused, exhausted, and not wanting to go back to the night-marish life in the crowded Dahmash Mosque, Shams kept quiet, as did her two sisters. She could no longer tolerate the repeated scene of Jewish militants who often came to il Dahmash Mosque and called on men, young and old, to follow them. Worse was the yelling and sobbing of the women and girls whose men were taken away with no promise of return.

It took a few minutes for the woman to register her name, her husband's name, the address of their home in il Lyd, and the names of her three "nieces" with the social worker, who took little note of the change of family name from Abu Ramadan to Nijim.

"OK, girls, let's go," said the woman, leading them away in a hurry as she held Nawal's hand on one side and Shams's on the other. This was the first time in a "month" that Shams had let go of the hand of one of her two sisters. But it was also the first time that an adult had held Shams's hand in more than a "month."

In the most instinctive way, and for the first time in a long while, Shams recalled what it meant for a child to hold the hand of an older person; the sense of safety and care made her cry, for only kindness can mend a broken heart. It was pure love and pure tenderness that Shams felt, as did her sisters.

It was only when she tightened her grip around the palm of the fair and plump woman who would become their surrogate mother that Shams recalled how her hand had slipped away from that of her real mother, Aisheh. Shams's eyes had fallen on a row of corpses, and she had let go of her mother's hand and jumped back. Shams had turned away, bent down, and vomited. By the time she'd regained her balance and stood up again, both her mother and her brother, Mohammad, were out of sight. She froze for a few seconds and looked around. In the midst of the crowds, Shams spotted her father, who was holding the hands of her two younger sisters.

"Where is your mother? Where is Mohammad?" screamed Khalil in a panic, as he realized what it meant to lose someone in this chaos.

"I think they went up the hill this way," Shams said, pointing in the direction of the corpses.

Khalil turned his head away and said, "I am sure Aisheh did not go in that direction," meaning in the direction of the corpses. "She either took the opposite road or went back looking for you, Shams."

With thousands of fleeing refugees around them, neither Shams nor her sisters could figure out what was up or what was down, what was left or what was right. All they wanted to do at that point was hold each others' hands and those of their father tightly and never let go ever again.

"We must go back to look for your mother and Mohammad," said Khalil.

Shams was happy to go in the opposite direction from the foul smell of death. "Just when we got our father back from prison, now we lose our mother and brother!" Shams complained. Little did Shams realize that events would take an even nastier turn.

"Come on in. . . . Come on in, *ya banati ya habibati,* my beloved daughters. Make yourselves at home," said the woman as she entered the house where she, her ten-year-old son, Mahmoud, and her husband, Abdul Hamid il Masri, also known as 'Abed, lived.

Since Shams and her sisters had been living under olive trees in the open fields and later in the courtyard of the mosque, they had forgotten what it felt like to be in a home. It was the coolness of the large crossed-vaulted room that made them recall their house in Salameh: the house they and their parents were waiting to return to once they were united and once the *shawasher* were over.

"Mahmoud, *habibi*, where are you? Come meet your sisters." From behind a curtain separating the living room from a tiny kitchen appeared a chubby dark-complexioned boy. He was about the same age as their missing brother, with a name also similar to their brother's. The shy boy came closer, shook their hands, and just stood there. Like his newly acquired sisters, he did not know what to do or what to say.

"This is my son, Mahmoud. Mahmoud, this is Shams and these are . . . ," said the surrogate mother, then stopped as she sought Shams's help to remind her of the names of the other two girls she had just adopted.

"This is Nazira and this is Nawal," added Shams.

Happy to know the names of her two daughters, the surrogate mother introduced herself: "Everyone calls me Um Mahmoud. However, you may simply call me Yamma."

"I see that you finally convinced the social workers to allow you to adopt a girl. You nagged them so much that they gave you three," said Mahmoud with a big smile.

"*Ilhamdulillah*, yes. I am thrilled. Mahmoud, why don't you go out and get us some wood? I need to give your sisters a hot bath."

The three girls were still standing close to the entrance door, not knowing what to do.

"Shams, *habibti*, bring your sisters and follow me to the back-yard. I need to clean your hair of lice with kerosene before I give you a hot bath. Here, take one of these combs. I'll comb your hair, you comb Nazira's hair, and Nazira will comb Nawal's hair. Don't be shy, girls. *Yalla,* go ahead and do it. It's like a train in motion."

Shams felt her head itch the minute Um Mahmoud poured the kerosene on it. "Don't touch the lice; they will fall out on their own. Just keep combing your sister's hair." Once their hair was free of lice, it was time to take off their smelly clothes and wash their itchy bodies, bodies that had not felt a drop of water since they'd left home in Salameh.

"Come, *habibati,* come, you must be starving and exhausted. Why don't you sit around the table while I prepare your dinner?"

With full stomachs and clean clothes, Shams and her sisters had a good night's sleep for the first time in over a month.

A *"Jewish"* Cow

(One Month Earlier, il Lyd, July 1948)

SHAMS COULD no longer recall if it was she or her new friend
Salma who spotted the cow first. Such a question wouldn't have
consumed Shams for the rest of her life had such a mundane and
insignificant incident passed without causing the macabre events
that followed.

Realizing the synergy between kids and animals, but also the
mystical ability of the latter to entertain children and bring them,
momentarily, out of their misery, Shams called on them to join her:
"Nawal, Nazira, Mohammad, Saleh, Ali, Laila, come and see the
cow. It's so huge, it is ten times bigger than our goats."

"I so miss our goat 'Afreet. When are we going back to feed
him?" sighed Mohammad, then asked, "Yamma, why didn't we
bring 'Afreet along with us? What happened to our puppy 'Antar,
cat Simsim, and also the chickens? Who's going to feed them?"

"Son, we hardly had time to bring you and your sisters along,
let alone carry 'Afreet or Simsim. Or would you rather we left you

behind and took the goat, cat, and chickens instead?" replied his mother, Aisheh.

A moment of awkwardness ensued.

Calling on the kids to come see the cow seemed to have triggered more nostalgia than excitement. To Shams's surprise, the number of grown-ups, both men and women, who followed her exceeded by far the number of kids whom she'd meant to entertain. Shams could only conclude that older folks and their friends needed to escape their despair as much as the little ones did, if not more. The sight of a grazing cow in the open fields seemed to have given everyone a bit of excitement, or a break from the misery they had been experiencing since they'd been expelled from their villages.

Like thousands of other people around them, Shams's family and their neighbors had been living under the olive trees in the open fields, waiting for the hostilities to cease so they could go back to their villages. But since the aggression had only intensified, more waves of refugees had been arriving in il Lyd and its countryside every day.

In order to survive not only the heat and thirst but also the starvation, everyone, depending on their age, had to take short or long walks in search of food. Some picked up vegetables from a nearby farm, others ventured into the open fields picking whatever goods the earth offered: mallow, chicory, dandelion, thyme, oregano, and wild endive. The lucky ones came back with some plums, apricots, or almonds. Young girls like Shams and Nazira accompanied their mothers, who took the risk of sneaking into some of the abandoned houses in the neighboring deserted Palestinian villages. They entered empty houses whose owners had, like them, fled. Thousands of homes were left with an abundance of stored food such as lentils, wheat, olives, olive oil, dried tomatoes, dried figs, raisins, flour, sugar, and jars of pickled cucumbers and turnips. Onions and garlic, which gave a bit of taste to the edible wild plants on which they survived, were the two items that Aisheh appreciated most. However, every time Aisheh entered someone's house, she wondered what had become of her own house: their goat, their chickens, their donkey, the horse that Khalil had bought just a few months before they left, and all that they had left behind as they fled Salameh.

It was not until later in the evening when her family and neighbors gathered around the huge vegetable pot that Shams realized that the cow was going to be the topic of conversation for the whole evening. Its appearance had led to much dispute and discussion.

"A little meat with the vegetables is not a bad idea. What do you say, Aisheh?"

"I don't know what to tell you, Khalil! For sure a bit of meat for the kids who have not had any for weeks would give them some nourishment. They have probably forgotten how meat looks and tastes. I bet you they're all anemic by now." Listening to her parents, Shams could not tell if their conversation was a serious one or if they were simply voicing an unattainable desire. On the one hand, Shams agreed with her mother: neither she nor her siblings—nor anyone around her, for that matter—had eaten meat for a whole month now. On the other hand, Shams had never forgotten how sad she was whenever her father and uncles gathered in the early morning of the big feast to slaughter the sheep, *il kharoof,* that she and her brother, Mohammad, had fed for a whole month before 'Eid il Adha. Somehow the cow conversation saddened her as she remembered the moaning of her *kharoof* before and while he was slaughtered.

She could never tell what made her cry more: his moaning or the sudden silence that followed. Except for Mohammad, no one else in her family noticed that she never ate the chunk of meat placed on her plate on the first day of the 'eid. Unlike Shams, Mohammad was thrilled to have his share of meat and that of his sister: "Mmm . . . yummy. We certainly did a good job raising the *kharoof*, sister." Shams never knew whether to laugh or cry at her brother's comment.

However, this time, circumstances made Shams sympathize more with her brother, her parents, and other meat seekers or meat eaters.

"Khalil, I beg you, don't go there on your own; have other men accompany you," Shams overheard her mother warn her father that evening.

"Of course I won't go on my own. I've already consulted with a few men, and both Ibrahim and Sami have agreed to come with me tonight."

Though Shams had been instructed by both her mother and her late grandmother not to intervene in older people's conversations, out of concern, she did this time: "But Yamma, whose cow is it?" she asked. Shams suspected—or, rather, knew—that the cow did not belong to the people of Salameh who had fled the village with them. They had in the meantime become like one extended family living together in the open fields.

In response to her daughter's question, Aisheh stuttered a bit at first, then replied, "It belongs to Abu Mohammad."

"Which Abu Mohammad?"

"Abu Mohammad il Yazouri," said Aisheh, referring to a man from the village of Yazour.

"Which Yazouri?"

"The displaced old man who fled his village with his cow."

"But how come the Yahud did not steal his cow the way they stole our money and gold?"

Shams was surprised that the Jewish militia, who had robbed the people of Salameh of all their belongings, had allowed this old man from Yazour to take his cow with him but she kept quiet. And she still wondered which Abu Mohammad, since every man and his mother (rather his brother) was called Abu Mohammad, including her own father. And which "displaced" old man, when everyone around Shams was a displaced person? The only identification that made sense to her was the village of Yazour, which she had visited once with her mother.

"And where is the old Yazouri now?" Shams persisted.

"He fled to Jordan and left his cow behind."

"Poor thing." It was not clear if the "poor thing" referred to Abu Mohammad, who had been forced to flee farther east, or to the cow that stayed behind! Knowing Shams's love for animals, it was probably the latter.

Shams did not sleep that night, nor did the grown-ups around her. Not only because the earth was their mattress, the skies their blanket, and a relative's arm or hip their pillow but also because of the hissing and the whispering of men. By now Shams was pretty certain that the cow's fate would not be any different from that of her *kharoof:* the sheep she fed, played with, and loved, but which was fated to be slaughtered and consumed.

The following night, like the hungry man from Yazour, many others—men, women, and children—begged for a piece of meat. Though the cow was ten times the size of Shams's goats, with so many asking for their share, it felt much smaller. With full stomachs,

Shams and the other kids slept deeply. Something about that meal brought happiness to everyone's heart. While the kids collapsed right after dinner, the men and women stayed up late chatting the night away but also joking, something they had not done in a while. But as the Arabic saying goes, *Allah yekfeena shar il dhuhuk*, "May God protect us from the terrible consequences of our laughter."

The Cow Interrogation

Big Crimes, Small Crimes

IT WAS THE YELLING in broken Arabic emanating from a staticky loudspeaker that woke up Shams, along with everyone else sleeping in the nearby fields. In a panic, she rose off the ground, trying to figure out what other disaster had befallen them at this early hour. Two days had passed since the slaughtering of the cow, and the sensation of a full stomach had by now vanished.

For a few seconds, Shams couldn't tell if the unsettling shouting that had shaken her awake was real or a nightmare. She had been having recurring nightmares since the Jewish settlers had tried to kidnap her sixteen-year-old cousin Alia, who was out in the fields picking almonds off her family's tree. Alia happened to be on her own when three Jewish settlers attacked her and dragged her in an attempt to kidnap her and scare residents out of the village. However, she screamed, kicked, and bit her kidnappers until her father, three brothers, and other men from Salameh saved her. As intended, the kidnap attempt filled people with fear, especially women and young girls. As a result of this incident, some girls did not sleep for days or weeks, while others, like Shams, began to have nightmares. Shams's mother could never figure out if her daughter's recurring nightmares had been triggered by this incident or by the horrific news of the Deir Yassin massacre a few weeks earlier. Shams belonged to the second category: those who dreamed of being one of the girls who was "exhibited" in the streets of Jerusalem.

Hearing shouts in broken Arabic made Shams's heart sink. It often brought tears to her soft eyes.

"Gather all men: old and young." Through the hissing loudspeaker, the head officer repeated his instructions to the six Jewish militiamen who had arrived with him in two British armored vehicles. In no time, as instructed, the armed men had lined up "all men: old and young," including young boys, against a rubble wall.

"Gather all men: young and old" was the phrase that terrified men and women, old and young. They had heard this command many times before, and they had experienced its frightful consequences.

Such a command could mean that the men would be punished and humiliated with a beating, or left to stand under the burning sun for hours at end.

It could also mean that they would be rounded up and taken as prisoners of war.

Or taken to hard labor camps.

In a few cases, it meant they would be executed.

But more often than not, it meant they would be taken to bury the dead.

Had they not been kicked out of their homes in Salameh, it could've meant that their homes would be searched for weapons, and the little food and furniture they had destroyed.

It could have also entailed their wheat fields being burned, their citrus trees cleared out, their livestock confiscated, and their horses shot. But now that they had lost their homes, their fields, and all their property, the options were fewer. Once the horrifying sentence was uttered, it was women of all ages, rather than men, who encircled the head of the Jewish militia and argued with him.

"What do you want from us this time? Isn't it enough that you threw us out of our homes and villages? Don't you fear God?" objected a woman who was instinctively defending her son Ibrahim, one of the three men who had slaughtered the cow.

"I said gather all men, not all women," replied the captain, ignoring Ibrahim's mother.

"Leave them alone. What do you want from them?" she yelled back at the top of her lungs.

"I need to know who stole the Jewish cow."

"Jewish cow! What Jewish cow?" replied Um Ibrahim.

"*Hajjeh,* old lady, don't act stupid. You all know full well what I'm talking about. The inhabitants of Ben Shemen filed a complaint that you stole their cow."

"We have stolen nobody's cow," insisted Um Ibrahim, then added, "Here, search me." She pulled her dress up to her chest, where she often hid her money in her bra. "You think we can hide a cow under our *thub,* our dress?"

"The Jewish cow that you stole has been hidden in your stomachs, that's where you hid it," responded the captain.

"Oh, *that* cow!" replied Um Ibrahim, realizing that the captain knew much more than she expected.

"Yes, that cow, *hajjeh.*"

"But the cow we slaughtered was not Jewish, it was a Palestinian cow that belonged to Abu Mohammad."

"Abu Mohammad! Which Abu Mohammad?" asked the captain

curiously, thinking that she had unintentionally revealed the identity of the thief.

"Show me which one is Abu Mohammad, the man who stole the Jewish cow and claimed it was his. This way I do not need to punish them all," said the captain as he stared at the men lined up against the wall.

"On your knees!" screamed the captain as he carried on his conversation with Um Ibrahim.

"Which one is Abu Mohammad?"

"Abu Mohammad il Yazouri."

"Abu Mohammad il Yazouri, stand up and come forward."

No one did.

"Abu Mohammad il Yazouri, stand up and come forward, or all men will be punished."

"Abu Mohammad il Yazouri fled to Jordan and left his cow behind!" screamed Shams's mother, Aisheh, as she came closer to Um Ibrahim. "The cow we slaughtered was his. Believe me, Captain Yossi, it was an Arab cow, not a Jewish cow." It was not clear why she addressed him as Captain Yossi, but she did.

"And who was the one who slaughtered the Arab cow?"

Taken by surprise by the captain's question, the women said nothing.

"I ask you again, who slaughtered the cow? Whether it was Jewish or Arab, I don't care."

Once again silence prevailed.

"OK, if no one wants to admit to stealing and slaughtering the Jewish cow, then follow me," said the captain, addressing the thirty-some men kneeling on the ground.

It was at this point that Shams's father, Khalil, stood up, came forward, and said, "It was I who slaughtered the cow."

"There is no way that a man can slaughter a cow on his own. Who else was with you?"

There was a nerve-wracking pause before Sami stood up and said, "I was with Khalil."

"Who else?"

"Me," said Ibrahim as he stood up.

And that was when Um Ibrahim began to sob.

"Who else?" asked the captain victoriously.

"That's it, no one else!" screamed an older man who could hardly stand up or walk.

"OK, then. You three follow me." Having been told that the men who stole the cow from the nearby Jewish settlement were three in number, the captain concluded his interrogation.

The minute Khalil, twenty-year-old Ibrahim, and eighteen-year-old Sami were arrested and dragged to one of two jeeps, a group of women, including Khalil's wife, Aisheh, and Ibrahim and Sami's mothers, along with the men's sisters and daughters, came running and surrounded Captain "Yossi." Not having any idea what sort of punishment awaited the three men, some reasoned with him, while others pleaded for mercy.

"I beg you, Captain, don't take my father!" screamed Shams, engulfed in a deep sense of guilt.

"Do you want us to die of hunger?" screamed Sami's mother.

"Just tell us where you are taking them and for how long," said Ibrahim's mother. Having already lost her husband and her youngest son in one of the frequent clashes that took place between the village of Salameh and its neighboring Jewish settlement, Um Ibrahim then totally lost it. She ran after the jeep in which her son was handcuffed and blindfolded and screamed her head off: "You sons of bitches, *ya wlad il kalb.*

"You son of whores, *ya wlad il sharmoutah*.

"You bastards, *ya 'arsat*.

"You fuckers, *ya manayek*.

"Have mercy on us!

"What crime have we committed to deserve all this?

"Tell me, what have we done to you?

"You're the ones who came to settle in our country, not the other way around.

"What more do you want from us?

"You have taken our country.

"Driven us out of our homes.

"Stolen our money and gold.

"You've shamed our honor.

"Killed and imprisoned our men.

"Isn't it enough that you killed my husband and my son Ali? Now you take my son Ibrahim just because we were hungry and wanted to feed our kids?

"Fuck you and fuck your JEWISH COW!

"If you punish us for stealing a cow, what punishment should you get for stealing a whole country?"

Um Ibrahim kept yelling and running after the armored jeep until she dropped dead on the narrow dirt road on which her son had vanished.

· 32 ·

Someone at the Door

I T WAS LUNCHTIME when someone knocked at the door. "Stay where you are. I'll get it," said Um Mahmoud. She rose from her chair, mumbling, "Who could it be at this hour on a Friday?" The unexpected knock at the door had interrupted a precious family gathering around the dining room table.

"Shhh. . . . Quiet," she whispered, placing her finger over her mouth as she walked toward the door, as if having second thoughts about opening it.

Since July 9, when il Lyd (the town where she had met, fallen in love with, and gotten married to her husband, 'Abed, some fifteen years earlier) had fallen into the hands of the Jewish militia, Um Mahmoud had felt overprotective of her family. Considering the violence that prevailed over il Lyd, she was the least vulnerable among them. 'Abed was a headmaster who had been accused of encouraging his students to take part in demonstrations against the British and the Zionists. And as such, he had spent more time in prison than with his wife and son. Like all Palestinian males, her ten-year-old son, Mahmoud, was also considered a "threat" to the "security" of the newly established state. However, what worried Um Mahmoud most was the false claims she had made about her relationship with her adopted daughters.

This Friday's gathering was particularly special. Not only because 'Abed had been released from a five-month imprisonment a couple of weeks earlier but also because he had, in the meantime, gained the daughters he had always wanted but never had. His long-term imprisonment had made it difficult for the couple to conceive.

"Who are these beautiful girls?" 'Abed had asked as he walked into the house, surprising his wife and his son.

"These are our daughters. The Salameh girls I adopted four months ago."

"Oh, how wonderful! I'm thrilled to see that our family has gotten larger and not smaller in my absence." 'Abed kneeled down and kissed the ground:

"Thank you, God. . . . Thank you, God," he said twice with a big smile. With such a warm reception, it was no surprise that humorous and gentle 'Abed became the father that Shams and her sisters had missed since their father, Khalil, was arrested and went missing.

FRIDAYS WERE the only days when Um Mahmoud had time to cook for her own family rather than for the bigger family she had adopted in il Lyd. With the help of Ustah, her Christian neighbor, her son, Mahmoud, and her three daughters, Um Mahmoud was able to provide daily meals for the needy and the elderly who were found in deserted homes or in the fields, many of whom were left unattended as havoc struck the twin towns of il Lyd and il Ramleh. This was the very first time that the newly established State of Israel had used its fighter planes to bombard Palestinian cities.

"Mahmoud, why don't you accompany Ustah to the fields while you girls get ready for our daily rounds?" Um Mahmoud gave the same instructions to her five-member team every single morning. While Ustah and Mahmoud went out to gather firewood and edible greens, Shams, Nazira, and Nawal accompanied their mother around the different neighborhoods collecting food from deserted homes.

"Only food, girls. Don't touch anything else. People's homes and properties must be respected and protected, even in times of war." This was the one sentence that Um Mahmoud repeated to her daughters day in and day out as they gathered flour, rice, lentils, onions, oil, olives, garlic, dried tomatoes, dried figs, and raisins from these homes.

"Yamma, Yamma, hurry up and come see what I found!" yelled Shams as she entered the home of one of the richer families that had disappeared. Stunned, Shams stood there looking at the gold bracelets left atop one of two chests of drawers in the living room. Though she was aware that leaving the gold bracelets behind for the Jewish militiamen who had been robbing people's homes day and night since il Lyd fell into Israeli hands was not a good idea, Um Mahmoud did not want to be complicit in a crime. She was still in shock about how most of the thirty-five thousand inhabitants of her town and il Ramleh had been driven from their homes by force. The same was true of the forty-some thousand refugees who had fled their homes in Jaffa and neighboring villages and who were waiting to go back. Only history would reveal, decades later, that Ben Gurion, the executive head of the World Zionist Organization, had made a hand gesture indicating "Kick them out" when he was asked what to do with the inhabitants of il Lyd and il Ramleh and the refugees in and around the two cities. Plan Dalet was an integral part of the Zionists' strategy to expel as many Palestinians as possible from their homes. Even from areas that had been designated as part of the Arab State according to the Partition Plan.

"Don't touch anything; leave everything as it is. Soon people will come back to their homes," said Um Mahmoud, doubting her own words. But there was no way that she would allow herself, or her daughters, for that matter, to play a part in the robberies taking place around them every hour of the day.

Once home, with the help of her three daughters, Um Mahmoud would prepare hot meals for the needy of her town, of which there were many.

"Shams, Mahmoud, Nazira, and Nawal, come here." She would call on her son but also on her neighbor Ustah: "Take these pots and go feed the people in the east neighborhood while I and the girls cover the western and Syrian neighborhoods." They would hand out pots filled with whatever combination of wild greens and beans Um Mahmoud and her team had gathered that day.

Except for the il Dahmash Mosque, where 160 Palestinians had been executed by the Palmach forces just a week after Shams and her sisters went to live with Um Mahmoud, Shams showed no hesitation entering places and homes to talk, joke, and, if need be, spoon-feed the elderly while hoping that their families would return soon. This remained the case until the day that Shams, her surrogate mother, and Mahmoud were walking in one of the alleys in a nearby neighborhood and heard someone moaning.

"Shams, Mahmoud, do you hear what I hear?" asked their mother.

"Yes, Yamma, I do," replied Shams.

What on earth is going on? wondered Um Mahmoud as she stepped into a shabby room whose door had been left wide open.

"Mmmmm, mmmmm, akhhhh," moaned an elderly fat woman whose hands, face, and legs were covered with wasps.

"Oh my goodness!" screamed Um Mahmoud as she handed Shams and Mahmoud pieces of cloth she'd picked up from a chair to chase the wasps away.

"*Habibi* Mahmoud, run out to the street and come back with two strong men, and if possible a wooden cart to carry her away to the Awqaf Social Welfare Department!" Like all members of his mother's army, Mahmoud followed her instructions carefully, and the woman was saved.

In spite of all that Shams had gone through in the last few months, this event was one she never forgot. Somehow that scene was imprinted in her mind for the rest of her long life.

TWO MIDDLE-AGED Palestinian men stood at the door as Um Mahmoud hesitantly opened it. Though momentarily relieved that they weren't the Jewish militia whom she feared might come at any moment to arrest her husband and son, she still felt her throat tighten as she asked, "How can I help you?"

"Is Headmaster 'Abed at home?"

"Whom shall I tell him is asking?"

"Tell him we're from the Social Welfare Department of the Muslim Awqaf and we'd like to talk to him."

Stop and say no more was all Um Mahmoud thought as her jaw dropped, her face turned pale, and her heart nearly jumped out of her chest. The moment she dreaded most had arrived at her doorstep much earlier that she had anticipated. Sensing the seriousness of the visit, 'Abed and her four kids had come to stand right behind her.

"Come on in . . . Come on in . . . Please," said 'Abed in his friendly way. In the same affable tone, he instructed Shams to take her siblings and go play in the garden.

"Don't send the girls away; we need to talk to them," objected one of the two officials.

"I am not sending them anywhere; they will be right outside," 'Abed said, then added, "Please come on in and have a seat." While the children reluctantly went out to the garden, the two men were ushered into the living room.

"Have you had lunch? Can I offer you something to eat?"

"We're all set, thank you, Headmaster." 'Abed's tone seemed to have calmed things down.

"Don't be shy." Since coffee and sugar were rationed during wartime, 'Abed was aware that offering the officials the family lunch they had interrupted would go a long way. Or so he thought.

Though she was getting impatient with her husband's placidity, past experience had taught Um Mahmoud that 'Abed's graciousness often worked to their favor. If anything, she needed his charm today.

"How do you like your coffee? Sweet, very sweet, I bet?"

"Yes, Headmaster, very sweet."

"*Habibti,* can you make us coffee or should I call on Shams to make it?"

"No, please keep Shams out of this. I'll make it myself." Um Mahmoud went to her kitchen to compose herself. Once behind the curtain, she took a deep breath so as to slow down her heartbeat. She knew that her husband's ways of beating around the bush before he came to the crux of a problem often paid off. From the little window of her kitchen, Um Mahmoud watched her three daughters playing hide-and-seek in the backyard, pretending to be indifferent to the situation. With the back of her trembling palm, she wiped her wet cheeks.

In the background was 'Abed's calming voice as he conversed with the two officials about postwar conditions. This gave Um Mahmoud the time she needed to think through all the arguments and explanations she was about to give the two men. Um Mahmoud stole one more glance at her daughters before she placed four cups of coffee on a brass tray. With shaky hands, she handed two cups of coffee to the two men and one to her husband before she took one herself and collapsed next to him on the two-seater.

Her presence made the three men address the subject head-on: "As you may have guessed by now, we are here in regard to the three girls from Salameh."

"What about them?" inquired Um Mahmoud as she tried hard not to let the tears drop from her wet eyes. The older official addressed 'Abed.

"Our respected headmaster, we aware that your wife, Rifqa—"

"You mean Um Mahmoud," 'Abed interrupted, trying to emphasize the name that his wife preferred to use since the birth of their son. His words went unnoticed.

"Rifqa was well intended when she claimed that the three girls from Salameh were her relatives. We are also aware that your wife has not only taken good care of the Salameh girls but also saved their lives by taking them away from il Dahmash Mosque a few weeks before the massacre. We're also thankful for all she does feeding the elderly and the needy in town. However, as you know, our respected headmaster, the Salameh girls are Muslims, and cannot be raised by a Jewish mother." Embarrassed by his own words, the official added, "I am truly sorry, Madam Rifqa, but we have been instructed by the director of the Awqaf to take them away."

"Take them away? Where? Come on, let's be reasonable about this," said Rifqa, who was visibly shaken.

'Abed piped in, "Wait, wait, before you talk about taking the girls away, let me explain. First and foremost, I am, as you well know, an Arab and a Muslim, as is my son, Mahmoud. And as you and your director know, according to Muslim law, children follow their father and not their mother."

"I am afraid that is no longer the case. According to Jewish traditions but also according to the laws of the new state, children follow their mother. Thus we must take the girls to a Muslim woman to be raised as Muslims."

As the shocking news muted Rifqa and 'Abed, the official carried on, "I am afraid this is no longer Mandate Palestine or Arab Palestine. This has become Israel."

It was at this point that both 'Abed and Rifqa became furious.

"But it is *you*, the Muslim Awqaf, that is objecting to this, not the new state!"

"What's wrong with you? You can hardly take care of your own problems; why add this now?"

"We know, we know, Headmaster. We can't tell you how embarrassed we are about this unpleasant situation."

"Unpleasant?! This is insane, it's really shameful," 'Abed responded, while Rifqa burst into tears.

Embarrassed but also touched by Rifqa's tears, once more the official addressed 'Abed: "Why don't you go talk to the Awqaf director tomorrow? I am sure he will be sympathetic to your argument. However, we have strict instructions to take the Salameh girls today and deliver them to a Muslim woman by the name of Mariam."

" 'Deliver them'! Is that how you handle three beautiful girls? And which Mariam is this? I know all the Mariams in town," said Rifqa angrily.

"I don't know."

"You don't know where you're taking my three daughters? What kind of cruelty is that?"

"*Habibti*, please, I beg you to calm down," 'Abed said, then went to his wife as he felt she was about to collapse. "I know it's truly shameful and tragic, but please, I beg you not to make a scene in front of the girls. This is hard on us all." 'Abed had tears in his eyes as he tried to comfort Rifqa.

Silence prevailed before 'Abed broke it with a few resigned words.

"OK, let me call the girls . . ."

But before he did, one of the officers looked at Rifqa and asked, "Have you and 'Abed told the girls that you're Jewish?"

"No, we have not."

"Do you think your son, Mahmoud, did?"

"I don't think so. This is utter madness. People are being thrown out of their homeland, out of their homes, their cities, their villages, and their farms, men are being imprisoned or executed in cold blood, women are being raped, and thousands of Arab refugees are dying from thirst and hunger, and all that you and the Muslim Awqaf are concerned about is taking my daughters away from me because I am Jewish! What shame, what nonsense!" Rifqa screamed, then collapsed on the coach weeping.

"*Habibti* Rifqa, take it easy, I will talk to the director of il Awqaf first thing in the morning. I will get the girls back to you the same day, trust me," said 'Abed.

With heavy steps and spinning heads, both he and Rifqa walked away from the Muslim Awqaf officials in the direction of the backyard. But before 'Abed stepped out into the backyard, Rifqa asked, " 'Abed, do you think it would help if I told the officials that we are both communists and atheists?' "

"Have you lost your mind, *habibti*? Don't you realize that for the Muslim Awqaf, two atheist parents are by far worse than a Jewish mother and a Muslim father?"

Rifqa was not in a position to do much but go back to her sofa and sob. It was 'Abed who went out to the backyard to carry out this painful mission.

Stiff as statues, Shams and her sisters stepped into the house. As instructed by 'Abed, Shams, Nazira, and little Nawal walked toward their mother, sat on both sides of the couch, and hugged her tightly.

In a state of shock, Shams and her sisters were once again fated to be separated from their loved ones. However, the three Salameh girls had learned at an early age that it is human kindness, rather than religion or nationality, that conquers the human heart.

33

A Muslim Mother

"HERE ARE the three girls who will be living with you, Mariam!" yelled the official who accompanied Shams and her sisters from the home of their Jewish mother to the shack of the Muslim woman the Awqaf had chosen to place them with. Nothing about the run-down surroundings or the chaotic entrance of the new foster home indicated that a human being might be living there.

In spite of her numerous rounds delivering food with Um Mahmoud, Shams had never been to this part of town. Like her two younger sisters, Shams was still in shock trying to handle the new situation and come to terms with the fact that her adored surrogate mother was Jewish. How could that be when Jews were the cause of every disaster that had befallen her and her family?

The separation from her surrogate family happened at a time when she believed that God had finally made up for her great losses by giving her a benevolent mother and brother, so close in age to her biological brother, Mohammad, in addition to 'Abed, their good-hearted and loving Egyptian father. What saddened Shams most was the loss of the sense of safety and security she was starting to feel being part of a family.

In spite of her bafflement, Shams still noticed that the Awqaf official had walked into Mariam's house without knocking, which was rather unusual.

"Here are the three girls we talked about," repeated the official. But once more he got no response. A minute or two passed before he yelled, "Mariam, where the hell are you?"

Having given up, he took the liberty of walking around the house in search of Mariam.

"By the way, you should know that Mariam is deaf and mute. But you'll soon learn how to communicate with her." Stunned on every level, the three sisters, who were zigzagging their way through a junkyard, went back to holding hands as they had when they lived all by themselves under the trees, and also later when they were transferred to live with hundreds of other refugees in il Dahmash Mosque.

Feeling insecure, Shams and her sisters followed closely behind the official, who had obviously been to this junkyard before. What intrigued the three dazed sisters most was the variety of animals they spotted inside the house. As far as their limited knowledge and experience was concerned, animals were to be kept outside the house, never inside. At least this was the rule for the animals they'd had in Salameh. As much as they adored their puppy 'Antar their parents never allowed him in the house. But here at Mariam's place, animals seemed to feel at home.

They had been brought into a barn that had been turned into a zoo with Mariam as a keeper.

"Perhaps the Awqaf officials thought we were animals and that was the reason they brought us here!" whispered Nazira to Shams.

"It looks like it," replied Shams, who paused, then added, "Don't worry, *habibti,* we'll get through this. Trust me." Though Nazira could not see the light at the end of this shack, she trusted Shams blindly. Once again Shams took the role of protective parent. Hoping to ease the mounting apprehension about their new mother and the uncanny foster home they found themselves in, Shams tried to busy herself and her sisters by asking them to count the animals they had seen so far:

"I see more than a dozen well-fed chickens, half a dozen or more lazy cats, a few rabbits here and there, and a goat that has climbed on a chair and stretched out his slim body and neck while munching on a green branch placed on top of a cupboard. Two sheep seem to be content inside the house away from the burning sun. That's what I have counted so far, but I'm sure there must be more outside the house," said little Nawal.

The three sisters were trying to find their way around the junkyard when their eyes spotted their new surrogate mother. Though Mariam was in her early forties, circumstance made her look like an old lady, more like a witch, with long curly gray hair that had never been combed and layers and layers of messy clothes that covered a skeleton-like body with no muscles to support a bent back. Mariam held a baby goat in her arms. Like a mother with her child, she was tenderly nursing it with a baby bottle because he was born too small and too weak to nurse from his mom. "Nana, dada," came Mariam's incomprehensible mumblings when she spotted her guests. Giving them little or no attention, Mariam carried on with her chores. Once done nursing the baby goat, she attentively placed it on a pile of rags. And that was when its mother stopped munching on the green branch, came running over, and began licking both Mariam and her baby.

Mariam showed no interest in the arrival of the three girls. She was now moving big and small items from one corner of the huge barn to another. The excessive accumulation of objects made the place seem more like a storage room than a foster home ready to receive three young girls. Shams, Nazira, and Nawal looked at one another in despair, not knowing what to do or say next.

Wanting to bring closure to his mission of delivering the three Muslim girls to their Muslim surrogate mother, the Awqaf official asked them to follow him.

"Mariam, these are the three girls we talked about. Now, you take care of them, and in return, the Awqaf will give you a monthly stipend. OK?" The officer stood there waiting for Mariam to respond.

"Taa, taa" was the only semi-word that Mariam mumbled in agreement. She pointed to the corner that she expected the three girls to occupy.

"Is that where you want them to sleep?"

"*Aaa*," said Mariam, nodding.

The three sisters turned around and stared at the spot in astonishment.

"I don't want to stay here. I'm afraid of this place, and I'm terrified of this woman." Nazira's comment made Nawal move closer to Shams.

"Don't say that," objected the officer in defense of the Awqaf's decision, then added, "Poor woman, she is truly good-hearted and kind. True, she may lack social graces, but deep down, she is gold."

"Why is she all by herself? Doesn't she have a family?" asked Shams.

"Of course she has a family. However, her family was thrown out of their home while she was out in the fields grazing her sheep. Her mother of course insisted she would not leave without her only daughter, but the Jewish officer threatened to kill her husband and her two sons if she did not go right away. The whole family was forced to join the crowds of refugees who were escorted east. A week or two later, Hashim, Mariam's youngest brother, came back to fetch her, but she refused to leave. She grabbed her goat, two of her cats, and a few chickens in her arms and mumbled that she was not moving without her animals—or, more accurately, that she was staying behind with her 'family.' So as you see, this is her family. We promised her brother, who came seeking our help, that we would take care of her until her family came back or until she is convinced to join them. So you are her family now."

"God forbid," said Nazira.

"Is that why she is mute? I mean, because she lost her family?"

"No, *habibti* Nawal, she was born deaf and mute. Poor thing, everyone made fun of her, and that's why she developed a special relationship and strong bond with animals."

"Maybe because they were the only ones that didn't make fun of her," added Nawal shyly.

Amused by Nawal's curiosity about Mariam, the official responded, "Good for you, Nawal. That is absolutely right." He took a deep breath, then joked, "Oh, well: animals are more human than most of us, after all."

Sure . . . See what you've done to us, Shams thought as the official carried on, "That's why Mariam has been going around town looking after deserted animals whose owners have fled. If she can't bring them to her house or her backyard, she goes out to feed them."

"I now understand why she keeps the animals inside the house, but I still don't understand why the house looks like a junkyard," said Shams.

Having succeeded in getting the girls to have some sympathy

for Mariam regarding her zoo, the official now tried to explain the chaos: "Well, she is a hoarder."

"A what?"

"A hoarder. Do you know what that is?"

"No."

"A hoarder is a person who collects junk and cannot get rid of it." Since both their biological mother, Aisheh, and their Jewish surrogate mother, Rifqa, kept their modest homes clean and tidy, it was not easy for Shams to understand or sympathize with a hoarder. Nonetheless, she later understood why Mariam was constantly collecting and adding to her mounds and mounds of odd objects.

Looking around her, Shams felt as if she and her sisters had fallen from a Jewish paradise into a Muslim hell. Realizing the sin he had committed, the Awqaf official looked into Shams's eyes and asked, "Is there anything I can do for you before I leave?"

Not knowing what to say, Shams was looking in the direction of her sisters when Nazira pleaded, "Take us back home, please. Please, we don't want to stay here."

"That is out of the question. Get it out of your mind, girls. You cannot be brought up by a Jewish mother. That is against Muslim laws. It is absolutely forbidden, it is *haram*."

Not wanting to deal with the sisters' tears, the official tried to exit the scene.

"OK, girls, I'll leave you now. As agreed with your parents, you'll go to school tomorrow morning."

"To the same school?" asked Shams.

"Yes, to the same school. I've informed your headmaster as well as your teachers that you've changed mothers, families, and houses. Goodbye for now. You know how to get to my office if you need me."

. . .

UNABLE TO FALL ASLEEP, or even close her eyes, with Nawal and Nazira on one side and a couple of cats and hens on the other, Shams reflected on all that had happened that day. As if she were looking at a film strip, she thought of Rifqa's Jewishness; of her new Muslim surrogate mother, Mariam; and of the idea of *haram* and *halal* (what was prohibited and what was allowed under Islamic law). In the dark room and grim situation she found herself in, Shams thought of the words her father 'Abed had whispered in her ear before she and her sisters were taken away: "Shams, *habibti*, I beg you to stop crying. Make it easy on your mother and your brother now and I promise I'll bring you back soon, very soon. If need be, I'll kidnap you from the Awqaf mother. Just insist on going to the same school and make sure to pass by Amin's shop every now and then. I will leave instructions for the plan with Ustah once I figure things out myself."

All of a sudden, she saw lightning and heard the rustling of paper blowing in the wind. *Am I dreaming?* She asked herself. Above the crumbling wall appeared strips of colored paper flapping around. *Kites,* she thought. Against the blue morning sky appeared the silhouette of an elegant boy with skillful hands making beautiful kites out of the crumpled-up paper sheets. Those same hands were now tenderly clasping her own hands, triggering a faint sensation of desire.

34

An Escape Plan

NOT A DAY PASSED without Shams's thinking about the words her father had whispered in her ear as they parted: *Trust me,* habibti, *I promise to bring you back. I beg you not to tell anyone. This is our secret.*

Meanwhile, for more than two months, 'Abed, Ustah, and Amin had been silently plotting. They were on the lookout. They had by now figured out who the "Muslim mother" was. They knew the exact location of Mariam's house, Mariam's daily movements in the fields and around town, the route that Shams and her sisters took to school, the hour they went to school, and the hour they came back from school. They had also figured out the day of the week on which Shams went to the Awqaf offices to collect their modest stipend of food, clothes, and pocket money. From a distance, 'Abed often watched Shams go in and out of Amin's shop, pretending to buy an item or two when in reality she was checking for the letter with instructions for the escape plan. "All you need to do is have the girls wait in your shop until the 2:30 bus arrives. Make sure to not only give Shams the bus fare but also help them get on that specific bus. Tell Shams to count five stations, then get off at the Grand Station, where I'll be waiting for them. Good luck to all of us," 'Abed said to the shopkeeper before he handed him the letter, some money for the bus tickets, and, more important, an envelope that had the cash Amin had requested for his services. Smuggling people from point A to point B had become the only source of income for the remaining Arabs in town.

Not wanting to raise Rifqa's hopes or cause her additional emotional distress, 'Abed hadn't shared his plan with her.

However, since the implementation of the second phase of the escape plan required Rifqa's approval and cooperation, 'Abed took advantage of being alone with his wife as she prepared lunch to let her in on it: "In order for the girls to come back and live with us, we must change houses and cities."

With a pot in her hands, Rifqa froze for a moment, then turned around and said, "Wait . . . wait, wait, 'Abed. Let me get this straight. Do I conclude that you've talked to the Awqaf director? Does that mean he's agreed to give us our daughters back provided we leave town?"

"No, Rifqa, none of the above. True, I've met with the Awqaf director more than once, but in vain. He's adamant that the girls must be raised by a Muslim mother. I tried to reason with him that Mariam needed a mother herself and that our daughters had been dumped in a junkyard, but it was like trying to reason with a mule."

"So?"

"So, I decided the only way out is to kidnap our daughters and go live elsewhere."

"What do you mean 'kidnap our daughters'? And where is this 'elsewhere'?" Rifqa repeated, trying to digest the new possibilities that were being thrown at her at a time when she was still trying hard to cope with her losses.

"Rifqa, I've given this a lot of thought. Believe me, I have not had a good night's sleep since the girls left us." Rifqa was well aware of this, as she herself tossed and turned in the same bed with 'Abed.

"Hard and risky as it is, the only way out is to take the girls and go live in Jaffa. As long as we are living in il Lyd, we stand no chance. However, if we take the girls and disappear, the Awqaf will not be able to find us."

"What if they report us to the police?"

"What police? Do you think the Muslim Awqaf would go complain to the Jewish police or Jewish militia? And what would they tell them? We've deprived a woman of her children because she is Jewish?" Though cautious, Rifqa was starting to see the method in her husband's madness.

"As you know, 'Abed, I'd do anything, *anything*, to get *my* daughters back. . . . I'd go to the ends of the earth, even to the moon, for their sake."

"First of all, they are *our* daughters, not only yours. Second, there is no need to go to the ends of the earth. Moving twenty-five kilometers might be enough. Mind you, living on the moon with you and the kids away from this hell seems like it would be the right move these days," 'Abed said in his playful way, then gave Rifqa a tight hug. His tenderness made her cry.

"I wish we could make it to the moon, as living on this land has become unbearable for people like us. And I fear that the worst is still to come. Anyway, forget about the moon for now and tell me what I need to do." Rifqa was ready to act.

"What you need to do, *habibti*, is go to Jaffa and rent us a house there. I wish I could save you the trouble and do it myself. But as you know, not only would I need two permits to get there, an Arab man with a name like 'Abed stands no chance of renting a house in Jaffa nowadays." Wistfully, 'Abed added, "Poor Jaffa, the biggest Arab town in Palestine, and look what has become of it."

"OK, 'Abed, stop wallowing for a second and tell me in which part of Jaffa I should rent a place."

"For sure we do not want to live in the Arab ghetto, do we?"

"Well, I don't know. Isn't it better to live in il 'Ajami than to live among the new Bulgarian immigrants whose language we do not understand?"

"But soon they will learn Hebrew."

"Soon? How soon? And what about Mahmoud and the girls?"

"I don't know what to tell you, Rifqa. I have a feeling there is no place left for people like us in this land."

" 'Abed, let's not get all depressed about what has become of Jaffa now. I'll go there right away and see for myself. But what about your job?"

"Ah, that is the biggest news I've hidden from you. I've gotten approval to be transferred to il 'Amirieyyeh school in Jaffa."

"Really? That is wonderful news! OK, off I go, then. But promise to take care of my son and feed him when he comes home from school."

"I promise to feed *your* son carrots for breakfast, for lunch, and for dinner. You'll find a big fat rabbit when you come back, as this country needs no men."

It was at this point that 'Abed noticed that neither one of them had touched their lunch.

"Come on, sit down, let us have our lunch," 'Abed said.

"I should get going," Rifqa replied as she sat down to eat.

"Wait, *habibti*. Why go today? We have time. You can go to Jaffa early tomorrow morning."

"I need to go and check out the house situation right now." With Rifqa, action was always faster than words. She rose from the dining table, put her plate in the sink, and rushed to her bedroom. In no time, she was standing next to the door with a small bag in her hand.

"Bye, 'Abed. You'll hear from me as soon as I figure something out." Rifqa was on her way to Bat Yam, the Jewish city south of Jaffa where her mother and sister lived.

Aware that traveling on the roads between il Lyd and Bat Yam could be dangerous, 'Abed said, "Be safe, *habibti* . . . Promise to be careful." He gave Rifqa a goodbye kiss, then stood on the sidewalk and watched her figure recede as she walked away from him along the narrow road shaded with eucalyptus trees on both sides.

WITH A FEARFUL HEART, Shams held Nazira and Nawal by the hands as they left the school grounds. The ten-minute walk between their school and Amin's shop felt like the longest march in history. Every step Shams took along that route seemed to pump more adrenaline into her bloodstream.

"For God's sake, Nazira, stop talking. I need your full attention for the coming hour," Shams snapped at her sister, something she had hardly ever done in the past.

"I have not uttered a word. All I said was 'I'll die if Shams's plan fails.'"

"That is a whole sentence, not a word," Shams retorted.

Terrified to be recognized by someone from the loveless world that had not seen her all this time, Shams kept her eyes on the pavement. Getting closer to Amin's shop, she gave her sisters their final instructions: "Once we're inside the shop, don't stand still like punished schoolgirls in a corner; keep wandering around, pretending you're buying something. The shopkeeper knows why we're there. He'll help us get on the bus. We do not want anyone to notice that we are waiting for the bus. Understood?"

Cautiously, Shams looked around her as she and her sisters stepped into Amin's modest shop. Sitting behind a raggedy small table, the shopkeeper ignored their presence. Though she was aware that he was acting according to the plan, Shams still worried he might be absentminded and ignore them when the bus arrived. While Nazira and Nawal went around the shop checking the few items on its shelves, Shams wondered if this was real or a dream. To be reunited with her mother felt more like a dream than reality.

Shams felt guilty that she had been thinking of Um Mahmoud much more than she had been thinking of her lost biological mother. Had she given up on finding her biological family? Or was she waiting for them to find her? Shams had no idea why her mind had drifted at a time when she should be concentrating on what the shopkeeper was whispering in her ear.

"Be ready. In a few minutes, the bus will arrive. It will stop right there." From inside his shop, he pointed toward the bus stop. "Here is exact change for the bus; you pay the driver as you board. Once you're on the bus, you'll find Ustah. Make sure to ignore his presence."

"Ustah? Really?" Nazira asked excitedly.

"Yes, your neighbor Ustah will be on the bus. Pretend not to see him. In other words, ignore him and don't talk to him. Sit a row or two behind him and not in front of him so you'll be able to see him. Count five stops and that's when you and he will get off the bus. Make sure to follow him, otherwise you'll get lost."

The shopkeeper had no clue of the impact his words "get lost" had on the hearts of the three girls who stood in front of him.

"The bus is here. Go out right now," Amin said.

Like small geese and their mother, both Nazira and Nawal obediently followed Shams to the bus stop and onto the bus. None of the girls could resist smiling when they spotted Ustah in an aisle seat in the second row.

Though he purposely frowned, it warmed his heart to see them. *God, I've missed them,* he thought. He tried to ignore their presence, as experience had taught him that things could go wrong at any moment. By the time he had calmed himself, the girls had passed him and settled into seats three rows behind him. They fixed their eyes on the back of his head, and Shams started counting stops, remembering the words from 'Abed's letter: *five stops, then get ready to get off at the Grand Station.* Each time the bus stopped, Shams felt more anxious. *What if the Awqaf director has been alerted that the three girls have gone missing? What if his officers get on the bus at one of these stops?* Fear was Shams's constant companion on the twenty-minute bus ride.

Shams could not hold back her tears when she spotted 'Abed from her window seat. She and her sisters followed Ustah, who got off the bus, then like three arrows, they shot across the road to meet 'Abed, who stood next to a black Plymouth. Tears brimming in his eyes, he hugged one girl at a time, then told them to get in the back seat of the car he had hired for this mission. Out of the corner of his eye, 'Abed took a glance at Ustah, who, by now, was waiting at the bus stop to catch a bus in the opposite direction.

Though it had been clear in his instructions to Shams that he and he alone would be waiting for them at the Grand Station, the first question the three of them asked was, "Where is Mother?"

"Rifqa is waiting for you at our new place in Jaffa," said 'Abed.

This was the first time Shams had ever heard 'Abed refer to Um Mahmoud by her Jewish name. She wondered if that was his indirect way of informing the Jewish driver who had been paid to smuggle them into Jaffa that their mother was Jewish.

35

Subhi

In Search of a Past, in Search of a Future

MUCH HAD HAPPENED the week Subhi beat Fawwaz the collaborator almost to death. Coming home with the shreds of his English suit pants in his trembling hands, Subhi thought of Shams and wondered aloud, "*Habibti* Shams, will I ever see you again? Or should I take this as a bad omen?"

He gazed at the strips of fabric and placed them on his single bed. He let the weight of his fatigued muscles pull him down. On his back, he stared at the ceiling for a while before he shut his eyes.

He was fearful for his life, fearful of Fawwaz's revenge, and fearful that the police might appear once more on his doorstep, pull him out of bed, and throw him in prison for assault. He could not imagine himself standing once again in front of Captain Obadiah to defend his actions. Having given up on winning any case in these kangaroo courts, and more important, having given up on finding Shams, Subhi felt a compulsion to get out of bed, out of his tiny room, out of the crowded house, the crushed community, the defeated city. He felt the urge to liberate himself from this series of confinements, which felt like a matryoshka of different-sized prisons. He so wanted to board one of the huge ships he saw daily in the port where he had been wasting his life waiting for a rare customer to pass by. He wondered what the point of pretending to have a life or a job on the port was, while in reality all that he and the other men did was get drunk on the cheapest arak and high on the worst hashish. With a foggy head, Subhi could not tell if this overwhelming compulsion to board one of those huge ships meant he was in search of a past or in search of a future.

Had it not been for the curfew imposed on the Arab ghetto until 6:00 a.m., Subhi would have by now been on the deck staring at the open sea and promising new horizons. *But how does one go about acting on such an impulse when one needs a permit to leave his ghetto, and another one to leave a city that has been declared a closed military zone?* Subhi thought. Nonetheless, in "gangland," borders were still fluid, smugglers reigned, and illegal trafficking was still possible. Even peasants who had been thrown out of their villages were able to sneak back in to work their land and harvest their fields.

However, much had happened to temporarily distract Subhi from boarding that ship. The same month that Uncle Habeeb was released from prison, Subhi's mother and sisters were smuggled back from Nablus into Ismael's orange grove in the eastern parts of Jaffa. Ismael and Subhi's brother Amir still lived in the orange grove in an effort to prevent the Israel Land Authority from confiscating it, an effort that ultimately proved futile.

Difficult as it had been to leave his city and his family, Subhi could not refuse when Uncle Habeeb suggested Subhi accompany him to Tiberias to work for a Jewish contractor there. Making use of old and new connections, Uncle Habeeb also had his dubious ways of getting himself and his favorite nephew the necessary permits to leave Jaffa. "Habeeb never ceases to be the source of evil," objected Ismael when Subhi went to the orange grove to inform him and his mother about his intention to go with Uncle Habeeb. Securing a job with a Jewish contractor was a golden opportunity, similar to that of working in the Jaffa orange industry pre-1948. While Uncle Habeeb's return gave Subhi the psychological and physical support he needed to face the potential consequences of beating up a collaborator, the return of his mother made it emotionally difficult for Subhi to break away.

WHEN SHE ARRIVED back in Jaffa, Khadijeh had not yet been informed about the death of her eldest son, Jamal.

"Where are the boys?" she asked the second after she hugged her husband, Ismael, and her son Amir.

"Both Jamal and Habeeb have been taken as POWs, while Subhi has found a new job on the port and is now living in il 'Ajami."

"Jamal is in prison? Where? Since when?" Khadijeh bombarded Ismael with a torrent of questions, to which he had prepared all the answers.

"Khadijeh, *habibti*, you and the girls must be starved and exhausted from the two-day journey on donkeys. Why don't you drink this?" Ismael handed his wife and his two daughters hot cups of tea with fresh mint, then added, "Come on, *habibti* Khadijeh, have a bite and we'll talk about everything tomorrow." Ismael was apprehensive about breaking the news of Jamal's death, but of course Khadijeh could not help but ask more questions.

"I don't understand, did you say Subhi was living in il 'Ajami? Why in il 'Ajami?"

"*Habibti,* take it easy on yourself. We will talk about it all tomorrow." Ismael hugged Khadijeh in a tender way that made her cry. "Did you like *allayet banadoura,* the tomato and onion stew that Amir labored over for a whole day to celebrate our family's reunion? Come sit next to me, girls. I missed you," Ismael instructed his daughters.

Khadijeh shook her head, then sighed, "What kind of family reunion is it when one child is in prison, another is living all alone in a room in il 'Ajami, and your parents and one of our daughters and her children were left behind in Nablus?"

"Don't worry, *habibti,* we will find a way to bring them all back once we have the money for the fees." Sad as it may have been, Ismael preferred to talk about his deserted elderly parents rather than tell his wife about the death of their eldest son, Jamal.

No one slept that night. They all feared what they'd have to face in the morning.

"Oh God, no. How? Why?" Khadijeh kept repeating as she collapsed on the floor. "How could you not send me the news about the death of our eldest son?" she accused her husband.

What pained Khadijeh most was having been kept in the dark for so long.

"I swear to God, I tried all possible means to get in touch with you. Believe me, *habibti,* things have not exactly been easy around here. I myself did not know about the loss of our child before I went to see Subhi at your mother's house."

Every time Ismael tried to explain something to his wife, he unintentionally revealed another tragedy. In this case, the death of her mother, Farida, and the loss of her family's house in the Old City of Jaffa.

There is nothing that a brokenhearted father can say or do to ease the pain of a mother who has lost a child.

"And my mother, and her house, and . . . and . . ."

"Exactly, *habibti,* and. . . . and. . . . has been the situation since we left our house in il Manshiyyeh."

"But didn't I warn them that they were too young to stay behind on their own? Didn't I say neither of them knew how to use a rifle?" Khadijeh said as she broke down sobbing again.

"Yes, *habibti.* You did. But who could've predicted the nightmarish events that befell us and our beloved city?" All Ismael could do was to absorb his wife's anger and grief.

Not having lived through the dramatic changes in her city, Khadijeh needed time to process, mourn, and come to terms with what had happened to her family and her neighborhood in the eighteen months she'd spent with her relatives in Nablus.

STILL MOURNING HER LOSSES, Khadijeh now struggled to accept Subhi's decision to accompany Habeeb to Tiberias.

But considering the current levels of deprivation, despair, and poverty in Jaffa, no Arab was in a position to refuse a job. And therefore, no one, including his mother, could change Subhi's mind about leaving.

As tiny and restrictive as his room was and as inconvenient as it was for his mother to live between two places (the orange grove and il 'Ajami), Subhi insisted that his mother and his two sisters take over his room before he left with Uncle Habeeb. This was partly because he, like many, predicted that it was only a matter of time before the Israel Land Authority would confiscate all Arab lands east of Jaffa and would kick their owners out of their orange groves. And partly because Subhi had secretly decided to turn his back on this devastated and traumatized place and never come back.

It was not clear who shed more tears, Subhi or his mother, as she stood with other members of her family at the gate of their orange grove and watched Subhi's back vanish in the haze of an early morning in December.

· 36 ·

A Few Knocks at the Gate

(Jaffa, 1950)

A FEW KNOCKS at the main gate of the *bayyara* right after sunset meant nothing but trouble. *Who could it be at this hour?* wondered Subhi's father, Ismael. Not that it was midnight, but the 7:00 p.m. daily curfew was about to be imposed. He looked at his watch. It was 6:45, meaning that in a quarter of an hour, the streets would empty and no Arab would dare venture out of the house.

The apologetic knock at the gate (atypical for the Haganah forces) made Ismael think it was one of his neighbors. For it was not uncommon for the few who still lived on their orange groves to seek out each other's help and provide one another with a missing item: a loaf of bread, a handful of tea or coffee, or a cup of milk for a hungry child. Having been engaged in the illegal smuggling of people in and out of Jaffa, Ismael feared punishment. But how else could he or others make a living under such circumstances? Apprehensively, he gestured to his wife and children to hide, in the back room of the storage house that had in the meanwhile become their home, as he expected the worse.

In front of him stood a tall and well-built man almost his age, an old-looking man who was barely in his forties. He was unshaved, with a long and untidy beard. His head and part of his face were covered.

"Hurry up, open the gate. It's me, Khalil."

"Oh my God, Khalil! I thought it was you the minute I heard your voice and saw your eyes. Hurry up, come in, come in," Ismael whispered as he opened the gate just enough for Khalil's slim body to slide in, looked around to make sure none of his neighbors had seen him taking in a *mutasallel,* an infiltrator, and bolted the gate once more. The two men looked at each another, hugged tightly, and then began to cry.

"Goodness, Khalil, look at you! You have become a skeleton. What happened to you?"

"The question is not what happened to me. The question is what *did not* happen to me since I saw you last."

Indeed, much had happened since the "Jewish cow" investigation. Ever since he had been released from prison and expelled to Jordan, Khalil had left no stone unturned in his search for his loved ones. He had been to every possible place under the sun inquiring about his wife, Aisheh; his son, Mohammad; and his three daughters, Shams, Nazira, and Nawal—but to no avail. He had toured every place where people from Salameh had taken refuge: from the village of Ni'leen, where he himself had landed, to the village of Birzeit. From Birzeit, he walked to Ramallah. Having no luck there, he ventured all the way to Gaza City, which had, in the meantime, become the largest refugee camp in the whole region. And when searching in an ocean of refugees failed, Khalil traveled all the way to il 'Arish on the border of Egypt. When all attempts there failed as well, he decided to sneak back to il Lyd.

"Ismael, I came to you thinking you might have heard about or seen my three daughters. Do you know anything about them? Have they come to you? Have you seen them? Do you have any idea where could they be?"

Khalil's torrent of questions made Ismael nervous. *But why would his daughters come to me when I don't recall their ever having been to my* bayyara? *Why would they come seek my help in Jaffa when all of Salameh's inhabitants took refuge in il Lyd, il Ramleh, and Jordan?* Ismael wondered, but of course he did not share his thoughts with the desperate father and his old friend.

"I am so sorry, Khalil, I am afraid they have not come here. No, I have not seen them or heard anything about them."

"Ismael, I am going mad. I have lost all members of my family."

"What do you mean 'all members' of your family? Also your wife and son?" Ismael couldn't help but think of the loss of his own son Jamal.

"God forbid, I don't mean lost, lost. I mean they've all gone missing."

"How on earth did you lose them all?"

"My wife, Aisheh, and my son, Mohammad, went missing first, and while I and the girls were waiting for them to come back, I was arrested and thrown in prison for fifteen months for slaughtering a Jewish cow."

"A Jewish cow? You must be joking."

"No, no, I swear to God, I mean it," said Khalil, then carried on, "And that was when I was separated from Shams, Nazira, and Nawal. Then they went missing." Khalil paused for a few seconds, then continued, "With the help of two men from il Lyd, I managed to sneak out from the village of Ni'leen and go to il Lyd, where I was told I would find my daughters. They hid me in the attic of a deserted house and they themselves went around il Lyd and il Ramleh asking about the girls' whereabouts. At the end of three days, the men came back to me with some terrible food and the weirdest story. A story stranger than our lives, Ismael." Again Khalil paused, then took a breath and added, "They claimed that my daughters had been kidnapped by an Egyptian man and his Jewish wife!"

"What's wrong with you, Khalil? A minute ago you told me it was a Jewish cow and now you tell me it was a Jewish wife! Have you gone mad?" Ismael asked, then noted his friend's pained expressions and red eyes and thought: *Poor man. Of course I, too, would lose my mind and start hallucinating if I lost all my children.*

Regretting that he had accused his friend of going mad, Ismael tried to make up for it by saying, "I know everything around us is becoming Jewish: our homes, our shops, our hospitals, our cities, our country, but I did not realize that Dutch cows have also turned Jewish."

Wanting to take a break from the absurdity of it all, Ismael said, "Khalil, let me call Khadijeh and the kids. Let's see if they recognize you. Meanwhile, have a seat. You must be starving. Let me get you something to eat."

"All I need is a glass of water."

"I will get you that too."

After dinner, the two men took a big pot of tea with fresh mint and two glasses and ventured out to sit under the orange trees in the dark.

"God, I missed these trees," Khalil said as he sat against the trunk of one of the orange trees.

They fell silent for a few minutes before Ismael said, "Khalil, did you say your daughters were with an Egyptian man and a Jewish woman?"

Becoming a bit hopeful, Khalil asked, "Have you heard of such a couple?"

"No. No, I've never heard of such a couple, though in the past, in the good old days, there were many mixed marriages in Jaffa, including that of Khawaja Michael. Anyway, why would I know them if they lived in il Lyd before they kidnapped your daughters? Khalil, I hope you don't get upset with me, but I am a bit perplexed about the 'kidnapping' of your daughters. Why would they have been kidnapped?" Ismael asked, unconvinced.

"I, like you, was surprised and did not believe the story at first, but then I learned that the couple had adopted them."

"Oh, adopted them! Why didn't you say that? That is very different from kidnapping them! Of course, my friend, many people adopt or take children into their homes until their families come asking for them. You're making more sense now. I swear to God, for a while I thought you had gone completely mad."

"But I *have* gone mad."

Ignoring Khalil's comment, Ismael added, "Though there are more villagers living in Jaffa now than Jaffans, Khadijeh and the girls, who spend some of their time in Subhi's room in il 'Ajami, got to know most of the people there. Schools are closed now, but I promise you once they're open, I'll go myself and ask about your daughters. I'm just afraid I won't be able to recognize Shams if I see her."

"I am afraid I would not recognize her myself. It has been close to three years, and as you know, girls change quickly at this age," said Khalil.

"But are you certain that the couple has come to live in Jaffa? I personally doubt that, or at least that they're in the Arab ghetto."

Khalil pondered this for a while, then said, "I tell you, Ismael, my biggest fear is exactly that. I dread the possibility that my daughters have been taken to live in a Jewish town or a Jewish neighborhood. And if that is the case, they're not going keep their Arab names. Who knows, perhaps by now they've acquired Jewish names such as Ruth, Lea, or Shulamit."

"Khalil, your thoughts are getting darker than this night. It is getting late." Ismael looked at his watch and saw that it was close to 1:00 a.m. "Let's sleep on it and revisit our plans first thing in the morning."

37

New Neighbors

(Jaffa, 1951)

"Guess what, Khadijeh? I've found the right bride for you!" yelled Henriette.

"For me!" Subhi's mother giggled, then added, "Never a dull moment in your company, dearest Henriette."

"Come on, neighbor. You know what I mean. I saw a beautiful bride for your son Amir," said Henriette, who had become Khadijeh's best friend. Except for Khadijeh, Henriette had a dislike of, or rather resentment toward, her neighbors, whom she blamed for the degradation of her neighborhood. Though Khadijeh was from a lower social standing and a poorer Jaffa neighborhood, Henriette liked her. For the last two years, since Khadijeh and her daughters had come to live in Subhi's room in 'Ajami, Henriette, who was sad to see her skillful mechanic go, had offered his mother and his two sisters her friendship. Having lost all members of her family and most of her former neighbors, Henriette found in Khadijeh the right companion for her morning coffee. The feeling was mutual, since Khadijeh also looked forward to taking long morning breaks away from her overcrowded house. More significantly, Henriette entertained Khadijeh and made her laugh, which was a rarity in such grim times.

Sometimes across from each other, other times next to each other, the two women sat on Henriette's balcony for an hour or two. Their first cup of coffee was often followed by a second and a third. Chatting, they watched the world stand still while their disoriented neighbors spun around them or came and went aimlessly.

"The worst thing that happened to us and our city was the arrival of the scum from neighboring villages. I used to think that the Hawranis were the lowest of the low," said Henriette, in reference to those from Hawran, the southern parts of Syria, "but it turns out these peasants are worse."

Perhaps out of affection for the two caring and loving peasant families with whom she shared a house or because many industrious peasants had worked for her husband on his orange grove before 1948, Khadijeh had more sympathy for the villagers. "Come on, Henriette, it's not the peasants' fault. The truth of the matter is that *kulna itsakhamnah,* we are all fucked."

"But no one has fucked me so far," Henriette said, breaking into high-pitched laughter.

"You have a dirty mind. How come with all your beauty and wealth you never found a man for yourself?"

"All the rich and educated Christian men are gone. I'm left with the riffraff. You want me to marry one of those?" Henriette raised her arm and pointed her finger at a shabby half-bent old man who was passing under her balcony. "But don't worry about me. I manage on my own. 'Desire is the mother of invention,' goes the saying."

"That is not how the saying goes. It is 'Necessity is the mother of invention.'"

"OK, OK, Khadijeh. Forget about me. Aren't you interested in the adorable bride I have found for your Amir?"

"You know what, Henriette? The Awqaf should hire you as a *mazouneh*, an authorized marriage clerk. I tell you, if you keep at it, there won't be a single man or woman in town."

"You're right. I will be the only spinster here. But you know full well, Khadijeh, that your Awqaf would never appoint a Christian woman as a *mazouneh*, would they?"

"The Awqaf wouldn't appoint a Muslim woman as a *mazouneh*, let alone a Christian. Anyway, tell me, who is this bride you have found for Amir?"

"She is a relative of mine," replied Henriette, joking.

"God forbid, a Christian!" said Khadijeh.

"Just kidding. I'm taking revenge on the Awqaf for refusing to appoint me as a *mazouneh*. I tell you, sooner or later, whether we like it or not, we Christians and Muslims will have to start marrying one another if we don't want to become spinsters. Or maybe worse, we might have to marry Jews!"

"You mean to tell me that with the thousands of Palestinians living in Jaffa, you could not find a Muslim bride for my son?"

"Would you like me to find him a peasant girl? If that is OK with you, I can find you ten of them."

"Oh no, God forbid!"

"Khadijeh. I told you I was kidding. The bride I have found you is not Christian and is not a peasant. She is the daughter of Mary's neighbors, and her father's name is 'Abed but I don't know his family name."

"And who's Mary?" Khadijeh asked, confused.

"*Walawo*, come on, you don't know my cousin Mary who lives in il Jabaliyyeh?"

"Why would I know your cousin Mary? Or for that matter the fancy neighborhood of il Jabaliyyeh? You seem to have forgotten that though I was born and raised in the Old City, I have lived almost all my life in il Manshiyyeh, which is . . . which is . . . which is now rubble."

"OK, OK, Khadijeh, let's not keep lamenting our situation. I am talking to you about the happy occasion of finding a bride for your son, and you're talking to me about rubble! We can't keep moaning and mourning. . . . Look at me, I am the only one left here from my family, so let's not compete in misery. All I know is, life has to go on," said Henriette, then added, "At least *sex* has to go on . . . so, my dear Khadijeh, do you want to know more about the bride I found or not?"

"Yes, yes, of course. Tell me who the girl is. Whose daughter is she again? And most important, how old is she? As you know, Amir is just fifteen," said Khadijeh half-heartedly, as her mind drifted from the rubble of her house in il Manshiyyeh to the death of her son Jamal and the disappearance of her son Subhi, whom she had not seen or heard from since he'd left Jaffa two years earlier. Habeeb had advised Subhi to give up on the futile idea of going to Jordan in search of Shams in an ocean of refugees, but one night Subhi vanished. Hoping that he would soon come back to Tiberias or Jaffa, Habeeb kept lying to Khadijeh, saying that Subhi was busy with his job, or did not have the right permit to move between Tiberias and Jaffa.

Khadijeh had no choice but to believe Habeeb and wait.

"Khadijeh, I can see you're neither listening nor interested in the bride."

"No, no, don't get me wrong, of course I am interested, but as you can imagine, thinking of happy occasions make me sad . . ."

"You know what, Khadijeh? Forget it. I thought this would warm your heart, but it seems to have done just the opposite."

"I was dreaming of dancing at Jamal's wedding, that's what I've—" thinking of the death of her eldest son, suddenly Khadijeh broke into tears and laid her head in Henriette's lap.

"Oh my God, Khadijeh, I am so sorry."

"I am the one who should be sorry, *habibti* Henriette. But as you know, time can heal all wounds except the pain of losing and longing for a lost child. Only death can make that kind of pain go away."

THE NEXT MORNING, Khadijeh appeared for coffee saying, "OK, Henriette, I am ready to hear more about Amir's bride. I went to see Ismael and Amir in our orange grove yesterday, and I am happy to report that they were both enthusiastic about the idea. Particularly because there are few Arab families living around our *bayyara* and Amir rarely sees girls."

"Your son will end up marrying a wolf out there in that wilderness. There are hardly any people left in Sakanet Abu il Reish, let alone girls! Anyway, thank God you're in a better mood today. I was worried about you yesterday. OK, *habibti*, what can I tell you? She is young, beautiful, and adorable. She might still be underage, but I'm sure Amir can wait a year or two, maybe a bit longer! Believe me, she is worth the wait. She is polite and well-mannered to a point you wouldn't think she's a Muslim," Henriette teased her neighbor, then cracked up laughing.

"Bite your tongue, Henriette. I'm sure one day you'll end up marrying a Muslim yourself."

"The important thing is to have someone in my bed. Christian, Muslim, or Jewish, I don't care."

"Stop it and tell me whose daughter she is."

"To tell you the truth, I don't know the name of their family; all I know is that her father's first name is 'Abed. But as I told you, her family lives up the road from Mary's in il Jabaliyyeh neighborhood."

"There are thousands of men called 'Abed. Anyway, I did not think there were Arabs still living in il Jabaliyyeh. I thought we were all crammed on top of one another in il 'Ajami."

"No, you're wrong. True, many Jews have already moved into 'absentee' Arab houses in il Jabaliyyeh, but a few Arab families have somehow managed to keep their houses and stay, including my cousin and Khawaja Michael, if you happen to know him."

"I told you I don't know any *khawajat* or big shots except for you, Henriette."

"Oh sure, I'm the big-ass woman, that's what I have become lately. Anyway, if you're interested, I'll go see my cousin Mary and arrange for us to go see the bride's family tomorrow or the day after."

"Make sure we see the bride. I want to be sure she is at least cute, if not beautiful."

"I know, I know. In the good old days when Jaffa had respected rich families, one only cared who the family was. But now that all Jaffans have become beggars, what counts is how sweet or well-mannered the girl is."

"Provided she is pretty."

"Yes, got it. I am sure you're going to love her as I did."

"The important thing is for Amir to like her, or at least find her agreeable."

. . .

"HAVE THEM COME over for a cup of coffee, though both her mother and I think our daughter is too young to marry," relented the bride's father. Henriette had so far visited them three times: once with her cousin and twice by herself that same week. "We must also consult with our daughter, either before or after they come. Probably after, as we don't want her to feel shy or embarrassed or rejected."

"Don't worry. Your daughter is adorable. The groom is also young, but why not plan ahead? As you know, the pool of eligible Jaffan girls has shrunk. Look at me. Would I stand a chance of marrying a respected Jaffan man? Or am I way past my prime?" Henriette burst into one of her high-pitched laughing fits again.

When she had left, Rifqa said to 'Abed, "A cup of coffee, then what? Then say sorry, she is too young? Why don't you nip in the bud and say that the girl is way too young to marry. Why don't you tell them to ask again two, three, or even four years from now?" Rifqa had no patience for her husband's courteousness.

"Take it easy on me, *habibti*, it's only a cup of coffee. Let me go make you one." In his humorous way, 'Abed managed to diffuse Rifqa's mounting anxiety. "If her biological parents do not show up—and by now I doubt they will—sooner or later, the girl will have to marry," said 'Abed in response to Rifqa's objections to the possible engagement.

"Sooner or later, like everyone, Shams and the girls and Mahmoud will all marry. But I do not see the point in marrying her off now."

"Rifqa, you know that I am in no hurry to marry off any of our children, but it is also impolite not to receive these people for a cup of coffee, even if the answer is no. Here, have some more coffee," said 'Abed, realizing that Rifqa was still unhappy about the potential groom's visit.

This too shall pass had always been 'Abed's motto in life, but more so lately.

ON THE AGREED-UPON DAY, Henriette, Ismael, Khadijeh, and Amir arrived for coffee. "Please, come on in . . . welcome . . . have a seat . . . you're most welcome, please have a seat," 'Abed kept alternating his two welcoming sentences until his guests, led by Henriette, were seated in his and Rifqa's modest living room. As often is the case on such occasions, awkwardness filled the air. Everybody, especially the men, tended to talk about everything under the sun except the subject at hand. 'Abed and Ismael, who sat next to each other, talked mostly about what had become of Jaffa, il Lyd, and il Ramleh, and the increasing sense of estrangement Arabs felt.

"I swear to God, I walk in the streets and rarely hear Arabic. There's not a single Arabic newspaper. Gone are the good old days when Jaffa had its own three daily newspapers," said Ismael.

"True, one does not hear Arabic, but strangely enough, one does not hear Hebrew either. I think it is time we all learned Yiddish."

"Bulgarian," Rifqa corrected her husband.

"Yes, I mean Bulgarian."

"I tell you, we're doomed: our city is doomed, and so are our people," responded Ismael, while the anxious three women and Amir waited for this part of the conversation to end.

"Hey, hey, men, please stop it . . . You seem to have forgotten the happy occasion that has brought us together," Henriette finally objected. Nervous smiles and laughter became the mode of communication for a short while, until silence fell over the room. They all looked at Ismael, waiting for him to say something. He composed himself, cleared his throat, put a nervous smile on his face, then said,

"*Bismillah,* in the name of God, my wife, Khadijeh, and I have come to ask for the hand of your daughter . . ."

"Shams," said Henriette, who realized that Ismael had forgotten the name of the bride.

"Yes, Shams," he repeated, then resumed, "We have come to ask for the hand of your honorable daughter Shams for our son Amir." Ismael looked in the direction of his son, who was now beaming.

"We are aware that your daughter is still underage, but as Henriette might have told you, we are prepared to wait a year or two."

"Good evening to you all. We're honored to have you in our modest home. And we thank you for your courteous visit," replied 'Abed, selecting his words carefully to please not only his guests but also, and more important, his wife. "You're absolutely right, our daughter is still very young. Both her mother and I want her to finish school before she marries. And that is why we did not inform her of your visit today."

Taken aback, Khadijeh and Ismael looked at each other, not knowing what to say. Not wanting Henriette to throw out one of her improper jokes, Khadijeh jumped in abruptly: "But we're here to see her. Can we do that today?" she asked in a rather demanding way. She was obviously annoyed, but also insulted by 'Abed's statement that they had not informed the girl that she had a suitor. Neither Khadijeh nor Amir was prepared to wait a year or two for a bride they had not seen.

"I am truly sorry, I did not mean to suggest that you will not see our daughter today. You will see all our girls today. But promise me not to reveal to them the purpose of your visit. Just ask Shams and her sisters mundane questions about school or whatever you want. Make it sound like a casual family visit," 'Abed said as he stood up and went to call Shams and her sisters.

It was a few minutes before Shams came into the room, followed by Nazira and Nawal.

"Come sit next to me." Noticing her daughters' shyness in a protective, motherly way, Rifqa moved sideways, making space for them next to her on the couch.

A few awkward moments passed as they all began to recognize or suspect who was who in the room, before Ismael had the courage to break the silence.

"What is your name, young lady?" he asked, staring at Shams.

"Shams," she replied in a shaky voice with an inquisitive look. She received a similar look in return.

"And what is your father's name?" Ismael's next question made Khadijeh, Henriette, and Amir laugh, thinking what an odd thing it was to ask in the presence of 'Abed. But 'Abed and Rifqa were alarmed by his question. Having her own doubts but also her own hopes, Shams replied, "My name is Shams Khalil Abu Ramadan."

Stunned that she had given him her full name, Ismael wanted to confirm what he had just heard.

"What did you say your father's name was?"

"Khalil."

"And your family's name?"

"Abu Ramadan."

"Abu Ramadan?"

"Yes."

"Are you from Salameh?"

"Yes." Happy to be recognized but afraid of the possible consequences, Shams drew closer to Rifqa, and stared at her seeking help.

"Shams, do you know who I am? Do you recognize me?" asked Ismael.

"No." The truth of the matter was that she did and did not.

"I am Ismael, I am Abu Jamal. Remember, your father, Khalil, worked for me in *il bayyara*?"

Not knowing what to do or say, Shams froze, as did everyone in the room. Soon the significance of the moment hit Shams, and she placed her head in Rifqa's lap and began to sob.

Was she ready for another dramatic chapter of her life? She was not sure.

Everyone in the room recognized the seriousness of the situation except for frivolous Henriette.

"Wait, I am at a total loss here! Isn't Shams your daughter?" She looked at Rifqa, whose jaw had dropped while her teary eyes were fixed on Ismael.

"Please, Henriette, wait. Do not interrupt," said 'Abed.

"Do you know where your father is now?" asked Ismael, trying to figure out what had brought Shams and her sisters to 'Abed and Rifqa.

"I don't know, maybe in Amman. The last time we saw him was in il Lyd, when he was arrested for slaughtering a Jewish cow."

"A Jewish cow!" repeated Ismael absentmindedly as he recalled his conversation with Khalil. "And your mother, and Mohammad, your brother?"

"They also got lost."

"Lost where?" Ismael asked, even though he had heard the whole story from Khalil.

"On the way to Jordan." Shams helplessly tried to control her tears.

"Did you know that your father came to look for you and your sisters a year or so ago?" asked Ismael.

"Really?" said Shams. "Is that true? What on earth are you saying?"

Thinking of everything he and Khadijeh had done to try to find Shams and her sisters, Ismael looked at his wife and smiled, then turned his eyes back to Shams and asked, "Would you like to see your father?"

"See my father? Of course!" Shams looked at 'Abed and Rifqa, seeking an explanation.

"OK, OK, let us stop here," said 'Abed, authoritative for once. "Shams, *habibti*, take your sisters and go to your room. Or you know what? You stay here with your mother, and Ismael and I will go outside. I need to talk to him privately." The two men stood up, and without uttering a word, Ismael followed 'Abed to a tiny balcony. 'Abed made sure to close the door behind him, leaving the stunned women and Amir behind. Disappointed in the way things had turned against him, Amir left the house.

Realizing the profound consequences of this development for her whole family, Rifqa wanted to protect her daughters. "Excuse me, ladies," she said to Khadijeh and Henriette. "I need to talk to my daughters in private."

Rifqa got up from the sofa, as did her dazed daughters. "Shams, Nazira, Nawal, come with me."

"My dear daughters, what marvelous news this is," she said when they were in the girls' bedroom. "As sad as I am that you will be leaving our family, I am thrilled that you will be reunited with your father. Finally, *Allah farajha 'alaykum*, God is merciful." Tears ran down her cheeks and those of her daughters as both apprehension and excitement filled the air.

"Mom, is it true that they can bring our father, Khalil, to Jaffa? I thought the Israelis wouldn't allow anyone to come back."

"That is very true. But, *habibti*, they can smuggle him in." Before Shams or her sisters could inquire who "they" were, Rifqa explained, "When the borders between Israel and its neighboring countries were still undefined and unguarded, it was easy for people to cross back and forth. However, now, after almost three and a half years of the creation of the Jewish state, the border police shoot at returnees."

"Oh no," said Nawal, fearing for her father's life.

"No, no, *habibti*, don't worry. Your father is going to be OK. Didn't you hear Uncle Ismael say that Khalil came looking for you sometime last year? For sure he will not take any risks. These smugglers know their way around." Rifqa regretted having scared her daughters, so she added, "The smugglers know the land much better than the Jewish soldiers. Trust me, they will bring your dad from one orange grove to another under cover of darkness. Come on, girls, let's go out and celebrate this happy occasion. Finally you're going to be with your father after almost what, three and a half years?"

"Three years, seven months, and twenty-three days" said Shams, who then went to her astounded mother and hugged her tightly. So did Nazira and Nawal.

By the time they went back to the living room, Henriette had disappeared like Amir. However, unlike the teenage boy who felt that destiny was fiercer than his desires, Henriette felt she had unintentionally accomplished a grander mission than she had set out to. Perhaps a family reunion was not as entertaining as a wedding, but she, who had been adamant about staying home while her family boarded a ship to Beirut, understood what it meant for her potential bride to once again be with her family; first with her father, then with her mother and her younger brother, whom Henriette had concluded were now living in Amman.

"*Mabruk, alf mabruk, habibati.* Congratulations, my dears."

'Abed moved swiftly toward his wife and daughters and caught them all in a group hug. "You see, *Allah kbeer,* God is great. You will soon be reunited with your father, who will arrive to take you to see your mother and brother in Amman."

"When?" asked Nazira, who had kept quiet all this time.

"Are you in a hurry to leave us *ya shaitaneh,* you little devil?" joked 'Abed, bringing tears to everybody's eyes, including his. Nazira looked perplexed for a second. She was about to respond to 'Abed's remark but decided not to at the very last minute. If there was anyone who was scared to venture to Amman, it was Nazira. Comparing the security she felt living with Rifqa and 'Abed to the unknown into which Khalil was about to take her made her almost admit she did not want to leave. Worried she would reveal her true feelings, Nazira went over to stand close to 'Abed.

"Hopefully within this week," responded 'Abed, trying to break the atmosphere that was charged with conflicting emotions.

No word, joke, or sentence seemed to be appropriate for this occasion.

38

A Friendly Request

A WHITE STREAK of light cut through the dark machinery room as its heavy iron door squeaked open. The light and sound struck Khalil, who was sitting crossed-legged on a straw mat placed on the floor against a gray wall. Over his head hung the rusty tools he had once used to water and prune the orange trees that stood half dead outside the door.

In the soft morning light appeared the silhouette of Shams, layered with the two silhouettes of Nazira and Nawal. Khalil jumped to his feet and rocketed toward the door.

"Oh God," he screamed at the top of his lungs as he rubbed his eyes a few times, slapped his face twice before he could utter his daughters' names: "Shams. . . . Nazira. . . . Nawal . . . is this for real or is it a dream?"

It was not clear if it was their father's long beard and skeleton-like body or the dark circles under his eyes that scared little Nawal and made her retreat a step or two backward before she came closer again.

But soon the three girls were glued to their father's body, weeping and laughing at the same time.

"Where is Mother? Have you found her? Have you found Mohammad?" were the first comprehensible words that Shams managed to get out.

Not wanting to disappoint her, Khalil responded, "Come on, sweetheart, let's rejoice in this precious moment. . . . Let's step out of this darkness into the light outside. With God's help, we will find your mother and brother soon. I never expected to find you, but here you are." Once again, he stretched his arms around his daughters and squeezed them tightly. Though saddened by her dad's confirmation that her mother and brother were missing, Shams had already come to that conclusion when Ismael told them about Khalil's visit to Jaffa a year earlier.

Ismael and Khadijeh were anxiously waiting for Khalil to appear with his daughters. Though curious about their encounter, out of respect, they gave Khalil a bit of privacy with them. Soon they were all sitting around a *tabliyyeh*, a low round wooden table, on top of which Khadijeh had placed the few dishes and sweets they could afford.

"Oh, Dad, how much we missed you. I can't believe we slept in the same town but in different places last night." Not wanting to admit to herself, but more specifically to her father, how torn she and her sisters had been about leaving their surrogate family, Shams hugged Khalil tightly and placed her head on his shoulder. "It is all Uncle Ismael's fault. He should've brought us here last night."

"You've been away from your dad for years. I thought a few more hours wouldn't make a difference," joked Ismael.

"Those 'few hours' were the longest and hardest in years," Khalil said.

It was at this point that Ismael felt the need to defend himself. "I hope you all realize that the curfew had already been imposed when Khalil and 'Ali, one of the smugglers, appeared from under the orange trees. Though I had been expecting them for forty-eight hours, I still jumped when I heard whispers and footsteps in the orange grove. Who knows, it could have been the Jewish militia who have been threatening to confiscate all the orange groves in this area."

"Why didn't you call us on the phone?"

"A phone call at that hour announcing the arrival of an infiltrator would've brought the Israeli intelligence unit to your father rather than brought you here."

"The important thing is that we are all united. Thank you, dear Ismael. My daughters and I are indebted to you for the rest of our lives."

"Yes, Uncle Ismael, thank you," said Nazira as she stood up from her chair next to her father and went to hug Ismael. Shams and Nawal followed.

"All right, all right, girls," said Ismael, embarrassed and not knowing how to reciprocate their love. He looked at Khalil. "Khalil, Khadijeh and I are going to town to do some shopping for tomorrow's supper with Rifqa and 'Abed. In the meantime, enjoy each other's company, and enjoy your lunch. I am sure you and the girls have a lot to catch up on until we come back around five or six p.m."

THAT NIGHT WAS the first time in years that Shams and her sisters slept next to their father and away from Rifqa. And like fish out of water, Rifqa, 'Abed, and Mahmoud tossed and turned in their beds. The next morning, they were up with the sun. Early-morning rays elongated their shadows as they made their way along the narrow dirt road that took them from their house in il Jabaliyyeh to Ismael's orange grove. Overwhelmed by the avalanche of events and coincidences, they, like Khalil, were speechless when they finally met him.

Feeling guilty about all the terrible things he had thought about the Jewish woman and Egyptian man who had "kidnapped" his daughters, Khalil knew there was only one way he could express his gratitude when words failed him: right after he shook hands with 'Abed and Mahmoud, he kneeled on the ground and kissed Rifqa's feet. The Prophet Mohammad said, "Paradise lies under the feet of mothers," and Khalil kept repeating this until he was helped up by Rifqa and 'Abed. "Neither my daughters nor I will ever forget what you've done; you will go straight to heaven." Realizing that Khalil was not aware that the concept of hell and heaven did not exist in the Jewish tradition, Rifqa simply smiled and said, "Since we are all living in hell these days, I do hope there will be only paradise at the end of this life."

THOUGH THE DAY had been emotionally taxing, everyone was running around the house lending a hand in the preparation of the last supper the three families would share together before the smugglers arrived later that night to guide Khalil and his daughters to the border of Jordan. Despite the buzz of activity, emotions were running high.

When the early supper was served, Shams sat next to Rifqa, while Nazira and Nawal sat on either side of 'Abed. *How can this be my last meal next to Rifqa?* Shams asked herself as tears welled in her eyes. Hiding her tears, she stood up and took a few steps away from them all. A few minutes later, she came back, sat close to Rifqa, and hugged her tightly.

In the hope of keeping her surrogate daughters a bit longer, Rifqa made a point of inquiring about the fate of their mother, giving a subtle (or perhaps not so subtle) hint that it might be better if they stayed with her until their mother was found. Terrified of once again being separated from his daughters, Khalil declined her offer. "I do hope to return home soon with Aisheh and Mohammad so you can meet. I am full of appreciation for all that you have done for my girls, and I am sure that Aisheh will be better at reciprocating your love and care."

In spite of Khalil's comforting words, they all knew they might never see one another again. They were all aware of the declaration made by Ben Gurion a month or two after his militias had forced the Palestinians out of their homes: "No refugee will be allowed back." And therefore Rifqa feared the worst for her daughters: an unknown and unsafe future, at best in a tent in a refugee camp in Jordan or in the Gaza Strip. *Who will take care of my daughters if their mother has fallen ill or died?* Rifqa worried, but she kept the thought to herself.

Having been on the sidelines during recent events, thirteen-year-old Mahmoud was hovering around wanting to know the fate of Mohammad, the brother whom he had never met but had had the psychological burden of substituting for over the last three years. Mahmoud could not grasp the sequence of events that had resulted in his losing his three sisters in the blink of an eye. He could not bear to think of going home alone, with no one to play with, tease, or fight with. And Shams's happiness about finding her father was overshadowed by her sadness about not finding her mother and even more so about having to say farewell to Mahmoud, 'Abed, and especially Rifqa. All of a sudden, Shams realized how much she loved Rifqa. She could not imagine a life without her. *Is it possible that I love Rifqa more than I love my own mother?* she thought. The idea scared her but did not stop her from wondering, *In the span of three years, have I forgotten how much I loved my mother? Or have I taken my love for her for granted?* Shams's head got all foggy. Considering the avalanche of emotions she was experiencing, Shams received the news about Subhi's disappearance, which was mentioned in passing by his father, with emotional numbness.

Seeing her two fathers, Khalil and 'Abed, sitting next to each other, Nawal wished she could also have her two mothers and her two brothers together. She wondered if there was some magical way she could have both families at the same time in the same place. *Why should we lose one in order to gain the other?* Nawal thought. She also contemplated the idea of having Khalil venture to Amman in search for her mother alone while she and her sisters stayed a bit longer with Rifqa, 'Abed, and Mahmoud. *And what if we went all the way to Amman and didn't find Mom and Mohammad?* Realizing the precarious situation of her father but also feeling sad about leaving her surrogate family, little Nawal asked, "Yaba, are we staying in Jaffa or are we leaving to search for Mom and Mohammad?"

"*Habibti,* I thought you knew the plan. We are leaving this evening for Amman to look for your mother and brother, but also to live there. I wish I could stay in Jaffa, but as you know, I am not a red ID holder like all of you," Khalil said.

"Red ID? What is that?" asked Nawal.

"The few Palestinians who remained were counted, registered, and given a red ID," said 'Abed.

"Why red?" Nawal asked.

"Not because they are communists like Rifqa and me, but because for them, red signals danger," 'Abed explained.

"Red gives a signal to the Israeli soldiers to beware of Palestinians whose houses, land, and souls they have stolen," added Ismael.

"*Habibti*, I am sorry for confusing you with such a long-winded answer to your question. In short, we are to leave in a few hours since I stand no chance of being able to stay here with my daughters. The Israeli governor would rather see the three of you leave than give one more red ID to another unwanted Palestinian."

"Even if they gave you a red ID that allowed you to stay in Jaffa but forbade you from leaving the city, how would you search for Mom and Mohammad?" asked Shams, who proved to be the only one grasping the complexity of the situation.

"There's that too," added Khalil, who was getting a bit tired of the futile conversation since he knew he had no other option but to pick up his three daughters and leave once darkness fell.

Though Rifqa contemplated once again bringing up the idea of keeping her daughters a bit longer, she hesitated to do so. But she felt the need to be alone with them, so she said, "Shams, Nazira, Nawal, why don't we take a little walk along the *bayyara*? We won't go too far, as I am sure both 'Abed and Mahmoud will also want to spend more time with you before you go away." It was the last two words that brought Rifqa to tears. For the first time in a week, she burst into loud sobs. *How is it possible that I won't see my three daughters ever again?*

Mahmoud asked to join his mother and sisters on their little goodbye walk.

"Don't be long. The smugglers will be here in an hour or so.

The girls need to prepare their luggage," said 'Abed, who also felt the urge to join his family on their last stroll. But being the courteous man he was, he stayed behind with Khalil and Ismael.

"What luggage?" giggled Ismael. "They are going to walk, or at best ride donkeys, for most of the trip. They have to travel as light as birds. A little bit of food and water and that's about it." Khalil, who had by now walked whole continents in search of his family, also found the discussion rather amusing.

ONCE RIFQA AND THE CHILDREN were back from their short but emotionally exhausting farewell walk, the unbearable last hours of being together were coming to an end. Ismael waited for the right moment to reveal his wishes. He excused himself and asked to be alone with Khalil. "Khalil, can we talk in private?"

"Sure," responded Khalil, and followed Ismael into the house.

"Khalil." Ismael paused for a while, gathered his failing courage, took a deep breath, and said, "I need a personal *favor* from you," emphasizing the word "favor."

"From *me*?"

"Yes, my friend, from you. I wish to ask for Shams's hand for my son."

"Shams's hand?"

"Yes, for my son Amir."

"For Amir." Repetition was Khalil's method of coping.

"Yes, for Amir," repeated Ismael, as his eyes met Khalil's.

In spite of the tightness in his throat and the unbearable thought of parting from one of his daughters after all they had gone through, Khalil felt indebted to his friend. Though they had become equally poor, Khalil was not in a position to say no to his old boss. Sensing Khalil's hesitation, Ismael increased the pressure.

"I gave you your three daughters back; can't you give me *one* in return?"

Realizing what it would mean to separate the three sisters but not wanting to disappoint Ismael, Khalil sought Shams's help.

"Shams . . . Nazira . . . Nawal, come in for a second."

Hearing the urgency in their father's voice, the three sisters stood before him in suspense. The two men exchanged glances before Khalil said, "*Habibti* Shams, as you know, Ismael is like a brother to me. He and his wife are like family to us. He has asked for your hand for his son."

"Amir." Ismael filled in the lost name, while Khalil continued to address his daughter Shams. "I could not but give my blessing. However, I first need your approval."

Not knowing what to say or do, Shams instinctively drew nearer to her sisters and put an arm around each girl. In a daze, she barely heard Ismael as he said, "You know, *habibti* Shams, you've always been like a daughter to me. You will be among family. Since you are still too young to marry, you and Amir can be engaged for a few years."

While everyone stared at Shams waiting for her answer, she was lost in her own thoughts: *God, what have I done to deserve all this? Now that I have finally found my father, it's time for me to lose Nazira and Nawal? And when I have finally come to terms with the thought of never seeing Subhi again, I end up marrying his younger brother?* Shams had the urge to inquire more about Subhi's disappearance but did not.

She froze.

No one could talk or reason with the speechless and expressionless Shams.

It was Ismael who went outside to bring Rifqa back into the house and into the conversation. If there was one person who could advise Shams at this pivotal moment in her life, it was her surrogate mother.

Having given her daughters one of her reassuring hugs, Rifqa took Shams by the hand and led her back outside for another walk around the orange grove. "*Habibti* Shams, I know how difficult it is for you to deal with all this: to separate from your father and from Nazira and Nawal for God knows how long!" Rifqa stopped herself from saying "forever."

"But you know, *habibti,* in life, we lose some and we gain some. Think of your father and how he regained the three of you and is now ready to have you marry and live your own life. Think of Ismael and Khadijeh, who all along wanted you to be part of their family. But most important, think of *us.* Think of *you and me* and how we will stay close to each other and try together to make sense of this cruel world. Please, Shams, why don't you say yes and stay close to me?" Rifqa pleaded.

Reflecting on all that Rifqa had done for her and her sisters, and fearing the unknown and unsafe world and future into which her father was leading them, Shams made up her mind. She would stay in Jaffa and marry Subhi's brother Amir.

Epilogue

(Jaffa, January 2018)

ON JANUARY 23, 2018, I met Shams in her home in il 'Ajami. I spent two days talking to her, about her life in general but more so about the events of the 1948 Nakba. What struck me most about the eighty-five-year-old woman was her peacefulness, her kindness, and above all, her ability to forgive. She was surrounded by her children and grandchildren, and I felt not only how much she was loved by them but also how loving she was toward them. Her affection engulfed everyone, including me, whom she had just met.

The contrast between the stories she told me and the softness of her voice left me in awe.

It was from her that I learned the following.

Shams and Amir were married in the summer of 1952 and lived happily together in Jaffa. They had six daughters. Nazira and Nawal were the names Shams gave to her first and second children.

Amir died in 2013. "May God bless his soul. He was a gentleman," Shams said.

Shams never saw her mother again. Aisheh got sick and died in Gaza while searching for her daughters.

After marrying Amir, Shams never saw her father again. In 1969, Khalil died in Amman.

Shams was never reunited with her brother, Mohammad. His mother left him with relatives in Amman when she went to Gaza in search of her daughters. In 1952, a few months after he arrived in Jordan, Khalil found his son in Amman. Mohammad lived in Amman the rest of his life and died there in 2003 at the age of seventy.

A year after the 1967 War, when Israel occupied the rest of Palestine (the West Bank, the Gaza Strip, as well as the Sinai Peninsula and the Golan Peninsula), both Nazira and Nawal got Israeli visitor permits, which allowed them to enter Israel. Arranging it with Amir behind Shams's back, they surprised Shams with a visit. They came for lunch with their kids. Shams did not recognize them at first. Amir had told her that some important businessmen were coming with their families for lunch.

Ismael died of a heart attack in 1963, when the Israel Land Authority confiscated his orange grove and cut down all his orange trees. He yelled and cried, then fell to the ground. Amir, who was with him, rushed him to a Jaffa hospital, where he was declared dead.

Finding it hard to live, move, or find a job in Israel, Habeeb went to live in Nahr il Bared Refugee Camp in Southern Lebanon. Like many other Palestinian refugees, Habeeb, who never married or had a family, joined the Palestinian Liberation Organization (PLO). In 1982, at the age of fifty-five, Habeeb was killed while fighting against the Israeli army that invaded Lebanon and stayed there until May 2000.

'Abed died a natural death in 1972.

Like many displaced Palestinians, Mahmoud migrated to Chile.

After 'Abed's death, Rifqa went to live in Bat Yam, a Jewish town south of Jaffa.

Rifqa and Shams remained in close contact until the last day of Rifqa's life. Shams's daughters adored Sitti Rifqa, their grandma. On their own, or together with their mother, they frequently visited Rifqa in her small apartment in Bat Yam. She also came to see them and have lunch with them once a week, on Fridays.

In 1988, Rifqa fell ill, and Mahmoud returned from Chile to be with his mother, who was hospitalized in Jaffa.

Rifqa died in the hospital a week later. Shams was cooking stuffed cabbage, Rifqa's favorite dish, when the phone rang. "My mother has just died," said Mahmoud, sobbing.

Rifqa's sister arrived from Bat Yam to claim Rifqa's body and bury it in the Jewish cemetery. Mahmoud objected. He insisted that his mother had converted to Islam and had asked to be buried next to her husband, 'Abed, in the Muslim cemetery of Jaffa. Resigned in the face of Mahmoud's insistence, Rifqa's sister gave in.

"And what about your love story with Subhi?" I gathered my courage and whispered in Shams's ear just as I was about to leave.

"Oh, that was *waldaneh*, that was childish," Shams giggled, blushing.

"Did you ever see him again?"

"No." she smiled.

A few weeks later, I went to see Subhi in il Mareekh refugee camp in Amman. He too was surrounded by numerous grandchildren. At the age of eighty-seven, Subhi was more interested in talking about his English suit than about Shams. When asked about the first, he rose from his chair, dragged his frail body toward a wardrobe, flung its left door wide open, reached up high, and, trembling, pulled out what looked like a gray rag with a thin red line and handed it to me.

He then went back to his chair and took a deep breath before he said, "This is all that remains of Palestine."

Giving us both a moment to swallow the lumps in our throats, I caressed the remnants of his English suit. Once I composed myself, I looked him in the eyes and asked, "And what about Shams?"

Subhi was quiet as he gazed out the window, revealing a touching vulnerability. Out of respect, I waited, my eyes fixed on the dark age spots on his hands.

"I never saw Shams again . . . but that doesn't mean she hasn't been on my mind all these years." With a sort of remote tenderness, he added, "Thinking that she, like most inhabitants of Salameh, had left with her family to go to Jordan, I went looking for her in every refugee camp there." He listed them one by one. It felt as if he was still hoping to find her. "I looked for her in the il Husn refugee camp, in the Irbid and Jabal el-Hussein camps, in the Jerash and Marka camps, and of course here in il Mareekh, but to no avail. I settled here and opened a machine repair shop in the hope of finding her or learning something about her. Though I doubted I would find Shams in Syria or in Lebanon, I looked for her in every refugee camp there too. However, on February 4, 1954, a gloomy winter day, Uncle Habeeb appeared on my doorstep. He had come from the Nahr il Bared refugee camp in northern Lebanon to find me. It was he who told me what had happened. . . . It turned out Shams had never left Jaffa." Subhi sighed. My tearful eyes met his when he added, "All I can say is, I'm happy she stayed in the family." Subhi paused for a while before he said, "To each his fate in this world."

Author's Note

Forty years have passed since I left Amman in 1981 and came to live in Ramallah. "Who in their right mind would opt to go live under occupation?" objected my mother as I stared at the Israeli visitor's permit that allowed me a one-month stay in Palestine. Though I was utterly thrilled, the fact that I could not read the Hebrew on the document amplified my anxiety. Amman was the city where my parents took refuge after the 1948 War, hence the city where I grew up. The one-month visit to Palestine ended up being a forty-year stay. A lifetime.

Though Ramallah was less than an hour's drive from my father's hometown of Jaffa, I never had the emotional courage to visit my family's home in il Manshiyyeh neighborhood. Dad's tears haunted me.

A year after the 1967 War, when Israel occupied the rest of Palestine, my father managed to get an Israeli visitor's permit that allowed him to visit Palestine. He planned to visit the house where he grew up, the house that he and his sister, my aunt Na'imeh, never stopped talking about: "Right next to the sea . . . every single morning, I would put on my swimsuit, throw a towel over my shoulder, cross the road, and take a dip in the sea." While Dad was fixated on his morning swim, Aunt Na'imeh had an obsession about the lemon tree. "The courtyard had a huge lemon tree, whose fragrance I can still smell. While your uncle Khaled and I lived on the ground floor with our five kids, your dad—unmarried then—and your grandmother lived upstairs. They had the sea view; our side overlooked the courtyard and the lemon tree." I could never figure out if this was a complaint or just a statement of fact. She never elaborated, and I never asked.

The minute he got to Jaffa, Dad hurried to the house. Though he had the keys in his pocket, the courtyard door was open. With much apprehension and a heavy heart, he knocked on the open door, then stepped into the courtyard. Not having seen a soul, Dad proceeded upstairs. He stood in front of the closed door, took a deep breath, and knocked. His hand trembled. It wasn't long before a middle-aged woman appeared at the door. He did not know whether to address her in Arabic or in English. Her fair features made him opt for English.

"My name is Mohammad Amiry." Never before had he felt that his first name was inappropriate. He paused for a second, then added, "I am the owner of this house." The combination of the name "Mohammad" and the word "owner" made the woman go pale. Seeing the fear in her eyes, Dad quickly explained, "I would just like to have a quick look around the house. And if possible, take my mother's photo from her bedroom wall."

"If you don't leave right away, I will call the police!" screamed the woman before she slammed the door.

Not knowing what to do or say, my father froze in front of the closed door. Tears rolled down his cheeks to his quivering lips. Back in Amman, Dad was silent for a whole month. I was seventeen, and it was the first time I had ever seen him cry. Those were the tears that stopped me from visiting my family's home in Jaffa all those years.

.

Though I have had access to Jaffa for the last four decades, it wasn't until January 2018 that I had the courage to try to visit my family's home. Accompanied by my husband, Salim, and a strong sense of estrangement, I walked around what remained of il Manshiyyeh, once the biggest neighborhood in Jaffa. I couldn't decide what distressed me more: the few remaining Arab houses inhabited by Israeli families, the vast empty lots of the razed Arab homes, or the high-rise office buildings and hotels of what had become part of Tel Aviv. I didn't know which fate I most feared had befallen my family's house. Being totally lost in the streets of what was supposed to be my hometown brought tears to my eyes.

Except for the train station, which had been transformed into yet another open space for trendy restaurants and coffee shops, and Hassan Bek Mosque, which I could see from a distance, I could not recognize any of the landmarks described to me by my late father, my late mother, and my late aunt Na'imeh. Having realized not only the impossibility of our ever finding my family's house but also how sad and agitated I had become, Salim gave me a hug, then suggested we try again sometime soon, which of course meant never. I hastily agreed. Having accompanied Salim to his family's home in the il 'Ajami neighborhood of Jaffa a few years earlier, I recalled the overwhelming sense of emptiness Salim and I felt as we stood in front of the house, which had become a rehabilitation center for drug addicts.

Utterly exhausted and disappointed, Salim and I took a taxi back to Ramallah. Listening to our conversation—the anguish I felt about my father's forced exile, the fact the he never saw his house again, and the lost opportunity of me writing a book about it—the cabdriver slowed down, turned around to face me, and said, "Why don't you come back to Jaffa and meet my aunt Shams. She has an incredible story." The minute he started telling it to me, I knew I had a treasure in my hands.

Acknowledgments

I owe an enormous debt of gratitude to the two people who inspired this story of Shams and Subhi. What touched me most was their ability to maintain their humanity and integrity despite the great losses they endured.

A very special thanks goes to my friend and editor Shelley Wanger, who generously gave me and my novel much of her precious time. And I am enormously grateful to her assistants, Tatiana Dubin and Morgan Hamilton, for all their hard work, as well as to Sibylle Kazeroid for her meticulous copyediting; to Melissa Yoon for her sharp eye on the manuscript through the production process; to Alisa Garrison, Elodie Quetant, and Susan VanOmmeren for their meticulous proofing; and, last but not least, to Jenny Carrow for her wonderful jacket. And many thanks to Greta Anderson, who read and edited the first draft of this novel.

This book would not have been written without Sami Abu Shehadeh, the son of Jaffa who reawakened in me a deep love I always had for my father's city but never dared to confront, hoping to avoid the emotional consequences. Thank you, Sami, for giving me the strength to gather my courage and narrate the painful story of Jaffa, "the bride of the sea," and its people.

Finally, no words—and I mean that, no words—can express my gratitude to Salim Tamari, my husband and closest companion, who has always been the great mind and supportive soul behind whatever I did, or didn't, do. Thank you, Salim.

Arabic to English Glossary

A

aaa: yes

abu: father of

akeed: for sure

alf: a thousand

'al fadhi: in vain

allayet banadoura: tomato and onion stew

amir: prince

ana: I and I am

araghil (sing. arghileh): hubbly bubbly

'arak: a distilled anise-flavored alcoholic drink widely consumed in the Levantine, very similar to the Greek Ouzo

'arees: bridegroom

'arous (pl. 'arusat): bride

'arous il lail: the night's bride

'ars (pl. 'arsat): bastard

ashawes: heroes

'asifeh: storm

awqaf: endowment

B

bahar: sea

bairaq: flag

banati (sing. bint): daughters

bannouteh: effeminate

bawarjeek: I'll show you

bayyara (pl. bayyarat): orange grove

bayyari: orange grove worker

bismillah: in the name of God

bittaliqni: you divorce me

bouri: sea bream

buraq: the flying horse believed to have carried Prophet Mohammad from Mecca to Jerusalem

C

casaba: historic center of
a city

D

dhaw: light

difa': defense

E

'eid: feast

'eid il adha: Muslim feast after
the hajj to Mecca

'eid il fitr: Muslim feast at the
end of the fasting month of
Ramadan

F

falastin: Palestine

falastiniyyeh: Palestinians

fallah (pl. fallaheen): peasant

farreq tasud: separate and rule

fasharu: no way

fawda: chaos

fi: in

foul: fava beans or stew of
cooked fava beans

G

gala gala: hanky-panky

ghaddar: treacherous

ghaleb: the victor

ghar: laurel

ghurbeh: expatriation diaspora

H

habibi (fem. habibti; pl. habibati):
my love or sweetheart

haddadeen (sing. haddad):
blacksmiths

hader: OK or right away

hai: neighborhood

hait: wall

ha'it al-buraq: the Wailing Wall

hajj: pilgrimage

hajjeh: a woman pilgrim but also
an old lady

halal: permitted

hammam: public bathhouse

haram: forbidden

harami: thief

hashish: hash

hijri: the Muslim calendar

I

ibin: son

ibni: my son

il: the

ilhamdulillah: thank God

inglese: English

inta (masc.): you

inti (fem.): you

isami: self-made man

J

jaha: group of elderly men who
formally propose or ask for the
bride's hand

jahsh: colt or ass but also means stupid

jallabiyyeh (pl. ghalaleeb): traditional men's robe

jarad: grasshopper

K

karakhaneh (pl. karakhanat): brothel

Karkouz (also spelled Karagöz): the lead character of a traditional Turkish shadow play popular among children of the Levantine

karkubeh: junk; in this context, old

karshat: a tripe dish

kazzab: liar

kbeer: big, great

khalas: stop it

khan: market or hostel

kharoof: sheep

khawaja (pl. khawajat): an honorific status used to refer to a rich Christian or a well-to-do Jew

khawal: a gay man

khhh khhh: snores

khirbeh: ruins

kisweh: clothes; the green velvet cloth that covers the holy tomb of the Prophet Rubin

knafeh: a traditional sweet made with semolina and cheese

L

la: no

lail: night

lamam: riffraff

M

mabruk: congratulations

madani: city dweller

mafkhoum: the Israeli Ashkenazi pronunciation of the Arabic word *mafhoum*, meaning "understood"

maghloub: the defeated

mahatta: station

makhyatah: tailor's shop

makhyatet: the *makhyatah* of

maleeten: red mullet

m'allem: master

manayek: fuckers

maqam (pl. maqamat): shrine of a holy saint

masagh: gold jewelery

masakhameen: poor or miserable

masrahiyyeh: play, performance

mawsim: season; festival

maylaweiyyeh: Sufi performance involving spinning dance, chanting, and singing

mazoun (fem: mazouneh): authorized marriage clerk

meen: who or who is

miskeen: poor thing

mtabbaq: a sweet pie

mushut: sea bass

muslim awqaf: Muslim Endowment

mutasallel: infiltrator

N

nabi: prophet

nakba: catastrophe

nas: people

Q

qahramaneh: the woman who manages a brothel; madam

qishleh: police station

quftan (pl. qafateen): robe or tunic, also known as a caftan

qumbaz: a traditional robe for men that opens from the front

S

sahayyneh: Zionists

sakanet (pl. sakanat): neighborhood

sakhra: rock

salat: prayer

salat il 'aser: afternoon prayers

salat il dohor: midday prayers

salat il fajr: morning prayers

salat il isha: evening prayers

salat il jum'a: Friday prayers

salat il maghreb: sunset prayers

saqqa (pl. saqqaiyyeh): water provider

shaitaneh (masc. shaitan): a devil

sharameet (pl. sharmutah): whore

sharmatah: prostitution

shattur: clever

shawasher: troubles

shilleh: clique

il sit: diva; used in this book in reference to the Egyptian singer Umm Kulthum

sitti: my grandmother

suq: market

T

tabliyyeh: a low round wooden table

taboun: a mud oven

temriyyeh: a fried sweet made of semolina

thub: dress

thub (pl. athwab) il malak: embroidered wedding dress

turuq: literally roads; also different schools of thought or sects

U

u: and

um: mother and mother of

um il ghareeb: mother of strangers

W

walad (pl. awlad): a child

walak: goddamn

walawo: of course or come on

waldaneh: childishness

Y

ya: you

yaba: my father

yabnel kalb: son of a bitch

ya 'ein: wow

yafa 'arous il bahar: Jaffa the Bride of the Sea

yahudi (pl. yahud): a Jew

ya ibni: my son

yalla: come on or let's go

yamma or yumma: Mother; also how children refer to their parents

ya sater: goodness (interjection)

Z

zawiyyeh (pl. zawaya): religious school

zboun: client

zilzal: earthquake

zu'ran: gangsters

Some phrases

ahlan wa sahlan: welcome

Allah akbeer: God is great

Allah farajha 'alaykum: May God make it easy on you

Allah yekfeena shar il dhuhuk: May god protect us from the terrible consequences of our laughter

habel il kizeb qaseer: Your lie will soon be revealed

inshallah: God willing, everything will be OK

kulna itsakhamnah: We were all fucked

la ya ibni: No, my son

walawo ya zalameh: Of course, man

ya banati ya habibati: my beloved daughters

ya bit rubini ya bittaliqni: You either take me to the festival of il Nabi Rubin or you divorce me

ya shaitaneh: you naughty one/girl

ya wlad il kalb: you sons of a bitch

ya zalameh: Come on, man

SUAD AMIRY is a writer and an architect. She is the founder of RIWAQ: Centre for Architectural Conservation in Ramallah, Palestine, and has won the Aga Khan Award for architecture. She is the author of six books of nonfiction, including *Sharon and My Mother-in-Law,* awarded Italy's Viareggio-Versilia International Prize in 2004. Amiry received the Nonino Risit D'Aur award in 2014. She lives in Ramallah.

A NOTE ON THE TYPE

This book was set in Fournier, a typeface named for Pierre Simon Fournier *fils* (1712–1768), a celebrated French type designer. His services to the art of printing were his design of letters, his creation of ornaments and initials, and his standardization of type sizes. His types are old style in character and sharply cut. In 1764 and 1766 he published his *Manuel typographique*, a treatise on the history of French types and printing.

Composed by North Market Street Graphics,
Lancaster, Pennsylvania

Printed and bound by Berryville Graphics,
Berryville, Virginia

Designed by Cassandra J. Pappas